They Said I Couldn't Do It: John Mercer Langston, Young Black Lawyer in a White Man's World

They Said I Couldn't Do It

John Mercer Langston, Young Black Lawyer in a White Man's World

Robyn R. Pearce

GettingAGrip Publishing

THEY SAID I COULDN'T DO IT:

John Mercer Langston, Young Black Lawyer in a White Man's World
Book 2 in the Freedom Series

First published 2022 by GettingAGrip Publishing
R.D.4, Pukekohe, 2679, New Zealand

This book is a work of historical biographical fiction. All references to historical events, real people, or real places are used fictitiously. All dialogue, other names, characters, places, and events are products of the author's imagination, and should not be construed as real.

ISBN 978-0-473-60062-4 Epub

ISBN 978-0-473-60060-0 Softcover POD
© 2022 by Robyn R. Pearce
First edition 2022

A catalogue record for this book is available from the National Library of New Zealand

Cover design by Nick Castle
For bulk supplies, contact the publisher.
Visit the author's website at https://www.robynrpearce.com

To my dear writing, editing and book marketing friends
Linda Coles, Kirsty Powell, Michele Zwillinger
Judith White, Pam Loan
Without your support, encouragement and advice,
I would have stumbled in too many ways to list!

'No one is free until we are all free'
Martin Luther King

Other Fiction By Robyn R Pearce
It Happened On Fifth Street: A tale of forgotten heroes

At https://www.RobynRPearce.com you'll find bonus material
about the story – maps, photos and other fascinating details I
discovered while researching John's remarkable true story. Also,
if you love historical novels and would like to keep up with my
future work, other authors' books, fascinating historical tidbits
and giveaways, you can request to be included on my newsletter.

CONTENTS

Dear Reader

ALLOW ME TO INTRODUCE myself. My name is John Mercer Langston.

I mislaid my parents while very young. Careless? Difficult to argue with the Grim Reaper!

I've lived through the best of times and the worst of times. I've been at the center of the most dramatic, nation-shaping events of my century. For the latter half of the nineteenth century, my name was on the lips of many, for they knew me as a leader of my race.

I've experienced advantage and adversity. Courage and cowardice. Delight and discrimination. Friendship and betrayals. Love and loss. Glorious achievements and gut-wrenching disappointments. Some triumphs. Many tragedies. War, peace and everything in between.

However, these days my name is not particularly well-known, for time has a curious way of changing history. We lose sight of some people, and highlight others who, in their day, were no more significant than those later lost to view.

The writer I've shoulder-tapped to bring you the tale of my early years thinks coincidence brought my name to her attention. She was investigating her ancestors, the Burnetts, and the history of Cincinnati, when my name popped off the page. Shh—don't tell her coincidence can be manipulated from beyond the veil.

You might think she's an unexpected choice, for she's neither black nor even American, but sometimes strangers see things more clearly than those close at hand.

So, set yourself down, get comfortable, and come with me on a journey. I've a tale to tell of the fight for black freedom and black rights.

PART ONE

CHAPTER 1

1842 CINCINNATI

BANG! THE DOOR CRASHED open. Three scary-looking men stormed into my brother Gideon's barbershop. Ugly. Loud. Waving pistols. Cracking whips. Chains clanging around their waists.

They rushed through the room, one heading to the back room, two for the stairs.

'Where's the black bastard?' shouted one. 'We know you've got a runaway here.'

I'd been sitting quietly at the back of the room, schoolbooks at my feet, hoping for a quick word with Gideon. Three men were reading newspapers while they waited for shaves or haircuts. Four others reclined in the well-padded chairs while my brother and his staff washed, snipped, razored, and pomaded them.

For a second, the room was stunned to silence. Then, with a roar of anger, the tall man in Gideon's chair jumped to his feet. It was Salmon P. Chase, local white lawyer and a true friend to all blacks. Draped in a protective oilcloth, his cheeks a-lather, in his loud courtroom voice he bellowed, 'STOP! Where do you think you're going?'

They turned in surprise, not expecting a white man to oppose them in a black barbershop. He towered over them, an angry eagle, ready to pounce.

'You have no right to barge in here. Where's your warrant?' he shouted.

They muttered amongst themselves. No warrant.

'Get out, or I'll see you in court,' he yelled, pointing to the door. They were inclined to argue. He marched toward them. They slunk out the door. Cursing.

We all gasped. The room erupted into a babel of noise.

Mr. Chase calmly took his seat. When Gideon tried to thank him, he brushed it off.

'All in a day's work, Mr. Langston. Glad to be of help.'

Gideon stepped my way. Spoke quietly. 'Better go, Johnnie. I'll see you Sunday.'

I grabbed my bag and scampered. I couldn't wait to tell Alf.

Alf Burnett and I had been friends since soon after I was sent to Cincinnati in 1841. Was it because we loved fishing? Or because we lived with people deeply involved in helping slaves escape north to Canada? Or was it because we complemented each other? I was the sober-sides; Alf turned everything into a joke.

Whatever the reason, though he was five years older than me, we'd become good buddies. Race was not an issue. I don't think Alf saw color. He and his family treated everyone with equal courtesy.

I wasn't his only young visitor. Few youngsters and children would go past his family's confectionary and bakery shop without calling in to stay 'hello' if they saw him at the counter. Even when he walked down the street, groups of urchins attached themselves to him.

'You're the Pied Piper of Fifth Street,' I'd heard a parent chuckle one day as Alf made funny faces. Three small children were rocking with laughter and nearby adults were joining in the hilarity.

I won't deny a healthy dose of cupboard love increased his pulling power. He gave a free candy to any child who entered the shop door. 'Happy customers equal good profits' was his motto.

Alf looked up in surprise as I raced into the shop, a short distance from Gideon's premises. When his father first set up business in Cincinnati in 1836, he'd secured one of the best spots in town, right outside Fifth Street Market House. Many house-wives and servants walked past their door every day.

'Where's the fire, youngster?'

I started to gabble, then realized he was serving a young woman. 'Sorry, Mam,' he smiled to her. 'My young friend's a wee bit excited.' He quickly handed me a cinnamon bun. 'I'll be with you in a moment, Johnnie.'

'Now, let's have it,' he said as soon as she and her basket of bread departed.

Brushing away crumbs, I blurted out my news.

He looked worried. 'I wonder if they'll try here next. I'd better warn Samuel and the boys downstairs. Bide here, Johnnie. If anyone comes in, tell them I'll be back directly.'

Within a minute, he returned. His white-haired father, Cor-nelius Burnett, was right behind, clutching some papers.

'I found Father downstairs. He'll do his writing in the parlor instead of downstairs in the kitchen, in case we need him,' Alf explained.

'Let the bastards try barging in here and they'll get the thick end of my tongue,' said his father. He turned to walk away. 'Now, back to my article. Dr. Bailey's wanting it for the next issue of *The Philanthropist*.'

'I've read your articles, sir,' I piped up. 'Mr. Watson takes that paper at home.'

He stopped. Looked back at me. 'You're a smart child, Johnnie Langston. A clever boy like you is bound to go far. You're a credit to your race.'

I looked at him, surprised.

He gave a genial smile. 'Do you think I don't notice youngsters, Johnnie? Anyone who helps the battle for black freedom and rights is worthy of attention, no matter how young. You and Alf do excellent work on lookout duty when our friends escape across the river.'

We both beamed at the praise as he headed to the parlor.

CHAPTER 2

1833 VIRGINIA

M Y CHILDHOOD WAS A disjointed affair. Death. Love. Interference. Abandonment. Good intentions. Devastating results. By the age of thirteen, I'd experienced them all.

My brothers say I was a pampered baby, but of that I have no recall. Perhaps they're right. My parents, old when I was born in December 1829, went to their long sleep within months of each other, when I was only four.

At the time this story starts, my brother, Gideon, was a man of four-and-twenty, Charles was sixteen, and I was still a few months shy of five. Apparently, I was the late in life surprise for Captain Ralph Quarles and his beloved, Lucy Langston.

A few disjointed memories of the time before my brothers and I left our home in Louisa, Virginia, still occasionally float through my brain.

I do recall, as a little boy, being lifted onto a wide bed piled with many pillows. The room was gloomy, candles flickered and there was a funny smell. Someone placed me beside a small brown woman who cried as she held me in her arms. She kissed me. Wiped moisture from my face. Were they her tears? I lay there quietly for a short time. Then I was taken away. I never saw her again. I'm told she was my mother.

Of my father, I have only a vague impression of an elderly man in an armchair. Perhaps he was too old and sick to be bothered with a chatterbox child. Gideon and Charles informed me, when I was of an age to enquire, that he'd been a fair and generous father, with a strong desire to do right by his mulatto children.

I also recall the sound of weeping. Grownups coming and going. A child's sense of things being topsy-turvy. Maybe my childish remembrance has linked two funerals into one.

My next memory took place, I'm told, a couple of months after our parents were carried to their last resting place. More wailing and tears. Women hugging and kissing me. My playmates being told to bid me goodbye. Men shaking the hands of my brothers and the four other dark-skinned men who stood beside us, then turning away. The seven of us standing together in the hot sun. I also have a vague sense of high steps and a blue door behind us. I think I used to play under the shady cool steps with other children.

Then, my friends and their families climbed into two high-sided creaky wooden wagons. The littlest children were lifted in. Bundles, sacks and big items were piled high in other wagons. Two white men I'd seen often at the house, my father's nephews I now know, climbed into their saddles and rode off alongside the wagons.

'Wave goodbye to your playmates, Johnnie,' said Gideon.

'Where are they going?' I asked, tilting my head to look up at my lanky brother. The sun was in my eyes. I had to squint to see his face. He looked different. Sad.

'To new homes,' he answered, but he didn't look down at me. Watching the wagons as they drove away, he said, 'Papa's nephews are their owners now. They're taking our people to their farms. New people will move in here soon.'

Bewildered, I asked, 'Who will I play with? Why can't I go too?'

Gideon sighed. This time, it was Charles who answered. He squatted down, wrapping his arms around me. 'Now Mama and Papa have gone to their eternal rest, your friends have to leave, Johnnie, and so do we. It's just us fellows now. But we're off on our own adventure in three days. It'll be exciting.'

The wagons went round the corner and out of sight. Dust rose in the air, then settled on the shrubs bordering the drive. I was left behind.

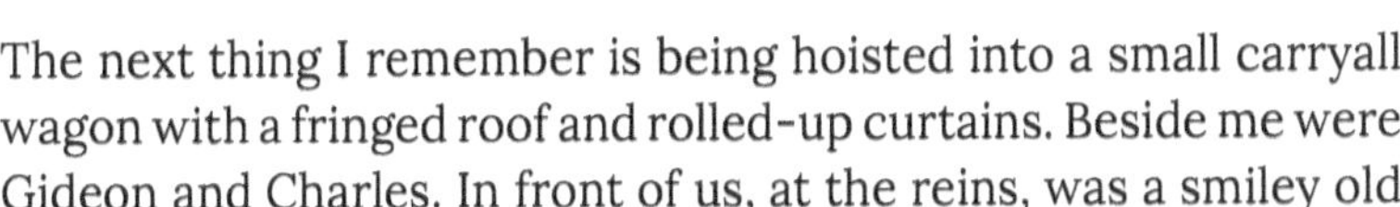

The next thing I remember is being hoisted into a small carryall wagon with a fringed roof and rolled-up curtains. Beside me were Gideon and Charles. In front of us, at the reins, was a smiley old black man with lots of wrinkles. Everyone called him Uncle Billy.

'Sit still, Johnnie,' growled Gideon as our wagon began to roll. I'd wriggled around to make sure the larger, canvas-covered wagon, with the three other fellows was coming along behind.

'Have they got my toys?'

'Don't fuss. They're aboard,' said Charles.

'Where are we going?' I asked after a few miles.

'All the way to Chillicothe, Ohio, little brother,' said Gideon.

'Will we be there by teatime?'

Gideon and Charles laughed. Uncle Billy laughed too, sounding like the bullfrogs I tried to catch in the lily pond.

'We're many days away,' answered Gideon. 'We have to go over the mountains to Ohio.'

'What's Ohio?'

'Another state, where there's no slavery. The others will have a better life there.'

'What's wrong with here?'

'It's like this, Mr. Twenty Questions. Papa freed them. They're not slaves now, and Virginia's a hard place for free blacks. Plus, we've got to take you to the Goochs in Chillicothe. They're going to be your new family Makes sense for us all to relocate to Ohio. That state is more friendly to people of our complexion.'

None of this meant anything to me.

'Can I have a cookie?'

By nightfall, I'd had enough of sitting in the wagon. Sometimes Uncle Billy let me ride up beside him. Other times, I had to stay between my brothers. I suppose I must have napped—I recall finding myself draped across a brother's knees at least once. Finally, as the sun got lower in the sky, we pulled in beside a little stream.

'There you are, youngster. See if you can find any shrimps or frogs while we set up camp,' said Gideon, lifting me down from the carriage.

I was mighty glad to stretch my legs!

That first night set the pattern for the close on three weeks we were on the road. I played until the sun was nearly gone. Then Arthur, one of the younger men, fetched me up from the stream.

'You all wet, Johnnie. It be dinner time, but we best get you outta dem wet clothes first.'

I shivered as the evening chill hit my bare skin. 'Stand still, boy,' he growled. 'Next time, try not to get wet when you play. You don' have no nursemaid to run roun' after you no more. We got other work to do.'

Once he'd helped me into dry clothes, he handed me a plate. 'Take this to your bruvver, laddie.'

Charles was stooping over the campfire, stirring something in a big black pan. The smells coming from it reminded me of my empty belly.

'Come, Johnnie. Vittles time,' Charles called.

Soon, all seven of us took our seats. Charles and Arthur, both short, sat on the ground with me. The others perched on logs they'd rolled close to the fire.

Sausages and beans. Yum. I went back for more. Then, eating done, I thought to play again.

'Not yet, Johnnie,' said Gideon. 'Everyone mucks in on a camping trip. No maids to clean up after you now, tadpole. Tonight, you'll help James with the dishes. Tomorrow you might be fetching firewood. We'll have you useful yet.'

James, another of the young fellows in the covered wagon, gave me my first lesson on washing dishes. Just as well the plates were tin!

Burrel, our fourth man, threw more logs on the fire. Sparks danced above the flames. The sky was black. Stars came out. The moon rose above the trees. I'd never sat by a campfire before. I was happy. Someone pulled out a banjo. The men sang. Told stories. Laughed.

Then came the words I didn't want to hear.

'Bed time, Johnnie,' said Gideon.

'Oh no. I want to stay up,' I pleaded.

Gideon looked over at Uncle Billy. 'You're a grandfather, Uncle Billy. I'm not used to playing nursemaid to a four-year-old. Will it matter if he's late to bed?'

Uncle Billy's tummy wobbled as he laughed. 'Childer get da sleep dey need. No harm for him to set awhile wiv us. It be a lovely night. Come here, young 'un. Set on Uncle Billy's knee a piece.'

The next thing I knew, daylight was shining through the tent wall and I could smell bacon frying.

Although we'd started with fine weather, it was early October, and fall was upon us. It rained—a lot! We rolled down the curtains if we saw it coming, but it sneaked through every crack and corner. We kept a horse blanket handy, draping it over our knees or shoulders, depending which way the rain came from. Uncle Billy had another one. The thunderstorms frightened me; I snuggled up close to Gideon when the bangs were close, but the sizzle and flash of lightning was exciting.

The rain caused other worries as well. After a downpour, the streams and rivers were often hard to cross. Little streams became big ones. Then the men looked worried as they tried to find shallow crossings for us to drive the wagons through. The bigger rivers had ferries, but some of them were dangerous too. One time, one of our mules put its hoof through a hole in the planking. Hollered. Reared up. Everyone yelled. I began to tip out of the wagon. My face was almost in the water before someone hauled me up by my braces.

Once we were safely back on the road, Gideon said to Charles, 'I've aged ten years! We nearly lost Johnnie! I shouldn't have tried to save time and money by fitting us all on to the same load.'

Charles looked just as concerned. 'You're not wrong! When I saw the narrow width of that excuse for a ferry, I wondered about your decision. No sides! Holes in the planks! And the ferryman was a disaster! Drunk and unhelpful.'

'It's quite a responsibility, being in charge,' said Gideon. 'Until we began, I'd never been further than a few miles from home. We've wasted a fair amount of time backtracking when I've read the map wrong, or else the map is out-of-date.'

'You doin' jus' fine, Master Gideon,' said Uncle Billy from the front. 'You doin' better 'n I could. I be no help wiv maps. Never been outa da county. All I knowed 'bout directions was how to git to Richmond from da farm when I delivered your Pappy's wheat and baccy. Dat be sixty mile de other way. No help in gettin' to Ohio, for sure!'

Soon we began to see big hills in the distance. The Allegheny Mountains, the men called them. We saw fewer people. The roads became rougher. Nearly every day, we had to push one or other of the wagons out of deep mud holes, or pull them back on the track.

Sometimes, we had to get out and walk. With my short legs, I couldn't keep up, so they left me in the wagon as long as possible. But, if a wheel slipped off the track, there was a risk of the rig falling into a gully, taking me with it!

'If we have to lose a horse and our possessions on this excuse for a road, that would be a big problem,' said Gideon as he lifted me out to walk with him one wet, miserable day. 'But if we lost you as well, little brother ... it doesn't bear thinking about. One close shave is one too many!'

No-one bothered about bathing and clean clothes. That I didn't mind.

CHAPTER 3

1833 VIRGINIA AND OHIO

WE'D BEEN ON THE road a week and were in the foothills of the Allegheny Mountains when Gideon was able to stop worrying about maps and wrong turnings.

As usual, we'd found a place to camp just before dusk. Burrel and James were watering the horses at a nearby stream and fetching water for cooking and washing. I'd gone down with them–it was a fine day, so I'd taken the chance to play. The others were pitching tents and preparing food.

Suddenly, Arthur called, 'A horseman's coming–fast.'

Burrel and James grabbed me and we all ran up from the stream.

The day before, when we'd stopped at a hamlet for fresh supplies, an old man had told my brothers about bandits in the mountains.

Gideon called to Charles, 'Fetch the gun from the wagon. I don't think a single man would attack six and a child, but let's play safe.'

As the horseman approached, he waved. Suddenly, the others all laughed. Charles dropped the gun. He and Gideon walked quickly towards the newcomer. The other four were right behind. The stranger jumped off his sweating horse, embraced my brothers, then shook hands with the other men.

Only I stayed by the tents, watching. Clearly there was no danger, but I did not know this person. He was darker-skinned than my brothers and me. Tall. Broad-shouldered. Big hands, with nicks and scars. Thick black whiskers.

He and his horse came to a halt in front of me. The horse snorted, lowering its nose to sniff at me. I reached out my hand, palm up and open, as Uncle Billy had taught me. Its whiskery chin tickled my hand. I giggled.

The stranger grinned. Crouched down to look me in the eye.

'So, you're the little fella I've 'eard 'bout. I be your half-brother, William, come all the way from Chillicothe to help take you to your new home.'

Puzzled, I looked up at Gideon and Charles. They didn't seem surprised.

Gideon spoke. 'Johnnie, you've not met William, but our Mama had three other children before us. William and his sisters were all grown up before you came along. They had a different daddy, but they're all Langstons. Our Papa helped them emigrate to Chillicothe some years ago.'

I frowned. A half-brother? Three other children?

'Too much detail, Gideon,' William said, noticing my confusion. He turned to me. 'De only important thing is, I be your brother too, little man.' I stayed close to Charles and watched both this new man and his horse, but especially the horse. She was pretty.

William noted where my interest lay. 'Johnnie, you wanna ride on my hoss?'

I couldn't believe my ears. How could he know? It was my dream! But any time I'd begged for a turn on one of our horses or mules, my brothers put me off, saying things like, 'The animals have to save their energy to pull the wagons,' or, 'When we stop, they need their rest,' or, 'You're too small.' That last excuse I especially hated!

So, there was only one answer to this stranger's unexpected question.

'Yep.'

'Right. First lesson t'morra,' he said.

His knees creaked as he stood up. He turned back to my other brothers. 'You be much further along the road than I 'spected, lads. I thought I'd reach you afore you left Louisa. I planned to say how-de-do to the other folks on the plantation, then help guide y'all to Ohio.'

'There's no one left on the plantation now,' Gideon said, 'but the families aren't broken up. Papa made his nephews promise to keep families together, and they're honorable men. I'm sure they'd let you visit our home folks, if you want to see them.'

'Not dat important,' replied William. 'It's been a long time since I left. You fellas an' this li'l tacker be my main concern. I figured none o' you'd probably been outside the county. I'm here to show you the way and help you wiv' the chile.'

The talk around the campfire that night was jolly. I didn't understand most of what they talked about, but I could see Gideon was glad.

The next day, good to his word, William lifted me onto his horse, shortened the stirrups, and let me hold the reins. I felt safe, though the horse was tall, for William kept a hand on the bridle or a lead rope. With no playmates, and the others in the party so focused on the details of our journey, it was grand to have someone happy to spend some time with me.

A few days later, I overheard him say to Charles, 'That lad'll make an excellent horseman one day. Worth teachin'.'

For the rest of the journey, William gave me a riding lesson every day. Told me I was doing well. Listened to my prattle. Helped put me to bed each night. I think he enjoyed having a little brother.

I liked my new brother–then.

The road became even harder after William joined us. High mountains loomed over us and big dark trees grew close to the road. Some nights, it was hard to find a spot to camp. I no longer ran off to play at the end of each day. Instead, I did my little chores, then waited quietly for dinner.

'Are you alright, youngster?' asked Charles one night. 'Not like you to sit so still and quiet.'

'I'm tired,' I answered, yawning. Although the men had walked a lot that day, for the road had been very narrow and rough, they'd left me riding in the little carryall wagon. I *think* it was easier than walking, but seated by myself, I bounced and banged all over the seat as it jolted over the bumps, rocks, and large potholes.

A couple of days later, as we sat at our evening meal, William said, 'We be over the steepest part of the mountains, thank the Lord! Not long now 'til we come down to the Kanawha River, where there be a ferry. The road on the other side flattens out. After dat, we only 'bout three days from the Ohio River. Once we cross the river, we be in Ohio, y'all be glad to know. Then, another three days to Gallipolis. I, for one, hope us can find lodgin's in Gallipolis. It'd sure be fine to sleep in a bed 'stead o' the hard, wet ground. I'm sick of wakin' up wet from rain leakin' inta ma tent fly!'

'Amen to that, brother!' said Charles.

Gideon was worried about something else. 'I'll be glad to find a general store so we can stock up on fresh food. I've had enough pancakes and jerky to last a lifetime!'

I wasn't much interested in their discussions. It was all grown-up talk as far as I was concerned. Our home in Virginia seemed a long time ago. The adventure wasn't fun anymore. When would it end?

I turned to Charles, sitting beside me on a knobbly old log. 'When we get where we're going, will we have a house?'

He put his arm around me.

'Different houses, Johnnie. You're going to have new parents. Papa arranged that if he and Mama died before you were old enough to look after yourself, Colonel Gooch and his wife and daughters would take you into their family. Three girls, two older and a young one still at school. They're good people–I remember them from when they lived in Louisa. The colonel was a particular friend of Papa's. Often used to visit the house. We'll get you settled, then Gideon and I have to find accommodation and work.'

'But,' my bottom lip quivered, 'won't you be there too? Don't leave me!'

Charles sighed. 'If only it were that simple, buddy. But no, sadly. The Goochs can't take us all. Gideon and I have to make our own way in the world now.'

Three days after leaving Gallipolis, we came to a small Negro settlement near a place the men called Berlin Crossroads.

Uncle Billy looked around as we drove into the hamlet. He pulled up in front of a small store, where white-haired black men were sitting outside on a bench, smoking pipes.

Turning to Gideon and Charles, he said, 'Can you lads water the hosses and give 'em the nosebags for a bit? I b'lieve this be the place I heard 'bout, that free folks like me an' the lads might find some land an' a welcome. I wanna discourse wiv these old-timers.'

The men talked. Others came. More talking. I became fidgety.

'Take your toys and go play under that shady walnut tree,' said Gideon, pointing to a spreading tree across the dusty road. 'But no wandering off. Stay where I can see you.'

People came and went into the store. Some children went in with their mothers. I know they saw me, but they didn't come and say hello. A couple of puppies ran up and I thought they might play, but a man called them away. I was bored.

At lunchtime, Charles called me over for a pie. Then I was sent back to play under the tree.

Finally, Uncle Billy, Burrel, James, and Arthur finished their talk. With smiles, they stood up. I heard Uncle Billy say to Gideon, 'Da boys an' me, we reckon dis place'll do. Peoples is frenly and they say the land's good 'nuf to make a livin'. We's not big city folks. This place 'bout da right size for us, an' da money your Pa give us will set us up jus' fine.'

There was a mighty bustle while everyone rearranged goods in the wagons. The men kept the bigger one. I made sure my toys weren't left behind.

It was hard to be brave when we waved them goodbye. I didn't want to cry, for William said it wasn't manly, but it seemed that everyone I knew went away.

———❀———

Two days later, battered, exhausted, and filthy, with our horses down to skin and bone and ourselves not much better, we rattled into the biggest town I'd ever seen. Gideon was at the reins, with William beside him, his horse tied to the back of our wagon.

William turned round to me. 'This be Chillicothe, Johnnie. Your new 'ome.' He seemed happy. Waved to some of the black people we passed. They waved back. Called 'Welcome'. Seemed to know who we were.

He proudly pointed out landmarks. 'Ain't that a grand two-story brick building,' and 'See how many big houses we got 'ere,' and 'Over there be the canal. Good for gettin' produce to market.'

Gideon tried to jiggle our two horses up, but they had no jiggle left. They just plodded along the wide, tree-lined street. Well-dressed people walked along the wooden footpaths. Clean buggies and well-groomed horses trotted past our tired animals. Passersby looked at our shabby rig with curiosity. But we didn't stop.

If this was my new home, where were we going?

Not far out of town, we turned into an open gateway and drove up a neat gravel driveway. Rounding a curve, we came to a grand two-story white house with a red door. Tall windows. Flowers crowding up to the sides of the steps. Tall thick-branched trees in the garden hinted at bird nests and possible tree huts.

At the sound of our wheels, three people came out onto the wide verandah—a tall white man with a wavy mustache that tilted up at the ends, a gently rounded, motherly-looking lady who clapped her hands when she saw us, and a fair-haired girl with ringlets.

Then, everything happened at once. All three ran down the steps towards us, broad smiles on their faces. Another white fellow, each trouser leg criss-crossed tight with string, came from behind the house and held the horses' heads while we dismounted from our wagon.

William began introductions. I heard 'Gooch' but the motherly lady didn't wait for him to finish speaking. She made a beeline for me. There was no time to be shy, or hide behind my brothers' legs. She picked me up, gave me a mighty hug, then put me down again, keeping hold of my hands.

'Johnnie dear, I've been so longing for you to get here. You were only a wee tot the last time I saw you, and now look at you. A big boy of four! You've got your dear Mama's beautiful brown eyes. And what lovely curls. Well, they will be, once they've had a good wash!' She laughed as she patted my head.

The girl bent down, her golden ringlets nearly touching my face. She gave me a sweet smile. 'I'm Virginia. I'm so excited. You're going to be my little brother, Johnnie!'

'Sweetheart, run and get the new clothes we've prepared for him. Bring them down to the kitchen,' said the lady. 'This poor child is in dire need of a bath!'

'Right away, Mama.'

Bewildered, I watched the girl disappear inside the red door.

The lady took my hand. 'Come with me, darlin'. I'm your new Mama, now your own dear Mama's gone to be with the angels.'

As she led me away, she called to my brothers. 'Don't you worry about Johnnie, lads. The colonel will look after y'all and we'll join you directly. Please excuse me—I must attend to this little fellow immediately.'

I looked back. They didn't appear even a tiny bit worried about me. Too busy talking and laughing.

Up the steps she took me. I had to take big steps to keep up. The door had a brass handle in the shape of a lion. I wanted to look at it but she didn't stop. We stepped into a wide hall with a polished floor. A wooden thing, taller than Gideon, stood by the entrance. It was covered with hats, coats, and umbrellas. A vase of white and blue flowers stood on a table. I could smell something yummy. Cookies maybe?

My new Mama tut-tutted as she trotted me down the long hall,

'By the look of you, darlin', you've not had a close acquaintance with soap since you left Louisa! Fancy coming over those mountains with only men to care for you! We'll soon have you spick and span again.'

We walked toward the delicious smell. I found myself in a spacious kitchen with light coming from two wide windows.

Two pots bubbled on a black stove. A basket with potatoes and another with green vegetables were on a table. A short round lady wearing a red head cloth, her skin darker than Uncle Billy's, was putting wood in the firebox.

And, on a sideboard, I spotted a cake!

'Sadie, look who's arrived! Our Johnnie! Can you fill up the bath while I get these rags off him?'

'Well, Lordy me. Look at the chile! We gonna fix you up in no time, sugar,' said the red headcloth lady. 'And we gonna get some food in you belly. You hungry, darlin'?'

I nodded. It had been a long time since breakfast.

'Get this piece o' pie inside you while I get yo' bath ready, liddle man.' She left me eating at the table while she took a tin bath off the wall and filled it with water.

And so began my new life with the Goochs.

CHAPTER 4

1833-1839 CHILLICOTHE

I T TOOK NO TIME for me to settle in. The Gooch family, including Virginia's two older sisters, made me their own. Even the people at church, and in the shops we visited, called me Johnnie Gooch. With my light skin, I think people soon forgot I was of mixed blood.

At breakfast about two months after my arrival, my new Papa said, 'Johnnie, would you like to come for a ride today? I'm off to see Mr. Lafferty.'

I looked up from pouring more cream onto my oatmeal.

'Yes please, Papa.' He often took me out in the buggy. It was one of my favorite things to do.

I noticed a smile pass between him and Mama, but thought nothing of it. Mama just said, 'Wrap him up well, Husband. It's a raw day today.'

Twenty minutes later, bundled up with mittens, woolen cap, thick cape, and new boots, I climbed up onto the buggy seat. There was a wooden box on the floor.

'What's this for, Papa?' I kicked the box.

'Might need to put something in it,' was all he said. He gave no further explanation, and I gave the matter no further thought. It made a handy footrest.

As we drove into the Lafferty yard an hour later, a pack of spaniels came running out, barking a welcome. Mr. Lafferty followed, calling them to heel.

'Good to see you, Gooch. So, this is the ...' Mr. Lafferty began. He stopped mid-sentence. I looked up, curious. Papa had a finger to his lips. The two men grinned at each other. Odd.

'I gather you want to look at my stables,' said Mr. Lafferty.

'Indeed. Come along, Johnnie.' Papa took my hand as we walked around the side of the house to the courtyard behind.

I spent a lot of time in our stables. Tom, our stableman, gave me little jobs, such as giving the horses their mash and helping to groom the quiet ones. I had to stand on a stool to reach their withers. Sometimes he let me ride Virginia's pony when she was at school, though he always held a lead rein. He reckoned I wasn't yet big enough to manage on my own. I suppose he was right, though it chafed me to be treated like a little boy.

As we walked into Mr. Lafferty's stables, one of the spaniels brushed past, whining. She ran into one of the horse-boxes. We followed. Dust sparkles lifted into the air as we trod on fresh straw.

When I saw what was in the box, I dropped Papa's hand and ran forward. There, amongst the hay, was a litter of puppies with fat tummies and floppy ears. Three had run to their mother, jumping at her. As we watched, she lay down and they jostled each other to latch onto her teats. Two others carried on playing chase, running and tumbling in a blur of black and white, giving little yips and growls of excitement.

I put my hand out to the two playing. One stood back, unsure. The other came up, licked my fingers, then cocked its head to look at me. I picked it up. Next thing, my face was being washed with a rough tongue.

I turned to look at my foster father. He was standing, one hand in a pocket, the other holding his pipe. He took a puff. Chuckled.

'Like that one, do you, son?'

'Oh yes! Is it a girl or a boy?'

Mr. Lafferty answered for him. 'A bonny wee bitch. Pick of the litter, that one. Bold as brass. She's my favorite too.'

'It's your fifth birthday today, Johnnie. Would you like to take her home?'

I couldn't believe my ears. I didn't know it was my birthday–no-one had given me a clue. I was beside myself with joy.

Papa handed over some money, chatted a little longer with Mr. Lafferty, then back to the buggy we walked, me cuddling my new love.

As he lifted us up into the buggy, Papa said, 'What say we put her in the box?'

'Can I hold her? Please?'

'Very well. But if she gets restless, in she goes. Can't have her falling off the buggy, or scaring the horse.' He wrapped the carriage blanket around me and my precious baby. As if she knew it was important to behave, she licked my face again, then snuggled into my arms. A short time later, she was asleep. We never did need that box.

My patchy memories of life in Louisa and the challenging journey across the Alleghenies slipped quietly into the back of my mind. I saw William and Charles occasionally, but Gideon I rarely saw. Charles told me he'd removed to the big city of Cincinnati to set up business.

However, I didn't miss my brothers, for life with the Goochs was full of fun. I played with my dog. Went fishing on the Ohio-Erie canal, which bordered the farm. Trotted round the property with Papa. Sweet-talked Sadie for a cookie or piece of pie whenever I felt hungry. Ran to my loving Mama with any minor problems. She was kind. Hardly ever growled about my lost buttons or rips in my breeches. And she gave me many cuddles, until I became too big to sit on her comfortable lap.

The older girls married during the years I lived with them, but Virginia, the one who'd run out to greet me on the first day, was my sister and first teacher. Although still a student at the Chillicothe Young Ladies Seminary, in her spare time she taught me to read, write, do simple sums and understand basic geography.

When I was seven the family decided I needed more instruction than Virginia had time or skills to give. They enrolled me in the local school.

At first, school was a shock. Except for a break for lunch at noon, I had to sit still all day. My teacher, Miss Annie Colburn, was very kind but the seating was painful. Problem was, with no school building in the community, the Methodist Church doubled as school during the week. We juniors were stuck in the church's gallery, where the seats were slabs of wood with no backs. Church-goers didn't have to sit there for six hours a day and it was fine for bigger children, but my feet couldn't touch the floor. We had no desks–a church didn't want school furniture taking up space.

I was stuck, squirming, on a hard pew. There was no way I could get comfortable. So, within a few days, I came up with a cunning plan. I told Miss Colburn I had to leave at noon, for my father needed me home by two o'clock to help get in the cows. For a week, I got away with this grand scheme. I'd sit with my classmates, eat the delicious lunch Sadie packed in my new lunch pail, then run home. It was only a mile and a half along the canal path.

A few days went by before Papa asked why I was home so early.

Truthfully, I replied, 'The teacher lets me come.'

A couple more days went by, with me continuing my 'escape-from-torture' plan. On the third afternoon my father said, 'Something doesn't add up, young man. Tomorrow I'm going to school with you to see what this means.'

I waited anxiously in the corner while he and Miss Colburn talked. I thought I heard them laugh, but I couldn't see their faces. Would I get a birching? Then Papa went home. All he said as he left was, 'Tonight, Johnnie, you come home at the same time as the other children. I won't need your help with the cows anymore.'

The teacher then called me to her desk.

'Johnnie, are you sorry you told such stories?'

I, taught always to be truthful, replied, 'No, ma'am!'

She turned away for a moment, making a muffled noise that turned into a cough.

She improved my seating as best she could and, in time, I learned to concentrate.

I was nine when the Goochs decided, in early 1839, that Saint Louis, Missouri, was the coming place. Their two married daughters and husbands agreed that, if the parents were leaving, they'd go with them. They asked if I'd like to go too. Of course! They were my family.

They sold their lovely canal-side farm and by early April we were ready to move. We took three days to load up the chartered packet that would transport us, and our household effects, the forty-five miles to Portsmouth. There, everything would be transferred to a paddle steamer for the longer journey–first on the Ohio River, then up the Mississippi to our new home in Saint Louis, Missouri. My job was to organize my fishing and hunting tackle. I also helped one of the farm workers make a special box for my dogs, for now I had two.

Sometimes the women looked tired and got a bit grumpy, but I was excited. I loved paddle steamers, and Papa told me we'd travel on at least two. We'd take many days, he said.

By nine o'clock at night we finally finished loading. We boarded, expecting to be nearly at Portsmouth by morning. The canal ran the length of the Gooch farm so our whole party–parents, daughters, sons-in-law and nine-year-old me, sat on deck to watch our beautiful home slowly disappear as the mules settled into their steady four-miles-an-hour pace. My mother wasn't the only one to wipe away a few tears.

We then went to our fold-down bunks, exhausted after such busy days. Imagine our surprise when we woke the next morning to find we were stationary and had only traveled fifteen miles.

'What's happened? Why aren't we moving?' I heard my father ask the packet captain as I clambered out of the narrow canvas bunk. 'I recognize this spot. We're still inside Ross County.'

'There's a break in the canal downstream. Sorry, sir, but we cain't go no further 'til they repair it. Help do be comin', I'm told. Hopefully, only a few hours.'

Papa came back down the steps into the cabin and saw me standing, ready to go up on the roof of the boat.

'You can hop off and play on the canal path, John. We'll be here awhile.'

This delay, keeping us still within the county boundary, had dramatic and life-changing consequences for me. Little did I know it, but this was the last hour of my happy childhood.

CHAPTER 5

1839 CHILLICOTHE

THE FAMILY HAD CARRIED their morning coffee to sit in the sunshine on the roof, and I was building a little fort of sticks for my lead soldiers on the side of the canal path, when we heard pounding hooves. Two horsemen were galloping toward us. As they grew closer, I saw one was William. How odd. I'd said goodbye to him only two days ago. I didn't know the other man.

As they dismounted, Colonel Gooch stepped across the gangplank and stood beside me, taking care not to stand on my fort or soldiers.

'Hello, Sheriff. And William. What brings you here at such a pace?'

Their horses' sides were heaving. Steam rose from their flanks and sweat dripped off them, making little puddles in the dust. Their rich smell reminded me of hours spent in the stables, grooming our thoroughbreds.

The men looked serious. William didn't greet me in his normal, jovial way. Suddenly I felt sick in the stomach. Something terrible was about to happen.

The sheriff spoke. 'Sorry to do this to you, sir, but I'm afraid I have to serve notice on you. You and your ward must accompany us to a hearing of the court–right now. It seems you're in breach of the terms of your guardianship by taking this child,' the sheriff looked down at me, 'out of the county, let alone out of Ohio and into a slave state.'

'What!! You're accusing me of not taking proper care of this precious child?' Papa grabbed me close, draping a protective arm around my shoulders. His voice rose in anger. 'He's like a son to us. We would *never* let harm befall him. And he's coming with us of his own free will. We gave him the choice.' I huddled so close to the colonel, I could feel him shaking with fury.

'I know you mean no harm, sir, but notice has been served. The court is in session today and they require your attendance–with the boy. We know you're moving from the district right now, but you can't leave until we settle this matter.'

'Who caused this interference?' the colonel angrily demanded.

William spoke. 'I did. I got to thinkin' 'bout it after I said goodbye to Johnnie the other day. Took my copy of the guardianship papers to a lawyer fella. He 'splained it all to me. You're breakin' the law to take 'im away. I know you an' your family done a grand job of raisin' 'im, but we cain't risk 'im goin' to a slave state. What if somethin' 'appens to you? 'Tain't safe for 'im.'

Colonel Gooch stood there, speechless. I looked up. I had never seen him so angry.

By then, the rest of the family had run down to join us. They heard the exchange. Mrs. Gooch pulled me to her, weeping. Virginia was crying as though her heart would break. A big boy of nine I might have been, but I couldn't hold my tears back. How could William do this to me? This was my beloved family.

The colonel was disputing the sheriff's demands. 'This is completely unreasonable. Our whole family is in transit. We've valuable stock on board, all our possessions are on this vessel, and you're expecting me to leave everyone and go back to town?' He glared at William. 'And how dare you question my honor!'

William didn't answer. Looked down at the ground.

'Sorry, Colonel,' said the sheriff. 'This will have to be settled in court. You and the child must come with me.'

Someone fetched a horse off the boat and saddled it. Papa mounted. I tried to hide behind Mama's bulky skirts, clinging to her. William dragged me, screaming, from her. Thrust me up behind my grim-faced father. Mama and Virginia cried out.

I matched their distress as we rode away, twisting backwards, reaching out to them. If I'd been able, I would have jumped off the back of the horse, but Papa held tightly to my other arm while managing his reins one-handed.

As their beloved faces grew distant, my father turned his head sideways to try and calm me. 'Hush, Johnnie. Please don't make this any harder. I hate doing this as much as you, but we must man up. There's naught for it; the law is the law.'

As we headed back to Chillicothe, William rode beside us, trying to talk to me. I turned my head away. Right then, I hated him. I sobbed quietly most of the way.

It was near midday when we finally reached the courthouse. A crowd of people–black and white–were shouting insults at each other. During the morning, word of the situation had spread. The blacks were all fired up. Someone had spread the rumor that Colonel Gooch was trying to kidnap me, that he was after my inheritance. The whites, who knew him to be a man of honor, were angry at such unjust accusations. The court was in session but the judge, a friend of the colonel's and knowing the family were already on their way, agreed to rearrange the docket and allow our case to be heard that afternoon.

No matter how much I wept and pleaded, the case went against the Gooch family and my wish to be with them. The lawyers William had hastily secured argued that the Goochs, in removing to a slave state, were putting me at risk, let alone that the colonel's authority as my guardian only applied in the state of Ohio, and the district of Ross County in particular. Unfortunately, the law was on William's side.

I only knew I was being torn from the arms of my family.

The court was left with a nine-year-old orphan boy on their hands. Two other decisions then had to be made.

They made William guardian. I suppose they figured he was concerned enough about my welfare to stop me from being taken to a slave state. That decision caused many problems in future years, but that tale will be told in its proper place.

The next problem was who would take me in, now they'd torn me from the only parents I remembered. William was a single man in lodgings and away from home all day with his carpentry business. Besides, I wanted nothing to do with him. Through term time, Charles, who had rooms in Chillicothe, was at school in Oberlin, 160 miles away in the north of the state. And because the legal paperwork said I had to remain in Ross County, Gideon in Cincinnati wasn't an option either.

I sat in the courtroom, heartbroken and sobbing, while a huddle of unknown men ripped my life to pieces. One thing they all agreed on, however, was that I should be with a family.

'Lad, would you like to go back to the home you lived in with the Goochs?' asked the stern-faced judge.

I nodded. I was frightened, confused, upset. The idea of being in a familiar place seemed like a glimmer of hope in a long, dark day, even if I couldn't be with the Goochs. Perhaps life would go on a little as before.

How wrong I was!

'The man who's bought the property, Mr. Richard Long, is an abolitionist,' explained one of the lawyers William had engaged.

'What's an abolitionist?' I asked.

'One who loves colored people and wishes them to be treated kindly.'

They sent someone to ask Mr. Long if he would take me on. He agreed.

So, less than twenty-four hours after leaving, I was back where I'd started, watching new people settle into my old home.

Nothing was the same. Mrs. Long was a pleasant and well-meaning woman, but Mr. Long was a very different stripe of man from Colonel Gooch. In going back to my old home, I'd supposed life would go on much as before. Big mistake! The new head of the household was a stern Presbyterian, originally from New England, who expected everyone, including his family, to work hard. He was also a very devout man. Lots of praying and no playing!

The first question Mr. Long put to me was, 'What, sir, can you do?'

I replied, truthful as always. 'I can't do anything.'

He looked at me, astonished. 'How do you expect to live?'

Equally astonished, I gazed back. What did he expect a nine-year-old to say?

One thing was clear. My leisurely life as a gentleman's son was at an end.

Mr. Long's highest praise of boy or man, including his sons, was that they were good workers. One of his lads was a gentle boy, but not practical. Took after his mother's interests in music, books, and art. Couldn't milk. Didn't know how to manage horses–neither to drive nor groom them. He couldn't chop, saw, or split wood. Didn't know how to do general farm work, and what was worse in his father's eyes, had no inclination to do such things. He caught the sharp edge of his father's tongue all the time. I got on better with his father than he did.

My first job was to drive a horse and wagon, hauling bricks from a kiln on a distant part of the farm to a new building in the yard. With my love of horses, it wasn't too hard to get into the way of it. By the third day, Mr. Long even praised me. Not long after my tenth birthday, in December 1839, I became the family's Sunday coachman, driving us all to church and Sabbath-school. And the farm manager, Mr. Long's nephew, whom he tasked with keeping me gainfully employed, was a reasonable man. He taught me to plow, hoe, and how to be useful around the farm.

In the house, the family always included me in their Bible study, praying, singing, and talk on spiritual matters. Luckily, Mrs. Long was regarded as one of the first ladies of the community, so living with them also exposed me to classical music and literary conversation. Although I missed the Goochs dreadfully, I was neither mistreated, nor did I suffer–on the outside. The practical farm work built my physical strength; the intellectual stimulation was good for my mind. However, life with the Longs was a serious affair. Inside, I felt lonely and unloved.

This state of affairs went on for nigh on two years. I no longer went to school. Instead, I was a laborer on the farm, unpaid apart from food and lodgings.

For the longest time, I was really sore at how William had upended my happy childhood. At first, I ran away to the back of the farm if I saw him coming to visit, but one day Mr. Long caught me doing my escape artist trick and forced me to be polite. Eventually, my attitude softened.

My lack of school attendance didn't bother William, for he'd had virtually no schooling, yet carved out a good living for himself. However, Gideon and Charles became increasingly concerned. They both knew our father had set funds aside for my schooling. Gideon and Charles applied to the Ross County Court to let me attend school in Cincinnati. It took some time, but finally, just over two years after the devastating split from my beloved Goochs, they were successful.

And so, again, others reorganized my life. This time, however, I knew what my brothers had in mind and there was no argument from me!

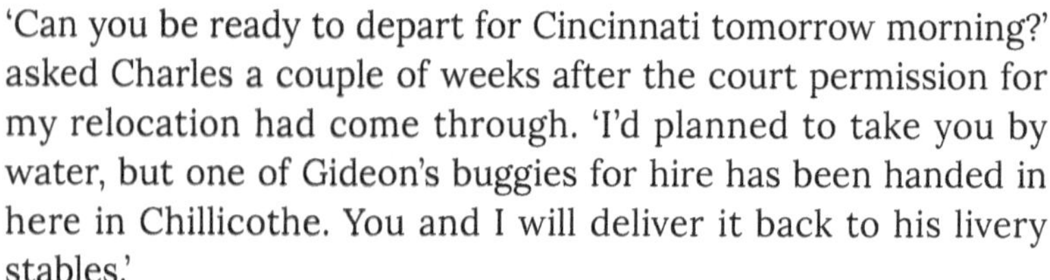

'Can you be ready to depart for Cincinnati tomorrow morning?' asked Charles a couple of weeks after the court permission for my relocation had come through. 'I'd planned to take you by water, but one of Gideon's buggies for hire has been handed in here in Chillicothe. You and I will deliver it back to his livery stables.'

Mr. Long clapped me on the shoulder as he left the breakfast table on the morning of my departure. 'Work hard, young Langston, and you'll amount to something.'

As Charles loaded my small trunk into the back of the buggy, Mrs. Long embraced me, taking care not to crush her elegant, full-skirted dress. Two of the younger children stood with her on the verandah and waved.

Once again, I was leaving the beautiful house on the banks of the Ohio-Erie Canal. But this time, there was no tugging of the heartstrings. No tears.

I was glad to go.

The one-hundred-mile journey to Cincinnati with Charles was an unexpected gift. The long two-day journey was the most time I'd spent with him since our exodus six years earlier.

The pair of good-looking bays jingled their harness and stepped out briskly in the pleasant fall sunshine. I was finally free of farm drudgery and new possibilities beckoned.

After a few miles, I started pestering Charles to let me take the reins.

Reluctantly, he handed me control. Within minutes, I'd convinced him of my competence. From then on, we took turn and turn about. All those Sundays driving the Longs to church had been useful after all!

We laughed, joked, and talked on many subjects as we bowled along. One of Charles' pet topics was how much he was learning at Oberlin Institute.

'But you're a grown-up. Why are you back at school?' I asked.

'I'm learning to be a teacher, John. It's the key to unlocking the poverty and ignorance that keeps our people repressed.' For the next hour, he talked passionately about the value of education.

Another question I had was the arrangements my brothers had made for me in Cincinnati. 'Will I live with Gideon?'

I hoped the answer was 'yes', for I was keen to spend time with my oldest brother. He was a tall, serious fellow with occasional flashes of humor and I knew he was deeply involved in helping runaway slaves, but did I know him? Not really. Once he moved to the big city and began his business endeavors, he seldom had time to visit me in Chillicothe.

Charles glanced my way, then back to the road as he guided the horse through a rough patch of road.

'I'm sorry, John, but he can't take you. Being a single man with two businesses, he's too busy to take care of a youngster. If he had a wife at home, you'd certainly reside with him, but after this last debacle, we both agree you deserve to be in a family of our own race.

'To start with, you'll lodge with Mr. and Mrs. Woodson. Then, when they get a vacancy, you'll move in with Gideon's close friends, the Watsons. They've a sizeable house and take in boarders. I hear it's quite hard to get a room with them. They treat their boarders like family and no-one wants to leave!'

This sounded promising. 'Do you know anything else about any of these folks?' I asked.

'I can only share what Gideon's written me, but I gather both families are leading members of the city's black community. Mr Woodson's a carpenter and joiner. Mr Watson, like Gideon, has two businesses—a flourishing barbershop, and also a bathhouse. I don't know either family personally, but Gideon vouches for them. He'll keep an eye on things, and you'll be able to visit him regularly.'

I felt a bit like a parcel, passed from hand to hand! But at least this change in my situation was finally giving me back my true brothers.

As we drove into Cincinnati at the end of the second day, I looked around me with some apprehension. It was known as the Queen City, but why? It was crowded, noisy, and smelly. After the pretty little town of Chillicothe, how would I ever adjust to living in this sprawling place with its dirty streets and squashed-together buildings? And so many people!

CHAPTER 6

1841 CINCINNATI

I QUICKLY FOUND I had no cause to be anxious about my new life in Cincinnati.

The Woodsons were genial hosts, and every morning I woke with anticipation, keen to get to school. What would I learn today? The black school was held in the basement of the Baker Street Baptist Church, and the teachers, Mr. Goodwin and Mr. Denham, scholarly white men, made me most welcome. I gobbled up learning like a drowning man after air. No longer were my intellectual horizons limited to the best way to plow a straight furrow, memorizing verses of Scripture, or soaking up random information as I served refreshments at Mrs. Long's entertainments.

The other benefit of my new location was getting to know Gideon better. With his firm chin, erect posture, and calm expression, he exuded quiet confidence and capability. At only thirty-two, was well on the path to being one of the wealthiest black men in Cincinnati. I was in awe of him, if truth be told.

One Sunday night, a couple of weeks after I'd arrived in the city, he invited me to dinner at his lodgings. Sunday was the only day he didn't open his barbershop.

'Tell me about our parents. I barely remember them,' I said as we sat in his cozy parlor. Even with the fire crackling to chase away the early fall chill, we could hear a blustery wind whistling around the chimney pots.

He gave the fire a poke and settled back in his easy chair before answering.

'That's a big topic, lad. Any specific questions?'

'Well, for starters, I sometimes hear people refer to the three of us as Quarles' sons. Why is our surname Langston?'

'Actually, I have Quarles as my middle name,' he said. 'When I turned twenty-one, Papa added it. He was proud I took after his side of the family in looks, temperament, and interests. But why Langston is our last name is a matter of the law. I'll tell it as Papa explained in one of my tutoring sessions.'

I looked at him in surprise. 'Tutored? You didn't go to school?'

'When I was much older, I took classes for a short time at Oberlin soon after their school opened. But when Charles and I were children, Papa was our tutor. From the time I was seven, every morning at 5 o'clock I had to show up at his office for lessons. Then he'd send me off to work in the fields with the slave boys my age. Papa wanted us to have practical skills as well as an excellent education. Eight years later, when Charles reached the same age, he began the same regime. Because I was the oldest son, Papa also taught me the business of the estate. But you asked about our name.'

'Oh, yes.' I'd become caught up in the story about tutoring and forgotten my original question. There was so much I didn't know!

'Our father was a very reluctant slave owner,' Gideon began. 'When he first became a plantation owner in Louisa, Virginia, he followed the example of his neighbors and purchased slaves to run his property. However, he grew to hate slavery. He believed owners should free their slaves, and he wanted to. Unfortunately for him, it was far easier to become a slave owner than it was to stop.'

'What did that have to do with us?'

'Patience, Johnnie. I'm getting there. It's important you understand the law on these matters.

'He acquired Lucy Langston as payment of a debt. To us children, she was just Mama, but I've heard people describe her as very beautiful when she was young. It wasn't too long before our father chose her as his companion. Her mother was a full-blooded Indian, from the line of Pocahontas, and her father had some African blood. In 1806, Papa freed her and our big sister, Maria, their first child. Maria was about twelve when I was born in 1809. Charles came along in '17, and late in their lives, you arrived in December '29. Because our mother was by then free, we were born free.'

'What about William?' I wanted to know.

'As you know, he's a half-brother. After she gained her freedom, Mama left the plantation for a time. Had three other children to another man. I don't know the whys and wherefores, but she then returned to the plantation, and we were born.

'Here's where the law comes in. Papa told me he would have married her if he could, but mixed-race marriages are against the law, as well as completely unacceptable in society. He didn't care about the scandal or how the tabby-cat matrons of the neighborhood would react. However, he did care what might happen to his family. He could have gone to prison, and the Lord only knows what would have happened to us if that had happened.'

Curious, I asked, 'Was that the only reason he hated slavery?'

'Not at all. He rebelled against the norms of southern society. He was a learned and thoughtful man who treated his slaves with respect and dignity, encouraging their self-respect and self-reliance. He used no harsh disciplines on our plantation and punishment was almost unheard of. I remember only one time when a young lad was given a whipping after repeated stealing. Papa associated closely with his slaves in a way none of his neighbors did. He hired no whip-cracking, harsh overseer to demand obedience and ensure profit. Instead, he gave his workers responsibility to manage themselves. Their chosen leader organized their work schedules and many of the farm details. Papa would have freed all his slaves if he could, but the law prevented that as well.

'When his management methods became known in the town, people scoffed. In the bars and clubs where men gathered, they laid bets as to when he would have to give up his nonsense. But our plantation prospered, and the bank manager was content. Father became one of the wealthiest men in the district, for he was an excellent businessman as well as farmer.'

I was agog with all this new information. 'Did they stop laying bets?'

'I believe so, though I'm told they were afraid his radical ways might plant seeds of discontent among their own slaves.'

'And did it? Make other people's slaves discontented, I mean?'

'Not that I heard. Papa was careful not to flaunt his unusual practices and success in the face of his neighbors. To be sure, he couldn't stop his workers talking to other slaves in the district when they got the chance, but he occasionally reminded them to be cautious about what they said. However, it wasn't the way he managed his slaves that made him a pariah in the eyes of the district; it was what happened indoors.

'No other white person lived on our plantation. Most men of his status in society, even if they had a Negro mistress and children of mixed blood like us, married a white woman. But he did not. Our mother was the only woman he wanted. As a result, apart from the homes of his nearby relatives and a few very close friends like the Goochs before they removed to Ohio, he was not welcome in the parlors and dining rooms of polite society in Louisa.'

'Did that bother him, do you think?'

'Not a jot. I'm sure our parents had a great affection for each other.'

'Tell me about them. ' I tried to squash a twinge of jealousy.

Gideon smiled. 'In the summer evenings, they often took a stroll around the garden, hand-in-hand. One particular time, when they were both still in good health, sticks in my mind. Something had caught Mama's eye. Papa leaned down—I have his height, while Mama was barely five feet, like Charles—to see what she was pointing at. She was wearing a yellow cotton dress with white lace and ribbons at neck and wrists. No bonnet. Having chatted about whatever she'd noticed, and about to step on, they shared a tender kiss. Mama lifted her hand and patted him on his cheek. I suppose I was about your age now—twelve or thirteen—and a little embarrassed to see my parents kissing, but I can still feel the love they shared.

'Papa was not one of those distant fathers who hardly bother with their children. I recall them often laughing at our childish pranks and the tricks our pets got up to. And in the evenings after dinner, we'd spend time in the parlor as a family. We'd play games and chat about the day's happenings. Often Papa would smoke a pipe while reading a book and Mama did embroidery or sewing. We made our own entertainments, and those who accepted our unconventional domestic arrangements regularly visited. We had a wonderful home until both parents became ill.'

'What else can you tell me about Mama,' I begged.

'I remember her as a contented woman,' he said. 'She hummed little tunes as she walked around or sat at her needlework. Often sat in the kitchen with our cook and the housekeeper, sharing conversation over the teacups. This is highly unusual in the homes of white people of substance; the mistress of a house doesn't socialize with her staff.'

'What did she look like?'

'There she is.' He pointed to the painting hanging near his dining table. 'This was on the wall in Papa's study.'

A smooth-cheeked young woman of comely proportions and high cheekbones, with tight black curls escaping from a topknot, looked down tenderly at a tortoiseshell kitten snuggled on her lap. Her pale green high-waisted dress highlighted her dark copper complexion.

'Oh, she's pretty.' A wave of longing washed over me.

Gideon looked sad. 'When they died within a month of each other, it was a great sorrow for everyone. It wasn't just we boys who were bereft. We'd lost our parents; the others on the plantation had lost their homes, security, and an excellent master. It was a truly terrible time. The future for us all was bleak and uncertain, for the estate had to be broken up and we all had to leave.'

'Why?' I was hungry for more.

My brother looked up at the mahogany-encased clock on the mantelpiece as it struck nine o'clock.

'Goodness, you should be getting to bed. Mrs. Woodson will have my hide if I don't send you home. School tomorrow. We'll talk more on these matters another time.'

A few weeks later, I was back again at Gideon's for dinner. His housekeeper, Mrs. Bird, served us an excellent beefsteak pie, baked parsnips and young greens. We were finishing it when the conversation returned to our early life in Virginia.

'Last time I was here, you said Papa wanted to free all the slaves, but the law prevented him. Shouldn't a man be able to do what he likes with his own property? Or at least free them in his will?'

Gideon frowned. 'You'd think so! But if he'd been too radical in his allocations, his will would have been challenged.'

'What do you mean—radical? And who would challenge it?'

'If he'd disposed of all his wealth by freeing all his slaves and giving everything else to his mixed-race children, people as far away as Carolina would have heard the uproar!'

'Why?' I was puzzled.

'Two reasons. First, Virginia had passed a law making it very difficult to free slaves. And second, his white relatives would have almost certainly taken the matter to law; they reasonably expected significant benefit. Note his clever compromise, Johnnie, for it may serve you in years to come. He could bequeath a portion of his wealth to us, but not all. Instead, he also left a lot of property to his nephews. This meant they had no just cause to contest the will. If he'd done as he really wanted, and they'd challenged it, the court would have almost certainly granted everything to them. We could have ended up with nothing. The one thing he wished, above all else, was that we have the education and the means to earn a good living.'

'Well, I don't like those laws. They're unfair. I think I'll be a lawyer when I grow up and get the lawmakers to change them.'

Gideon laughed. 'Good luck on that, little brother. Blacks don't become lawyers. There's no such thing in this country.'

I tucked that information away. I hated being told I couldn't do something.

'So how *did* he arrange matters? I've never been told.'

'By the time he died, Charles and I already had some education, and I was well-advanced in useful business skills. We would have managed even if he'd been unable to leave us anything. For you, however, it was a very different matter. You were only a couple of years out of clouts and still in the care of Lucky, your nurse.

His wisdom secured your future, John, and you must make the most of it. Once you reach your majority, you'll have far better resources to call on than almost all your classmates.

'He left we three boys one of his farms, with its livestock and other farm-related items, plus all his cash and a portfolio of shares. The rest of his land and possessions, including the slaves he couldn't risk freeing, he gifted to his nephews who lived nearby. However, he had them agree not to split up the slave families.

'Your inheritance is being held in trust until you reach twenty-one. Charles and I received ours at the same age. That's how I could set up my barbershop and livery stables. It's no small thing to purchase a string of horses and a selection of conveyances for hire.'

'Did he leave anything for Maria? I don't know anything about her.'

'She'd left home long before you came along and was already well provided for. Papa taught her to read, and other useful skills. Then, when she was of age, he gave her a plantation. He also bought and then gifted her Joseph Powell, the slave she wished to marry. Their family is thriving.'

Gideon gave a big sigh. 'I still miss our parents, even after all these years. It's been good to talk about them. I'm glad you asked, Johnnie.'

'I'm glad too,' I replied. 'The Goochs occasionally mentioned them, but as I grew older, I never thought to ask more. As far as I was concerned, I was a Gooch. After the court dragged me away, I began to wonder, but there was no point in asking the Longs. They didn't know our parents or anything about our history. William has shared a few memories of his childhood in Louisa, and told me a bit about Mama, but very little about Papa or the things you've just explained. I've been wanting to know more for ages.'

Just then, Mrs. Bird came in with a delicious plum pie. The conversation turned to school, then it was time to go home to my host family.

CHAPTER 7

1841 CINCINNATI

Although I'd had some little school mates when living with the Goochs, I'd lost touch with them once I was placed in the custody of the Longs. No more frivolities. No more play. My childhood vanished like early spring blossom after a storm.

My new situation changed all that. I quickly made friends. Alf Burnett was one such.

I first met him through Underground Railroad business.

Soon after my arrival, Gideon had said, 'Would you like to earn some money, Johnnie?'

I was keen. I'd never had cash in my pocket, but now I was walking past shops every day and wishing I had pennies to spend. The following Saturday, I began working for my future landlord, Mr. Watson. The work was varied. Sometimes I was at the end of a broom, or shining shoes, or running errands in his barbershop. Other times I'd be picking up towels and cleaning at his equally popular bathhouse. Mr. Watson paid me, and I was also allowed to keep my tips. The best barbershops, like Gideon's and Mr. Watson's, attracted the cream of white Cincinnati society.

One morning, while I was sweeping the scatter of hair and whiskers around Mr. Watson's chair, a well-built white youth, about sixteen at a guess, came in. Although his curly mop of brown hair could have done with a trim, he didn't take a seat.

Instead, he walked purposefully toward us. Mr. Henry Boyd, a well-respected black businessman who manufactured quality beds, was having a shave.

I glanced up as he approached and noticed a look of alarm flick between the two men. Before the youth could open his mouth, Mr. Watson said to me, 'John, here's young Alf Burnett. Probably come to see if you'd like to go fishing. Take him out the back and give him a drink of water while you have your chat. He looks like he could do with it.'

For a fraction of a second, I was perplexed. In the nick of time, with both men trying too hard to look normal and the boy looking confused, I cottoned on. Gideon, the Woodsons, the Watsons, Mr. Boyd and others I'd met since living in the city were conductors on the secret network known as the Underground Railroad. They helped many slaves escape to Canada. Some white folks were also involved, the Burnetts among them. I'd seen this boy behind the counter as I looked in the window of their confectionary and bakery on Fifth Street. I'd also read his father's name in the papers Mr. Watson took for his customers to read. The pro-slavery *Enquirer* and the *Cincinnati Daily Gazette* described him scathingly as a trouble-maker and a 'damned abolitionist'.

Perhaps this Alf was bringing a message about a delivery. I beckoned him to follow me.

As soon as we got into the back room, I whispered, 'Whatever you were about to say, I think Mr. Watson wants you to tell me.'

He stuttered for a moment. 'But I don't know you.'

'I'm John Langston, Gideon's brother. I know your family are friends to our people.'

He was standing there, indecisive, when we heard Mr. Watson say loudly, 'Excuse me, Henry. I don't think John can reach the water jug.'

He walked in, bent low so only Alf and I could hear him, and said, 'Alf, have you got a message for us?'

The young fellow nodded.

'Don't say anything here. Sheriff Doty is waiting his turn out there. I'll send John over shortly to get it. You can trust him.'

Then, in a carrying voice, he said, 'Here it is, boys,' and bustled back to his anxious customer.

That was the beginning of a grand friendship. A couple of young fellows with fishing gear were invisible to suspicious slave-catcher eyes. We ran many errands that helped get frightened, exhausted runaways on the next stage of their dangerous journeys. It was no hardship to be down by the Ohio River with a fishing pole and a humorous friend. Sometimes we caught fish, though we didn't try too hard if we had to sit downstream of the filthy effluent flowing into the river from the many pork abattoirs. No wonder our city was scathingly nicknamed Porkopolis!

One day we got into a conversation about our futures.

'What would you do if you weren't selling cakes and candy?' I asked Alf.

He looked at me in surprise. 'That's a mighty fine question! It's always been expected that Burnett men be bakers.'

'That's not what I asked,' I replied. 'What would you *really* like to do?'

'I won't ever be allowed to do what I really want,' he said, looking sad.

I waited. When he didn't reply, I tried a different tack. 'What do you like best about what you do now?'

'That's easy,' he said. His face lightened. 'It's the people. It's always jolly in the shop. I enjoy giving the old biddies a laugh, entertaining the children with my silly faces, and flirting with the maids sent to do the shopping.'

I grinned. 'I've seen you do it.' You've got such a rubber face—people can't help laughing when you do your naughty impersonations.'

He chuckled. 'Like this?' He poked his fishing pole firmly into the bank and turned to face me. 'Here's our minister.'

Puffing up his cheeks, he lowered his chin to make a fat neck and hunched his shoulders. 'He's so boring! I keep awake by watching his mannerisms and thinking about how I can copy them.'

I giggled.

'And this is Mrs Worthington. She's always poking her nose into other people's business. Mean as a snake. Not popular in the neighborhood.'

Pretending to hold a basket in one hand, he hobbled a couple of steps, his mouth pulled tight as a drawstring bag. He stooped forward and squinted his eyes into gimlets, giving me a nasty glare.

I laughed out loud. 'More, more!'

He grinned. 'That's what the customers say. Sometimes, when I've a young family in the shop and the children are begging me to pull my faces, Samuel comes up from the bakery to see what all the racket's about.'

'You're such a comedian, Alf. Have you thought about being an actor?'

'You've found me out! I would dearly love to make a career on the stage. But my Mama would hatch a canary if I attempted such a thing. Thinks actors are the spawn of the devil and I'll go straight to hell if I even step foot on a stage. She's such a hypocrite. She enjoys going to plays and other stage performances. Just doesn't want anyone from *her* family to be on the other side of the lights.'

I made sympathetic noises.

He sighed. 'I really *really* don't want to be stuck behind a counter all my life, John.' He picked up my fishing rod, serious again, but continued to unburden himself.

'Mother doesn't know it yet, but I've started going to a Drama Club every week. We read plays and perform scenes. They've asked me to take part in a public performance and I'm dashed well going to do it. The proceeds are going to an Orphan's Fund she supports. She won't be able to stop me for fear her friends will think she's mean. And I'm constantly reading works by great playwrights. Going full chisel in my study of the craft of acting. Even quote lines from plays for the customers when it's appropriate.'

'Keep on it, Alf. Maybe one day you'll get away from your mother's apron-strings.'

Then he turned the tables on me.

'What about you, John? Have you given any thought to your future?'

'Indeed. Something in the professions is what I really want to do. Maybe a lawyer. I so admire Mr. Chase. He goes out on a limb for us blacks. If only I could be like him. People take notice of attorneys.'

'What about that! A most noble ambition!' Just then, his line jiggled. He flexed the rod. Just an opportunistic nibble. He went back to my last comment.

'Can blacks be lawyers?'

'I don't know,' I replied. 'But I intend to find out.'

CHAPTER 8

1842 CINCINNATI

I T WAS SATURDAY, ABOUT a year after I'd located to Cincinnati, and I was now living with the Watsons. As well as attending school through the week, I continued to work every Saturday for Mr. Watson at either his barbershop or bathhouse. Barbering was a profitable business for black men and he and my brother were two of the best, and wealthiest, in our big city.

We were having an early breakfast together and Mr. Watson and I were due to head off to work in ten minutes.

'You're looking rather down-at-mouth, son. Anything wrong?' he asked as he buttered a piece of toast.

I took a deep breath. Rubbed my left ear, a habit when faced with troublesome matters. Tried not to cry. At nearly thirteen, I wanted to be manly. But, a sneaky tear escaped.

'What's the matter, dear?' Mrs. Watson shifted chairs. Wrapped me in a motherly hug. That didn't help. More tears joined the first.

'Goodness me. What's happened?' Now they were both worried. I'd been living with them for some months and they'd never seen me like this.

'I miss the Goochs,' I sobbed.

They looked at one another. 'What brought this on?' asked Mr Watson.

'Colonel Gooch came to see me yesterday.'

'Wasn't that a good thing?' said Mrs. Watson. I nodded, but was too upset to explain.

Mr. Watson pulled out his pocket watch and frowned. 'Tell you what, sonny. Take the morning off. I don't have time right now to sort this out, but you're clearly not the bubbly young fellow we like to see. Can't have you frightening my customers with your doleful face, can we now!' He said the last with a smile.

'See if you can get to the bottom of the lad's troubles,' he asked his wife as he rose to his feet, smoothing his well-fitted suit and adjusting his bowtie in the mirror over the highly polished walnut sideboard.

As he walked out into the hall, I heard him greet a couple of other boarders coming in for their breakfast.

'Come with me, love,' said Mrs. Watson, quickly whisking me through the other door. In the hallway, she said, 'Let me sort something in the kitchen, then let's have a chat. Would you like to wait in the parlor, or go back to your room for a couple of minutes?'

I wiped away my tears. 'Thank you, but I'll go for a walk. I might call on my friend Alf. He always makes me laugh.'

When I reached the Burnett family's shop on Fifth Street, I found Alf wiping fingerprints off the big glass jars of candy on their counter. I'd often seen small children poke grubby fingers at their favorites. Every morning, one of the staff had to wipe off the children's love marks.

'Good morning, Johnnie. No work today?'

'Mr. Watson gave me the morning off.'

'How come?'

'He felt sorry for me.'

'Why?' Alf sounded surprised.

I said nothing. Scuffed my feet on his wooden floor. Tried not to cry again.

He took a closer look. 'You don't look like your usual happy self, buddy. Will a candy help?'

I shook my head. 'No thanks.'

Now he looked really worried. I'd never turned down a sweet before.

He leaned over the counter, tipped my chin up, and looked at my sad face.

'Out with it, Master Langston. Something's up. Tell Uncle Alf.'

I placed my elbow on the counter, propped my face on my hand, and took a deep breath.

'Yesterday, I was working on my arithmetic when Mr. Goodwin called my name. Said there was someone to see me. This surprised me, for the teachers are really strict about interruptions during class. I immediately feared something was wrong with Gideon or Mr. Watson. But no. When I stepped outside, there was my old foster father, Colonel Gooch. I'd not seen him since I was nine.'

'I don't know anything about this Colonel Gooch. Was that not a good thing?'

'It was wonderful to see him after so many years. We had a grand talk.'

'So why the long face?'

I struggled to speak. Another unwanted tear threatened to spill out.

'Hold up, youngster,' he said. 'Sister Sarah will be here right soon. We've a delivery of confectionery to make across the Miami Canal–I was going to send one of the apprentices, but you and I'll do it and you can start from the beginning.'

Sarah bustled in moments later and was easy to convince. I think she liked me too.

'I'll be back as soon as I can, but get Thomas up from his baking to help if you get too busy,' Alf said over his shoulder.

Down in the hot kitchen we stepped carefully around the men, one kneading a large white blob of dough, another throwing wood into the wide jaw of the hot stove, and the third stirring a tall pot of what smelt like toffee. Together we grabbed the handle of the already loaded cart, and set off down the back lane and into the crowd of Saturday shoppers heading to the nearby Market House.

Once we were clear of the crowd, he said, 'So what's the story about this colonel fellow?

I took a deep breath. Explained about the Goochs, my life with them, and how the sheriff snatched me from their arms as we were on our way to Missouri.

'I just miss them all so much. Seeing my dear foster father yesterday has right cast me down. You're so lucky to have your family. I've only got Gideon here, and I can't live with him.'

'At least you're in the same city, and you see him often,' said Alf. 'And the Watsons are good to you, aren't they?'

I nodded. 'They surely are. Look after me like one of their own.'

Conversation paused for a moment while we swerved to avoid a smelly heap of pig droppings and a team of pigs running to a fresh pile of vegetable scraps. A housewife had just thrown a basinful out her door. Then, speaking loudly as the cart rumbled over a patch of rougher cobbles, Alf said, 'I can't understand the logic of taking you from the Goochs. From everything you've said, they only had your best interests at heart.'

'I know they did. It devastated me. I understood later, the big problem was their new location. If some tragedy happened to the family, such as Colonel Gooch dying unexpectedly and his property sold, there was a real danger that, without a powerful protector, I could be kidnapped and sold into slavery, even as pale-skinned as I am.'

'I've seen that happen in this city, and we're not even a slave state. It's terrible,' said Alf grimly. 'The first time was a light-skinned girl, dragged out of Dumas House on McAllister Street by four filthy-mouthed slave catchers. She and the people who knew her kept shouting she was free, but the bastards ignored them. No-one dared get near their whips, guns and snarling, snapping bloodhounds. If such a thing can happen in free Ohio, how much more likely for it to happen in a slave state like Missouri? If there was a risk of that happening to you, John, I regret to say, William did you a kindness.'

I let out another sigh. 'Yep. Reluctantly, I now accept he was worried about my safety.'

While I'd been engaged in my tale of woe, we'd crossed the bridge over the Miami Canal to the German part of the city. The smell of richly seasoned bratwurst wafted out from a butcher's shop. Inside, I could see a glowing brazier with sausages sizzling. The window displayed fancy cuts of raw beef and pork, several glazed hams, and many types of sausages. I'd been too upset to eat breakfast and the delectable aromas were hard to ignore, but Alf headed for a shop two doors along.

'Here we are, John. Mr. Hagen's grocery.'

'Guten morgen, young Mister Burnett,' boomed a big-chested fellow with a cheerful face as we pulled the cart into his shop. Colorful displays of bottled sauerkraut, tins of herrings and sardines, a vast range of mustards and sauces, and many other delicacies loaded the shelves behind him. Below the shelves were large pull-out bins with flour, sugar and other dry goods. In pride of place on the highly polished wood counter sat large almost-empty jars of chocolates, bulls-eyes, peppermint sticks, licorice, and lollipops.

Mr. Hagen patted the counter. 'Just load them here, danke. Straight in the jars they will go. Very popular are your sweeties, even if not German specialties.'

He carefully counted out the paper bags of treats and made a note on his ledger; it tallied with Alf's reckoning.

As we left the shop, Alf stopped. 'How about we get a sausage, Johnnie? I reckon you've worked up an appetite now.'

Sharing my story had eased the knotted black hole in my stomach. Suddenly I was hungry. I nodded gratefully.

As we headed back across the Canal, each munching a spicy, moist sausage, Alf returned to our subject.

'John, what happened after the court said you couldn't go to Missouri?'

I told him the rest of my sad tale and ended up with yesterday's unexpected visit.

'So, was it a happy visit? What did Colonel Gooch have to say?' Alf asked.

'It was fantastic! I was beyond delighted. Mr. Goodwin gave me leave to step out of class and, for the next two hours, we stayed on a seat under the elm in the yard. It was wonderful to feel my father's arm around me again. We exchanged news. He'd returned to Chillicothe on business related to the final settlement of his property and, naturally, inquired for me. Imagine his surprise, after all the fuss of making me stay in Ross County, to find I wasn't there.

'The family is doing well in St Louis, Missouri, but he said the sad spot in their happiness is that I'm not with them. That fair warmed my heart, I can tell you. His message from Mrs. Gooch and Virginia was that they demand I come and visit just as soon as ever I can. I promised I would once I was old enough to take charge of my destiny.

'Then he had to go. The pain of being dragged from my beloved family and thrust into the care of strangers came flooding back as I watched him walk away. I tried to be brave about it, but I couldn't stop crying. It seems I've turned into a leaky tap this last twenty-four hours! I asked my teacher to be excused for the rest of the day with a sick headache. Truth to tell, it was a sick heartache. And I woke up this morning no better.'

We'd been rolling the empty cart down Vine and the junction of Fifth Street was up ahead. Alf slowed down. Turned to me.

'Johnnie, that is some tale! You've lost not just one set of parents, but two, yet in all this time we've known each other, this is the first time you've said anything. I'm in awe of you, my young friend. You're tough; you'll go far.'

It *had* helped to tell Alf. After a generous snack in their family kitchen, I headed to work with Mr. Watson.

PART TWO

CHAPTER 9

JULY 1843 CINCINNATI

I WAS WITH GIDEON on Sunday afternoon, July 30, 1843, when a message came for him to attend an Underground Railroad emergency meeting in half an hour. It was to be held at what most of us still thought of as the Burnett's shop, though it was now run by Alf's brother-in-law, Samuel Alley. Alf's oldest brother, Joseph, the previous owner, had sold to Samuel before taking his family back to England in 1842, but most of the Burnett family still worked there, including Alf.

Two days before, a mob of men had tried to break into another white abolitionist's home to recapture a runaway slave girl they thought to be sheltering there. The determined band of abolitionists repelled the attack. The mobsters then decided to teach a lesson to the man they believed was the leader of the resisters—none other than Alf's father, Cornelius Burnett.

'We'll fix that bloody Burnett once and for all,' their leader, Scanlan, had been heard to say. 'He's the ring-leader. Let's get across to Kentucky and find some more fellas to deal with him. Stealing our niggers has to stop!'

The black community was abuzz with the drama, and Gideon had been expecting some such invitation. I went with him—in any Underground Railroad activity there were almost always jobs for nimble youngsters.

White-haired, big-beaked Cornelius Burnett chaired the gathering.

He looked at us all from under his bushy eyebrows. 'Thanks for coming, everyone. We don't know when it will happen, but we've heard they're raising a mob in Covington and Newport. We must prepare for a siege. What youngsters have we?'

Eight hands went up, including mine and that of my school friend, Peter Clark. His father was another successful black barber.

Mr. Burnett nodded approvingly. 'Could you lads, in twos for safety, immediately get out round the streets to be our eyes and ears?'

We all nodded, delighted to be part of the excitement.

He continued. 'Especially keep a watch on the Public Landing. If you see a posse assembling on the Kentucky side, or rowing across, run back to us like the Devil's on your tail. Also, look round town for any men gathering. If you can get close to any groups of rough-looking fellows, try to eavesdrop. But avoid attention. Don't put yourself in danger. Let us know of *anything* that might be helpful.'

I teamed up with Peter. The streets were quiet–nothing to report. We checked in as night was falling and found pails of water and sand to put out fires, planks and boards ready to reinforce doors and block windows, barrels with ammunition, and a stash of rifles. Upstairs, large piles of bricks and rocks were in each room, ready to rain down on attackers' heads.

'What's your job, Alf?' I asked him as he dashed by with a bucket of rocks.

'I'm in charge of the Brickbat Brigade upstairs. I can't wait to teach those bastards a lesson,' he said fiercely. 'Remember last time, Johnnie? No more hiding in terror. This time we're *not* running away.'

Peter looked at me in surprise. 'Last time?'

Just then, Gideon spotted Peter and me. 'We've got men on the street patrols for the night, boys. Time for you two to go home. You can get back out again in the morning; I'll square it with the teacher.'

'Will we be here to help defend the building?' I asked.

'No. It's been agreed that none of us colored folk will do that. If we're spotted, they'll come for the black homes and businesses if they can't break in here.'

As we walked back to our homes, Peter asked again, 'What was that about last time?'

'He's referring to the 1841 riot.'

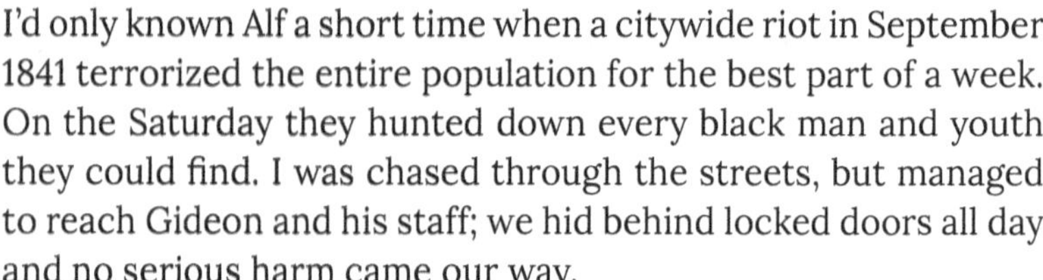

I'd only known Alf a short time when a citywide riot in September 1841 terrorized the entire population for the best part of a week. On the Saturday they hunted down every black man and youth they could find. I was chased through the streets, but managed to reach Gideon and his staff; we hid behind locked doors all day and no serious harm came our way.

We were some of the lucky ones, though everyone in the black community suffered. Men were imprisoned, women shamefully treated, children terrified, and homes and livelihoods damaged, sometimes beyond repair. Even though they were free, many families left for Canada or other locations. They were afraid to risk further hate-fueled attacks.

The mob targeted white abolitionists too, and first on the list had been Alf's family. Apart from Dr. Gamaliel Bailey, editor of *The Philanthropist*, the abolitionist newspaper for Ohio, Cornelius Burnett was one of the most strident advocates in our city for the end of slavery. He never backed down from an argument and was constantly in the press, speaking out for black rights.

During the riot, the Burnetts suffered as much as any of our black community. The mob completely trashed their home and business. Alf, at the time only sixteen, had to look after his mother and sisters. His father, brothers, and brother-in-law, Samuel, at the time the printer of *The Philanthropist*, ran for their lives. Friends hid them for ten days before it was safe to return. They had to use the escape routes they'd set up to help others, and vigilantes and bloodhounds came close to discovering them several times. If they'd been caught, they would likely have been killed.

The mob tried to capture Dr. Bailey, but he was out of town. However, the printing press he paid to produce his paper was an easy target. The mob trashed Samuel's premises on the same night as his in-laws' property, smashed his machinery to smithereens, and threw it in the river. It nearly broke him financially.

In the eyes of many of the civic leaders and businesspeople, the greatest sin of the abolitionists was the impact on the commerce of the city. With the slave state of Kentucky only a few boat lengths across the Ohio River, Cincinnati flourished when slave owners, bringing their personal slaves, came to town. When they took their business elsewhere, for fear their attendants would run away, the businesses of the Queen City lost income. As a result, many townspeople hated Cornelius Burnett, and the pro-slavery press constantly vilified him.

In the two years since the 1841 riot, freedom fighters of all skin colors had become more organized, and we were part of it. Exciting? Yes. Scary. That too. But we were glad to help.

Peter and I went back straight after breakfast the next morning. We knew the situation was serious, but it was also fun wandering the streets as we watched for trouble spots. Finally, late afternoon, we heard raucous shouts from down near the river. We ran to investigate. What we saw there had us turning tail and running up the cobbled streets to Alley's in Fifth Street.

We burst into the shop. 'They're coming. Ten boats, full of men waving weapons, just left Covington, and another six boats are rowing over from Newport. And we've spotted rough-looking men, carrying sticks and implements, heading down to the landing. Looks like they're waiting for the reinforcements from across the river.'

'Thanks boys. Champion work,' said Mr Burnett, who'd been at the shop all day, checking details and keeping track of reports. 'Go straight home now. We don't want your blood on our conscience.'

Reluctantly, we did as we were told. We knew we'd be in big trouble from multiple sources if we didn't obey. The danger to the entire black community was too serious.

For three days, fifteen determined men and lads defended the bakery against two thousand. Guns pointing at them from every window, every sortie repelled, a constant barrage of rocks and stones on their heads–finally, in disgust, the mob gave up.

We colored folk breathed a collective sigh of relief when they dispersed. Perhaps they'd run out of steam; they didn't vent their anger on the black community—this time.

And what help did the besieged defenders get from the civic authorities? Nothing. The police were a disgrace. Most were supporters of the anti-abolitionists, and happy to let the violent mob create mayhem. Their strategy rebounded on them, however. Every time the authorities failed to keep the peace and freedom of speech was threatened, it brought more right-thinking people over to the abolitionist view, and the Ohio Anti-Slavery Society gained more members.

CHAPTER 10

SEPTEMBER 1843 CINCINNATI

A FEW MONTHS LATER, Gideon called in to see me at the Watsons' well-furnished brick home. We'd finished dinner and were in the large family parlor. Mrs. Watson and her daughters were mending garments or doing embroidery. Along with three other student boarders, I was bent over my homework at the circular table near the window. We spent most of our at-home evenings together in this spacious room, the heart of the house. Some of the adult boarders regularly joined us, as did close friends of the Watsons.

Mr. Watson looked up from reading *The Philanthropist* as Gideon was ushered in by the maid.

'Gideon, how pleasant to see you. Is this a social call or are you here on other matters?' This was code for our illicit Underground Railroad activities; had that been Gideon's purpose, he'd probably not have sat down.

'Tonight I'm here on family business, my friend,' Gideon replied.

I dropped my pencil and jumped up with delight, then paused. At nearly fourteen, I was too grown-up to run across the room for a hug; the other boys might tease me for childish ways. Instead, I walked across the room to offer him my hand.

'Ruthellen,' he said, turning to Mrs. Watson, 'I declare you're feeding this boy growing beans! He's grown half-an-inch since last week!' She gave us her generous and motherly smile.

'Soon you won't be able to pat me on the head, brother,' I replied, stretching to my fullest height. 'Look, I'm up to your shoulder.'

Laughing, he tousled my curls, flung a casual arm over my shoulders, and led me to a chintz-covered sofa.

Once courtesies were out of the way, with him balancing a cup of tea, he turned to me.

'John, I suspect this won't be news you want to hear, but you need to go back to Chillicothe.'

I looked at him, surprised. 'Do you mean for a visit? To see William? Are you coming too?'

He looked awkward.

'No to all those questions, I'm sorry. The court allowed me to bring you to Cincinnati for school, though technically it was outside the letter of the law. I hoped they'd allow you to stay longer, but they're now saying that to protect your inheritance, you must go back to live in the county in which your guardianship is vested, at least for a year or so.'

'What! I don't want to go!' I wailed, momentarily forgetting my dignity. 'All my friends are here. I'm one of the two top boys in my class. And I'm *not* going back to live with the Longs.'

'The Longs we agree on,' he said firmly. 'You're not going back there to be his farm boy, no matter how godly the man.' He sighed. 'My heart is heavy, and it's not what I want, but return you must. The law is the law.'

Mr. Watson chipped in. 'What will happen?'

Gideon frowned as he rubbed his glossy, well-trimmed black beard. 'Basically, the court requires him to have a guardian in the county nominated in the will , or John risks losing his inheritance. That we won't allow. And he's supposed to be living under the care and observation of that guardian.'

'So, who should it be?' I asked. 'William? Charles?'

'William's the only option,' replied Gideon. 'He has your best interests at heart, John, and Charles is still away studying in Oberlin. I have a concern, however. William's not one for advanced schooling. Thinks you've already had enough. Says at almost fourteen it's time you were making your way in the world. I don't agree, but he's a hard man to argue with. He can't read and write himself, but he had his pastor compose a very firm letter on the matter.'

Yet again, my happy world was tumbling down around me. 'It's not fair, Gideon!' I burst out. 'I really enjoy school. I don't want to go. And where will I live?'

'We all agree you should be in a family. It can't be either William or Charles, with them both in lodgings and Charles away much of the year. William's good friends, Mr. and Mrs. Harvey Hawes, whom he describes as a warm-hearted elderly couple of our race, are delighted to board you in their home.'

He glanced over to my hostess, listening to our conversation with some concern. 'You've been a wonderful foster-mother to him, Ruthellen. I trust Mrs. Hawes will be as kind as you.'

I bit my bottom lip to stop it quivering. It wasn't fair. Yet again, William was tipping my life upside down.

'I understand the importance of securing his inheritance, Gideon, but limiting his education?' said Mr. Watson. 'He's a quick learner and has an excellent brain. Is there any way you can persuade your brother to let him continue his studies?'

Gideon looked glum. 'William's almost as immovable as Niagara Falls when he's set on a course.'

'What's the schooling like at Chillicothe?' asked Mrs. Watson.

'Pretty basic, I'm afraid. That's why I insisted he come to Cincinnati. At their colored school, the children only get a teacher in the winter, when it's difficult for them to earn pennies to help feed the family.'

'I know this is common in smaller places,' said Mr. Watson, looking even more concerned. 'So many of our people can't afford to educate their children at all, and this winter term scheme at least gives them basic book learning. But with your father's bequests, that's not an issue for our John. It's ridiculous to take him away from an excellent school to go to an inferior one.'

Gideon sighed. 'You're preaching to the choir, friend. But, to be fair, many of us haven't had much formal education. Look at you and me—we've done alright. Barbers with excellent clientele and other businesses, as well as the properties we own. We make far better livings than probably 90% of the white people in this city. Although our father gave Charles and me an excellent grounding, I only had one year of formal schooling at Oberlin, when I was an adult.'

'I hear you, Gideon,' said Mr. Watson, 'but we mustn't let that be the reason we don't constantly strive to raise the standard. Until our children are properly educated, our people will always struggle to take their rightful place in society.'

While the adults in the room debated the merits of practical skills versus higher education, I sat, miserable at yet another upheaval looming over me.

A few weeks later, with a sorrowful heart, I prepared to farewell my many Cincinnati friends.

The two families who'd opened their doors to me, the Woodsons, who'd boarded me for the first few months, and the Watsons, promised I'd always be welcome if I could return. My teachers, looking sad, said many kind things. And I couldn't leave without bidding farewell to Alf.

Mrs. Watson, knowing my wish, sent me to collect some delicacies from Samuel's shop; she'd ordered them for my farewell dinner.

Sarah was at the counter when I arrived, asking for my friend.

'Hold there, John.' She left the counter for a moment, and I heard her call down the stairs for Alf.

A minute later he walked into the shop, brushing floury hands on his white canvas baker's apron. I took a good look as he approached, knowing it might be a long time before I saw him again. He was quite the young man about town now, with his broad shoulders, twirly mustache and square-jawed friendly face.

We stepped out into the fall sunshine to chat.

'So, will you continue with your schooling or become a working man like me? You're just the age I was when I started working here.' He waved at the shop behind me.

'My brothers are arguing about that. William thinks I've had enough education. Gideon and Charles disagree with him. But they can only get him to agree to school for the coming winter.'

'What do you want?'

'To continue my studies, for sure. I love learning.'

Alf looked bemused. 'Sooner you than me, my young friend. Tell me about this new school. Will the teacher be as good as Mr. Goodwin and Mr. Denham?'

'I'm told so, at least for this coming winter. Until now, the Chillicothe Colored School had to make do with whoever they could get, but now they hire student teachers from Oberlin Collegiate Institute. According to Charles, school trustees around the region compete for Oberlin teachers; they're very knowledgeable, even though not qualified teachers.'

Alf asked, 'But if they're still students, why aren't they also in school?'

'It's the Oberlin way. They want their students to have practical knowhow *and* an excellent education. With no classes in the winter term, they're free to hire themselves out. This way they earn enough to pay for the next year's classes, as well as learn useful skills. Some go teaching, others work on farms. Whatever work they can get.

'I'm told my teacher will be George Vashon. He's expected to be the first colored man to graduate from Oberlin with a degree.'

'I've heard good things about Oberlin,' said Alf. 'Both the school and the philosophy of many of its residents. You know it's regarded as a safe destination for runaways, as well as those who need a safe haven before continuing on to Canada, don't you?'

I nodded. 'I do. And not just fugitives. My brothers were the first two blacks to have some schooling there when it started, and Charles has just done a further two years. They want to send me there one day. They'll have to persuade William, though.'

'I can see you graduating in a few years, buddy. You'll be too smart for poor old Alfie Burnett.'

He hunched his shoulders, made a gloomy face, and said in a whiny voice, 'Mr. Langston, don't you remember me? Your boyhood friend, Alf. I know you're such an important man now, but for old times' sake, please may I shake your hand?'

I laughed at his antics. 'You are a silly. Of course I'll always remember you.'

'I wish you all the very best,' said Alf, reverting to his normal cheery look as he shook my hand. 'Advanced studies were never for me, but you're such a diligent scholar, I predict you'll go far, my friend.'

As I walked away, I wondered sadly if we'd ever go fishing together again.

CHAPTER 11

WINTER TERM 1843 CHILLICOTHE

'HERE BE YOUR DINNER box, John. Aunt Patsy's packed you some of last night's pecan pie, given as you love it so much. I declare that woman looks after you like you her own grandbaby! Too bad if I'd wanted it for *my* midday dinner.'

I looked up from tying my shoelaces, concerned at Mrs. Hawes' words. She saw my anxious face and gave her jolly belly-laugh.

'I be teasing you, son.' She patted her well-padded hips. 'We'll not go hungry in this house, not while Aunt Patsy's in charge of the kitchen. You run along to school, dear. I wish you well for the geography test.'

I thanked my kind landlady, picked up the dinner box and schoolbooks off the hall table and scampered down the steps of their small brick home. She'd offered to accompany me on the first day. I politely but firmly refused! I was on the skinny side, but I didn't want to start off being teased as a weak ninny.

Now into the second week, I'd made a couple of friends, though I'd known none of my classmates when I arrived; they hadn't attended the white school in the Methodist Church. And people who'd known me as Johnnie Gooch didn't seem to recognize me now I was one of the Langston boys and living with a black family. Had I changed that much in four years?

As I walked along the road, I thought about what William had said a couple of days earlier.

'You're a man now, John. This winter term I'll let you 'ave, but don't get any ideas of more schoolin'. I'll not have it said that my brother cain't do an honest day's work. Over-edicated fellows spend too much time indoors. Soft hands, soft muscles, too much talk and not 'nuff action.'

'I'm well used to working hard,' I'd replied crossly. 'I worked long days for Mr. Watson–nearly every Saturday 'til close to midnight in one of his businesses. It was always busy. Often, we barely had time to eat.'

He humpfed into his bushy thick beard. 'Mebbe. But dat weren't physical work, like buildin' things.'

I thought of all I'd learned with Mr. Watson. He insisted on excellent customer service. Plus, I'd become well informed on political matters by listening to the men talking. Lathered up and relaxing in a barber's chair, or soaking in the bathhouse, they had time to talk over the small doings of the week, as well as the bigger issues. As a result, I'd become well-informed about the politics of not only Cincinnati but also the nation. When the Watson businesses were closed, I'd learned even more as staff discussed what we'd heard and how the topics of the day affected our race. The same thing happened at home.

I didn't bother saying this to William.

He continued his rant. 'Mr. Long got you in good work habits when you lived wiv 'im, and I don' doubt you earned your keep at the Watsons. But now you old enough to earn a proper livin', not jus' tips rich folks throws you.'

I quickly settled into the new school. It was my teacher, Mr. George Vashon, who made it special. Some of the older students had looked sideways at such a young man, for he was only nine-teen–a year or two more than the oldest of us, but in days the grumbling stopped.

It wasn't his pleasant manner and kind eyes that drew us to him, so much as his sharp mind and the ideas he exposed us to. I couldn't wait to get to school in the mornings. Even the reluctant learners sat up and listened. Like Alf, he knew how to capture our attention, but while Alf used his comic faces and impersonations to entertain, Mr. Vashon engaged us with gripping tales of ancient heroes. He even made their orations interesting as we learned the basics of Greek and Latin. His teaching talents didn't stop there—regular subjects such as mathematics, geography and English were also alive and interesting, at least for me.

School had been going about ten days when I dropped by William's carpentry shop one afternoon. The tangy smell of paint and fresh-cut wood met me as I opened the door.

He looked up from pushing a hand tool across a thin plank of golden wood. Smiled.

'Come in, lad. I was wonderin' when you'd come by. Put the pot on the stove and we'll 'ave a brew. I'll jus' finish dis 'ere planin'.'

As the tea brewed, he dusted off a couple of stools.

'So, how's dis fancy teacher doin'? Learnin' anythin'?'

I went into raptures about my new hero. William frowned.

'Greek and Latin! Humph! Does it 'elp anyone earn an honest dollar? Don't be thinkin' to follow in his footsteps, little brudder. Come spring, you're comin' to be my apprentice. Don' go fillin' your head with foolish ideas 'bout dat high-falutin' learnin'. Dat's for the whities, not the likes of us. We cain't do nothin' wiv it. Cain't vote. Cain't get fancy jobs. What's the use?'

I looked at him, horrified. 'But I love learning. I don't want to be a carpenter.'

William didn't like that. He muttered something rude. Just then, a customer came in, inquiring about a cabinet. I quickly finished my tea and left, slamming the door angrily on my way out.

I raced down to Charles' lodgings. Now twenty-six, he'd finished at Oberlin just as my classes began. He was taking a break before beginning his long-planned-for teaching career. His face darkened as he listened to my story.

'Leave it with me, John. I'll write to Gideon. Between us, we have to persuade William of the folly of his plan. What a nuisance the court appointed him as your guardian. With him the only family member here at the time, I daresay it seemed logical. We're suffering the consequences now, that's for sure!'

With that, I had to be content. I trudged home to Mrs. Hawes. The sparkle had vanished from the day.

Three days later, Charles arrived at school as we were doing our end-of-day tidy-up. One of my friends, Jeremiah, was coughing from chalk dust as he cleaned the blackboard and I was putting books away. Other fellows were stacking our chairs on the battered old tables, emptying trash cans, and sweeping the floor. Charles waited at the back of the room until Mr. Vashon dismissed class, then stepped forward, signaling for me to wait while he talked to the teacher.

'George, it's good to see you in my hometown,' I heard him say. I looked up in surprise at the greeting. I had no idea they were friends. 'Do you like our new school building? John's host, Harvey Hawes, and I helped build it a couple of years ago. The black community of Chillicothe is very committed to giving our children the best education we can.'

'I really appreciate it,' replied my teacher, looking around the large room. 'It's great working in a classroom designed for that purpose. Many schools, even for white children, make do with churches and often don't have proper desks.'

I knew that from personal experience!

They continued to chat for a few minutes about things and people I didn't know, then Charles asked, 'How's my brother doing? Behaving himself?'

Mr. Vashon gave me an encouraging wink before replying. 'He's a pleasure to teach. I wouldn't be surprised if he tops the class, even though not the oldest.'

I tried to look modest.

Charles nodded. 'How do you think he'd go in the Oberlin Preparatory School? Do you think he has the makings of a scholar? And could he continue into the senior academic program in due course?'

'Absolutely. He's bright. Picks things up quickly. The standard of his work is excellent, and he's looking set to become as good an orator as you.'

Now it was Charles' turn to try looking modest. He brushed the praise aside. Turned the topic back to me.

'I'm wondering if you'd come to dinner at John's lodgings next week. Our half-brother, William, who's his guardian, is fixed on John having no more schooling after this winter term. Wants him to work for him in his carpentry business. I've tried talking to him and he won't listen. So, we need all our ammunition. You'd be a valuable ally. We *must* change William's mind.'

Mr. Vashon frowned. 'Of course I'll come. For John not to get higher education would be a waste of God-given talents. This boy has the makings of a lawyer, or doctor, or some other high profession.'

A spark of excitement ignited in me. Could I?

Aunt Patsy outshone herself with a splendid dinner of roast pork and all the fixings, followed by a peach pie. Afterwards, the Hawes escorted us three Langston brothers and our guest to the parlor, which in their house was not the regular room the family sat in after dinner. With a cheery fire and the curtains drawn against the early winter chill, it was a pleasant enough room, though a touch too formal to be relaxing.

'We'll leave you gentlemen to your discussion,' said Mr. Hawes. Charles had given them the nod that serious matters were to be considered.

At first my brothers went toe-to-toe, for and against my having more education. Charles was the more eloquent, but they were evenly matched in stubbornness.

'William, our little brother's got a good brain. It would be a crime not to give him a chance to further himself. Think what a well-educated black man can do for the future of our race.'

'I seen too many of our kind 'ave hopes smashed by whities that don' let 'em use their skills,' said William. 'Better not to 'ave 'is hopes raised, jus' to be crushed into the dust by rules and laws fixed so's only white people succeed.'

'I don't agree with you, brother,' said Charles. 'It's less than ten years since James Calhoun sneered at our intelligence. At Oberlin, his crass comment is held up as a goad to push us to study even harder.'

William frowned. 'Since I've not the benefit of your fancy edication, you best 'splain your meanin'.'

Mr. Vashon, who had requested I call him George at home, tried to settle the tension between the two.

'Many people don't know this, William, but it's commonly quoted at Oberlin. A few years after Calhoun became vice-president to John Quincy Adams, while addressing an audience of white men, he said: "If I can find a Negro who knows the Greek syntax, I will then believe that the Negro is a human being and should be treated as a man".'

William scowled. 'What an arrogant divil! But what's that to do wiv our Johnnie? And what's the point o' Greek anyways?'

Charles picked up the thread. 'A classical education is the basis of all our higher learning academies, William. Anyone who can write and read both Greek and Latin is regarded as fit to serve in high office, and to take on positions of responsibility for state and other governance.'

'Fancy learnin' don' make a man more or less worthy. An' if we ain't got the vote, none wiv even a tinge o' black blood'll ever git any govmint job,' countered William. 'For the life of me, I cain't see 'ow fancy learnin'll put more bread on the table than a good craftsman, or even someone who cin run a business profitable-like. Look at Gideon. He only 'ad one year o' learnin' at your precious Oberlin. He's makin' a fine livin'.'

Gideon wasn't able to attend the meeting, but he'd written. Charles read the letter out. 'As the oldest son of our father, I know he wished John to receive a good education. He set money aside for it. I request you let him attend Oberlin Preparatory School.'

William scowled. 'The courts made me the lad's guardian. It be my job to decide what's right for 'im. Your father ain't here, seein' what I see every day. I don' want 'im beaten up for ideas 'bove 'is natchil place in life.'

The three men debated back and forth for some time. The more Charles and George spoke of the benefits of education, the more William became entrenched in his opinion. I sat there saying nothing, alternating between hope and despair.

Finally, George said, 'What say we ask the lad his preference?' He turned to me. 'What do you want to do, John?'

I didn't wish to upset William, for I'd be working with him through the summer and, as my legal guardian, he had the final say on my future. Also, deep down, I knew he wanted the best for me, according to his way of thinking. But I yearned for Oberlin; it had become a siren song to me.

I leaned towards him, pleading with my hands, my body, my words. What could I say that might help change his mind? I thought of the debating skills I'd learned at school in Cincinnati. The teacher always told us to use story and practical examples to open people's minds.

'I know your workmanship, William. Everyone says you're more a craftsman than a plain carpenter and joiner. Suppose you've been commissioned to make a table. You've got quality wood that, if cut correctly and put together with care, will become a work of art, showcasing your skill. You'd use the best piece of wood, with the most attractive grain, for the top. And, for the legs, you'd look for straight grain and strength, wouldn't you?' He'd explained this to me on my first visit to his workshop.

I paused. He nodded.

I continued. 'It's the same with us. We all have unique skills. I hazard I'd only make an average carpenter, for I don't have a natural aptitude for tools. However, I do have a love of learning and I pick up new knowledge fast. My brain and memory are my particular gifts; your hands and design abilities are yours. I *really* want to continue my education. Please, William.'

He slumped back into the chair. I couldn't work out whether he was disappointed in me, or worried about me. For a moment, he said nothing. George and Charles looked at each other, eyebrows raised, but kept quiet.

I tried one more time. 'I remember very little of our parents, but I'm told that both of them stressed to those left to raise me, that I was to be given every opportunity to realize my potential, whatever that might be. If I've been blessed with a gift for study, don't you think it would be wrong to ignore that? Putting me to manual work would be like using the fine-grained wood for the legs of the table.'

With a sigh, William said, 'I think they're right 'bout your speechifyin' skills, young fella. Here's what I'll agree to. We'll talk again after your winter school term. Then, ifn you still wanna keep on wiv this edication nonsense, I'll allow a year at Oberlin. That should be plenty o' time to knock this Greek and Latin nonsense out of your head.'

The three months passed quickly. I had stiff competition from my fellow students to be top of the class, for almost all were diligent with their studies. I was thrilled when Mr. Vashon gave me the honor of addressing the assembled families, school trustees, and interested parties at the close of our school term. Charles and William came, and Gideon traveled from Cincinnati to attend.

As the four of us walked back to the Hawes' place after the event, I rejoiced when Charles said, 'You have in you, John, all the elements of an orator.' Even William gave praise.

CHAPTER 12

MARCH 1844 OBERLIN

THURSDAY MORNING, MARCH 1, 1844, dawned cold and wet, but I didn't mind. I was leaving Chillicothe yet again, but this time it was by my choice! I was off to Oberlin with my teacher, George Vashon, returning for his final year.

Conflicting words from my brothers floated around in my brain as we boarded the packet boat that would take us, via the Ohio-Erie Canal, to Newark, Ohio. At Newark we had to take to the roads.

William stated firmly as he farewelled me the night before. 'It's for one year only, Johnnie. Don't get no fancy ideas 'bout a fancy edication. You'll thank me in years to come that you'll 'ave a useful trade.'

I'd buttoned my lip. Had he known it, his resistance lit a fire in my belly to prove him wrong. I *would* succeed.

The next morning Charles said to George, as he bade us good-bye at the landing stage, 'This lad is smart and promising, and should be as thoroughly educated as might be. I trust you to ensure he's in the right classes.'

George nodded. 'You can leave that with me, my friend.' I noticed a significant look pass between them.

Four days later, I wasn't so jaunty.

The first two days, by boat and coach, were reasonably easy traveling. However, a day south of Oberlin, our problems began. The snows had not long melted, washed away by heavy rain. The roads were deep in mud and almost impassable.

We dismounted at Mansfield on late afternoon Friday, expecting to take another coach north to Oberlin the next day.

'Sorry, young fellas,' was the response when we ducked out of the steady rain and entered the coaching depot to book our passage. 'Roads be closed. No coach'll get through 'til the rain's stopped for at least a day. Mebbe longer. Ye'll have to wait it out here.'

'Oh no! We have to be at Oberlin by Sunday latest. We start school on Monday,' exclaimed George. 'There must be some way of getting there.'

The man behind the desk scratched his head. 'Weeell, only two things I can suggest. Either hire a horse each, or a wagon and team.'

'We've got our trunks. It'll have to be a wagon.'

He directed us to the livery stables. Thankfully, they had a couple of strong work horses and a suitable wagon available.

I looked up at my guide's anxious face as he paid. 'Can we afford it, George?' William had allocated enough funds for our planned mode of travel, but there was precious little for extras.

He shrugged. 'We've got no choice. I can dip into my earnings from this last winter, and I'm sure your guardian will reimburse me. Here's hoping the rain eases overnight, or we're in for an uncomfortable day.'

Early next morning, as rain beat a tattoo on the tin roof of the stables, we watched while the ostler harnessed the horses and hitched up the wagon. In went our heavy trunks. Mine carried schoolbooks Charles had given me on long-term loan, as well as my clothes for the next nine months, carefully packed by Mrs. Hawes and Patsy.

As the burly stableman threw a heavy canvas over our trunks, George asked, 'Do you have any waterproof capes we can also hire? We've got our heavy coats, but we didn't expect to be traveling all day in the rain.'

Thank the Lord, he did!

By five o'clock, with not even the cocks crowing, we drove out of Newark. George was at the reins, and I perched beside him on the wagon bench. I won't ever forget that day! Twenty hours and forty-eight miles later, we finally drove into the dark and sleeping town of Oberlin–cold, wet, and exhausted. We headed to the town's only reputable hotel. It took a while for the host to respond to our desperate banging. At one o'clock in the morning, he looked less than enthusiastic to find two drowned rats and a tired team of horses on his doorstep.

⁂

Oberlin was a surprise.

I'd assumed we'd lie abed that Sunday morning to recover from the rigors of the journey, but no. Loud chatter from the street below woke me from a deep sleep. I hopped out of bed to discover a crowd of people below, all dressed in their Sunday best, moving in both directions on the boardwalk set above the muddy street. They chatted to their companions and greeted passers-by as if this was a normal occurrence.

I turned to my companion, who was stirring. 'Is there something special going on, George? Why are so many people out on the street at this hour of a Sunday morning?'

He rubbed his eyes open. 'What?'

'The noise outside. All the people. Why?'

He reached for his timepiece on the bedside table. 'Nearly nine. Oh, they're off to prayer meetings and Sabbath-school. And we need to get up. We must be in church by half ten.'

I yawned, looking longingly at my pillow. I was still tired. And stiff.

He grinned. 'Welcome to Oberlin. This is a normal Sunday. I can see I've not explained enough about the way of things here. The founders built the community upon Christian principles, worship, and right living. Sundays are devoted to prayer and church and only a very few godless people ignore that expectation. It's those foundations that make it possible for we of color to gain an education equal to any college in the land.'

By half past ten, we were entering the doors of First Church. Here I was in for another surprise. The early morning crowd was nothing in comparison with the many hundreds of students and residents who poured in.

I caught a whiff of freshly sawn timber as I entered. 'Is this building new?' I asked George, looking around in awe at the vast space.

'Indeed. It wasn't quite finished when last year's commencement was held. They've been working on it through the winter term, I see. With the growth of the town and school, every building we'd previously used for worship, or big events like commencements, quickly became too small. This can seat 2,000 and squeeze in another 500 at a push. We've already seen it full.'

My first day passed in a blur of new experiences. The mighty hundred-voice choir stirred my soul. A scholarly-looking fellow, whom I later learned was Professor John Morgan, gave a powerful reading of the day's scripture lesson. And then Rev. Charles Finney, whom even I had heard of, kept the congregation transfixed for an hour and a half with his sermon .

I confess to being glad when lunchtime came. Then, forty-five minutes later, to my surprise, back to church we all went for more of Finney's spell-binding oratory. I had never heard such preaching. At the finish of the service, I walked away in silence, overcome with the power of his words.

That first day in Oberlin made a lifelong impression on me.

CHAPTER 13

1844 OBERLIN

MONDAY WAS AS OVERWHELMING as Sunday, but more as I'd expected.

'First, I'm taking you to meet Mr. Hill,' said George. 'He's the treasurer and secretary of the Institute. He'll take your money and organize your study program.'

I was here—at the college of my dreams!

The imposing entrance of the administration block struck me with awe; I was used to the humble building of our Chillicothe Colored School.

We were ushered into a cluttered office. The bespectacled man behind the desk looked up with an abstracted air, which instantly switched to a beaming smile when he saw my companion.

'George, great to see you back. Your final year, hey? Incredibly significant for you and the college! Our first colored graduate. And who have we here?'

George pushed me forward. 'I've brought you a promising youngster for the Preparatory School, sir. John Langston, brother to Gideon and Charles.'

Mr. Hill shook my hand warmly. 'It's a pleasure to have another Langston with us.'

Courtesies exchanged and fees sorted, Mr. Hill then asked, 'What branch of study do you plan to take, John? The English one, or Latin and Greek?'

I took a breath, about to ask a question. As I hesitated, George quickly spoke up. 'Latin and Greek, starting straight away.'

In that brief exchange, they arranged my future. Had William been the one to enroll me, the choices would have been vastly different; my mentor deliberately ignored William's edict that I was there only for one academic year. Along with advanced arithmetic and algebra, Bible studies and rhetoric, George set me on the path taken by students preparing for examination and entry to the regular College course.

The next and equally important detail was my housing and care. Charles had arranged that I board with a mathematics teacher, Professor Whipple, and his family.

As we approached a picket fence and turned in the gate of a wooden two-story house that spread over most of the lot, George said, 'John, I know you're a sensible lad. You'll do well in this home. The Whipples are generous and upright people. They have several other student lodgers. Apart from you, there's only one other colored person, a young lady, living with the family, but you'll find that of no consequence in this house.'

He was right.

I'd been well looked after by William's friends, the Hawes, and loved them for their generous care of me. They were people of a similar education and life experience to William. The Whipple household was of a very different stripe. Here, education and culture were the norm.

To my delight, their daughter was taking the same classes as me. At least I'd know one person when I started the next day.

Mrs. Whipple showed me to my room on the second floor, my trunk was delivered, and then it was time for dinner. At the table, I found myself seated between my hostess and a lady teacher. I felt shy and tried very hard to make a good impression by not eating when the ladies quizzed me about my history. To my embarrassment, they asked so many questions I couldn't finish my meal before a maid cleared the table. But within a day or so, the shyness evaporated; everyone was inclusive and encouraging. I soon ate and talked with the same ease as my housemates.

My first week at Oberlin passed in a blur. Overwhelmed, I was grateful when George invited me to take a walk the following Saturday.

'George, I keep hearing Cincinnati mentioned. Are some of the staff from there?'

'Indeed. Our president, Reverend Asa Mahan, and Professor Morgan, whom you heard in church last Sunday, are two who used to be part of Lane Theological Seminary in Cincinnati. And a good number of our first students also came from there. You must know of the Seminary, surely?'

'Oh yes. Everyone in Cincinnati knows of Lane, up on Walnut Hills. Dr. Beecher is president. I've heard him preach. And my friend, Alf Burnett, sometimes took me when he was delivering special cakes for functions at the Beecher household or the Seminary.'

'Do you know about the revolt they experienced in 1834? It nearly caused the seminary to close.'

I looked at George, startled. 'No! It's a theological college. What kind of revolt?'

'The students and some of the professors decided to put on a series of debates. The topics were about the evils of slavery, freedom of speech, emancipation of all slaves, and the pros and cons of colonization. But their choice of subject wasn't popular in some quarters. It became known as the Lane Revolt. This is what I know about it.'

1834 Cincinnati

'What do you mean by staging these debates?' The roar of combined fury from the trustees of Lane could just about be heard across the river in Kentucky. 'You have no right to threaten the commerce of our city in this way!'

The seminary students stood their ground.

'You, sirs, have no right to try to muzzle us,' retorted Theodore Weld, the students' charismatic leader. They were half-way through their scheduled eighteen lectures and debates, had established an Anti-Slavery Society and pledged to work on *"the minds of slaveholders [with] the truth, in the spirit of the Gospel"*. They also wanted to improve the lot of the colored people in Cincinnati.

The men who formed the hastily convened special sub-committee of the Lane board weren't backing down either.

'Do you have any idea how your ill-conceived ideas threaten the very foundations of not only our society, but even the safety and funding of this college?' bellowed the chairman. 'You've chosen a fine time to spring this nonsense on us, with Dr. Beecher and half the faculty away on summer vacation. And you're causing disruption in the town. This city relies on friendly commerce with our friends from the south. Abolition of slavery is **not** a suitable topic of discussion at this institute. We've only narrowly avoided being mobbed by the riffraff of the city because of your actions. Not appropriate behavior, sirs. We will not tolerate it.

'Here are the terms this committee has agreed on. If you want the privilege of being educated here, you will obey them, starting now!'

1. No further discussion about the policies of the Colonization Society.

2. No mention of immediate emancipation anywhere on campus, including in students' rooms—it diverts students from their studies.

3. No more public debates.

4. Your campus Anti-Slavery Society is to be abolished and no other such societies are to be formed.

5. From now on, your focus is to be only on your own studies instead of working in local black schools and helping the black community in other ways.

6. Professor John Morgan is dismissed. He has usurped his authority in supporting this dangerous nonsense.

Weld and his supporters were furious.

'Wait 'til Dr. Beecher returns. He's never forbidden us to discuss the plight of the blacks. Surely, he'll see this is God's work we must do. Slavery is an evil curse on this land.'

They misjudged. The next full meeting of the trustees ratified the interim decision.

'That's it! We're leaving. Those terms are unconscionable,' was the decision of the Lane Rebels, as they'd become known.

Thirty-nine scholars, Reverend Asa Mahan, the one trustee prepared to publicly side with the rebels, plus Professor Morgan, now without a job, began their own school a few miles away.

Oberlin, tucked away in the wilds of Northern Ohio's Western Reserve, had been struggling for funds, staff, and students. The founders, Reverends Shipherd and Stewart, had begun the community in 1833, only a year before the Lane Revolt, and quickly attracted other hard-working and intrepid pioneers, many from the Eastern states. The shared vision was to create a Utopian, plain-living settlement free from the vices and temptations of larger towns and cities. Many also shared an abhorrence of slavery.

Rev. Shipherd soon found his way to the Rebels with a proposition.

'If we agree to come to your institute,' said fiery Theodore Weld, once again spokesperson for his seminary friends, 'we must have freedom of speech, be allowed to discuss slavery and abolition in any way, and blacks must be admitted as students.

'You've said you need a president. Our Rev. Asa Mahan will make an excellent appointment for that position. Also, our Professor, John Morgan, must be given a faculty position. Lastly, we want you to invite the Rev. Charles Grandison Finney to take up the theology chair. He may not want to leave his pulpit in New York, but, given the aims of your establishment, he might accept the call.'

It took time to negotiate these wide-sweeping and radical conditions. The idea of blacks being educated side-by-side with white people, even in such a liberal town as Oberlin, stuck in the craw of many. The trustees, residents, and students were frightened of an influx of people markedly different from themselves. Throughout the country, people believed blacks weren't equal to whites in intelligence, physical stamina and ambition, and weren't capable of sharing political and social equality with whites.

The problem was, even the unconventional settlers of Oberlin with their enlightened (or unusual, depending who was speaking) views on so many things had limited experience of relating to blacks on an equal footing. But Weld and his cohort were inflexible. It was all or nothing. Money helped too; wealthy New York abolitionists, brothers Arthur and Lewis Tappan, sweetened the deal with serious funds if the institute accepted the conditions.

It took nearly a year, but the Oberlin trustees, by a majority of one, finally and reluctantly agreed. Thirty-two ex-Lane students, including Weld, and supporters Mahan and Morgan, were installed. Within two years, the institute had become 'abolitionized'—every man and woman in the school was, to some degree, committed to the cause of ending slavery.

'So, now do you understand why Cincinnati is so often mentioned, John?' asked George. 'A number of the Lane Rebels are still here in some capacity, as well as Professor Morgan and President Asa Mahan. And you already know, because you've heard his sermons, they got their wish with Rev. Charles Finney.'

I looked up at my mentor, a head taller than me. 'That's amazing! A lot of white people put their careers on the line for us blacks and our right to education.'

He added a note of caution.

'Not everyone in the town is against slavery, as you'll find if you're here long enough. However, this town is one of a handful of places anywhere in the United States where we blacks are encouraged to rise to our potential. Neither the town, nor the institute, existed when your father died, but if it had, I'm sure he would have specified you and your brothers were to be educated here.'

I grimaced. 'That would have stopped all the trouble with William! Never mind. I'm here now, and will do my darndest to make the most of it.'

The nine months of 1844 passed in a blur of work. I studied hard, and that fall I bade goodbye to friends and teachers. I so wanted to come back next year.

But—the obstacle was still my guardian.

CHAPTER 14

WINTER 1844-45 CHILLICOTHE

CHARLES HAD WRITTEN JUST before the end of school. 'When you get home, come and have a two-week holiday with me before William puts you to work.'

I was still enjoying that welcome break when Charles received visitors. A deputation of colored men from Hicks Settlement, eight miles out of town, came seeking advice, for they knew him as a advocate for black education. They'd hoped to have their community school open from the first Monday of November through to the end of January, but time was running out.

I was reading in the next room and the door was ajar, so couldn't help but hear the conversation.

'We cain't find anyone to teach our childun,' I heard one man say. 'We ain't wealthy folks and cain't afford much, but we can promise ten dollar a month an' lodgin's. Each family'll take a turn to house an' feed the teacher for a week.'

'I'm really sorry, but I don't know anyone suitable,' said Charles. He didn't add, 'that would be prepared to work for such a low salary,' but I'd heard him discuss teacher salaries; I knew that was nothing like the going rate.

For a moment, there was silence. Then another fellow asked, 'Ain't your young bruvver just back from Oberlin? What 'bout him?'

'He's had an excellent year at the best school in Ohio, but he's too young–not quite fifteen. And he's small for his age. What about the discipline? How can he be expected to manage a class of children? Many of the students will be bigger and some older than him.'

'We can promise the girls an' boys won't give 'im no trouble. They be diligent childun, an' keen t' learn. He'll just 'ave to hear recitations an' teach 'em the basics o' spellin', writin', readin', sums, an' geography.'

'Well, let's ask him,' said Charles.

He called me into the room.

They put the proposition to me. Me–a teacher! The idea began to bubble. I would certainly know more than the students. I'd had an excellent grounding in debate at Oberlin that year. Knew how to carry an argument. The men watched my face, hopeful. They saw my growing interest.

'Charles, I reckon I could do it. And William won't demand I work with him if I'm earning something.'

Charles was right in one thing. I *was* the smallest in the classroom, bar one boy, but the men were right too—the behavior of the students was exemplary. The children soaked up the lessons like dry land after rain, excited to be learning. Perhaps they were also glad not to be at their normal tasks in the harsh winter weather. Our simple classroom, which doubled as their church on Sundays, was kept well supplied with firewood and every few days, one of the parents stopped by to make sure we had sufficient supplies. I wondered if they also came to make sure I was up to snuff with teaching and discipline, but kept that thought to myself.

The one thing I wasn't over-thrilled about was having to move lodgings each week, for I quickly realized I'd be sharing beds or bedrooms with my students in their humble and mostly cramped homes. Still, that was the way of things in many working-class homes, not just those of color; I figured I'd get by. And then, into the second week, I had an unexpected visitor.

I had just set the class some arithmetic problems when I heard a noise outside. Even on tiptoe, I couldn't see out the small high-set windows, so walked on to the porch to investigate. A stranger was tying his horse to the hitching rail. Knocking the mud off his boots as he reached the top of the steps, he introduced himself.

'Morning, young sir. I'm John Jackson, one of the elders of this community.' That he'd ridden rather than walked suggested he was more prosperous than many of his neighbors.

'I've a proposal for you. My son be too small to walk to school, for we live five mile from here. An' I want to improve my readin' an' understandin' of the Bible. If I give you board and lodgin' for the rest o' your time wiv us, an' care an' stablin' for your horse, would you school us at home? It'll save you the inconvenience of havin' to move each week, and I've a bigger house than some of our folk. You'll have your own room at my place.'

The arrangement worked well. Every morning before leaving for school I gave Mr. Jackson and his son a lesson and exercises to do during the day. After dinner, we reviewed the day's work, and once their younger children were in bed and his wife was sitting with her needlework, he and I would discuss the meaning of the scriptures we'd read together after dinner. My horse, or, more correctly, Charles' horse, was housed in a well-built stable and I was delighted to have a bed to myself–no more wriggling children kicking me in the night.

Every month, one of the three men who'd engaged me came to inspect the school and bring my wages. Because the state of Ohio made no contribution to schooling for colored children, the people of the settlement had to find every cent of the ten dollars. My pay arrived in small coins, mostly five- and ten-cent pieces, which made it seem like a larger amount than it really was. I didn't mind. I was proud to see the pile of coins grow. And grow it did, for I had nothing to spend it on.

Some weekends I visited with either Charles or William, a short ride away in Chillicothe, but others I stayed at Jackson's place and caught up with lesson preparation and marking, and worshiped with my students and their parents on Sundays. I loved being with these good people. Many couldn't read and write, but they hungered for their children to have better opportunities. The tiny contributions each family made to my salary were hard won, for most earned very small wages. It deeply reinforced in me the immense value of education as the only way our race would rise from poverty to prosperity.

With only a brief break for Christmas, which I spent with my brothers, the winter term passed quickly. Finally, Graduation Day arrived.

Once the children had finished their recitations, songs and other presentations of work, family after family came up to shake my hand. 'John,' they repeatedly said, 'we're so glad you came to us. Our young 'uns done good.'

I rode back to Chillicothe, well pleased with my first experience as a country school-teacher and carefully carrying my big bag of coins. I couldn't wait to tell Charles how well I'd done. He looked amused.

But another surprise was coming round the corner. I'd only been home with Charles a few days when Mr. Deveaux, that winter's teacher at the city's colored school at which I'd been a student the year before, came looking for help.

He said to Charles, 'I'm in urgent need of help, Langston. My Pa is near death, and I must go. They're many miles the other side of the state, and my Mama has sent urgently for me. I expect I'll be away from school for two weeks, maybe three at the outside. Could you step in for me?'

Charles replied, 'I'm truly sorry for the situation. I would help if I could, but my other responsibilities prevent me. However, I have a better idea. My young brother is the teacher of the family now. He tells me he's very good at it. The students at Hicks Settlement have apparently made remarkable progress under his tuition.'

Deveaux turned to me. 'John, I'd be most grateful if you could help. I'm plumb out of options.'

'I don't know,' I demurred, embarrassed by Charles' not-so-subtle scoffing. 'I was their classmate only a year ago. There's a few I didn't get on too well with. They used to tease me for being a know-it-all. And,' pointing at myself, 'you can see I'm not exactly a big fellow. I'll still be smaller than your older students. I doubt they'd take me seriously.'

Mr. Deveaux ignored my protests. It seemed he really was desperate. 'I'll pay you ten dollars a week,' he said, 'and I'll give the troublemakers two weeks' vacation. You won't have any problem with the others.'

My jaw dropped. Ten dollars for a week's work, where I'd had to labor a month to get the same amount at Hicks! It sure was tempting. If the ratbags who'd bullied me were on leave, it might work.

To my delight, the two weeks went very smoothly, except for one smart but very naughty small boy. He refused to sit down when asked, repeatedly pulled the girls' plaits, and was a general disruption in the class. I had to do something or my control of everyone was in jeopardy. A conversation with the birch hanging by Mr. Deveaux's desk sorted him out.

I was delighted to finish the winter with fifty dollars, useful experience, and increased confidence.

———❈———

Late winter 1844/45 Chillicothe

"Now, young John,' said William toward the end of winter. 'It's time for you to come and work with me. I told you one year, and that's what you've had. Plus, I've let you play at school mastering over the winter.'

My heart sank. I absolutely did not want to be a manual worker, not even a well-paid craftsman. With every fiber of my being, I hungered to go back to school. Nine months at Oberlin had merely fueled the desire for more.

Charles spoke up. 'William, we've had this discussion before. I know you're the boy's guardian and you think he's had enough learning, but you're not doing your job right if you don't consider his father's wishes. And don't forget what Professor Whipple said in his letter.'

I knew my Oberlin host had written, for not only had I delivered the letter, but I'd had to read it to William—that I was well-suited for an academic and professional education. He'd strongly urged my guardian to allow me to return to Oberlin, not only for the final preparatory year but then to continue with the four years of college. However, William was always reluctant to change his mind once he settled on a course of action. Because he didn't read himself, he thought my passion for learning was a waste of time and money. and whenever he saw me with my head in a book, he scoffed.

Even though he was normally a man of few words, the debate between him and Charles raged for upwards of an hour. Finally, he threw his hands in the air and, as he'd done a year earlier, said, 'John shall decide for himself.'

I jumped up with joy. 'Oh, thank you. I really, really want to get a professional qualification. You won't regret it, brother. I'll make you proud of me.'

He looked worried. 'I cain't understand you, boy. What can you do with all that learnin'? There's no opportunities for edicated blacks.'

Charles spoke up again in my support. 'Time will take care of the boy's interests! Let us do our duty!'

I was beyond excited to finally have a straight path to my shining future–or so I thought.

CHAPTER 15

1845 COLUMBUS

'ARE YOU SURE YOU'RE fine to travel on your own?' asked Charles as we waited for the coachman to strap everyone's luggage on the back of the stagecoach. It was the first day of March and I was on my way back to Oberlin. The four big horses stamped with impatience to be off, their breath frosting white in the chilly spring air.

Flushed with the success of my winter's activities, I drew myself up to my entire five foot one, feeling very manly. 'I'll be fine, brother. I've done this journey twice now. Stop fussing!'

'Listen up, people,' called the coachman. 'When I calls your name, take ya seat.' We'd booked early, so I was first called and chose a spot by the window. In the few times I'd traveled by coach, I'd quickly learned that being close to a window was the best position; the air in a tightly packed vehicle is pretty ripe.

It was a long and bumpy ride over the forty-five miles of badly formed roads north to Columbus and everyone gave sighs of relief when we finally pulled up outside Neil House, the staging post and chief hotel of the city. We all disembarked. I was right glad to stretch my limbs. Much smaller than my fellow passengers, I'd been squashed in the crowded and stuffy interior. Our luggage was unloaded and everyone walked through the imposing entrance, carrying their hand luggage and eager to seek rest and refreshment. As I made to follow, an arm was thrust out in front of me.

A scowling fellow, with a stomach suggesting many ample dinners, barred my way. Thrusting his bulk across the doorway, he glared at me. 'Where d'ya think y're goin'?'

'Into the hotel,' I answered, surprised at the challenge.

'Oh no y're not! We don' entertain *niggers*! You need to find a nigger boardin' house,' he snarled. 'Get ye gone.'

'My ticket entitles me to lodgings,' I protested.

'I don' care what ya ticket says. Yur kind ain't welcome here.' He stepped inside and slammed the door in my face.

It was cold, raining heavily, and I was exhausted from the long tiring day. I stood on the step with my trunk, looking out at the rain, a friendless outcast and on the verge of tears. I knew no-one in Columbus and had no idea where to go or who might help me. I'd been cast aside like kitchen scraps, an object of no worth in the eyes of that horrible fellow.

Just then, a black man walking by, seeing my distress, stopped. 'What's the matter, lad?'

I pulled myself together and, full of hurt and indignation, told my tale to the sympathetic fellow.

'We can sort that,' he said, looking concerned. 'I'll take you to my place. You'll be well-cared for there.' I looked up at him with caution, for I'd been warned to be wary of strangers. He had an open, friendly face. I could discern no malice, and what option did I have? I nodded with gratitude.

'One thing we need to fix before we go,' he said. 'Wait there a moment.'

He walked over to the stables, where the black coachman was measuring out oats to his horses. They exchanged a few words. 'Leave it with me,' I heard the coachman say.

'Come with me, son,' said my good Samaritan. Bending down, he easily gathered up my trunk and we headed off along the dirt street, stepping carefully to avoid the worst of the mud and puddles.

His wife was surprised to see him arrive with a wet, bedraggled companion. 'Who have we here, Abraham?'

Her husband quickly explained my plight.

'Eh lad, you're most welcome to our humble home. Let's get you to the fire.' She helped me off with my damp coat and pushed a chair up to the bright fire. 'You're lookin' right weary, love. You bide there and one of the girls'll bring you a bowl of stew.'

The next morning, breakfasted, well-rested and my spirits restored by their generosity, I expected to be taken back to the hostelry, but at eight o'clock, to my surprise, the coach pulled up at my host's door. The same objectionable man was with the coach. It seemed he was the local agent.

'Up there,' he commanded roughly, pointing to the outside seat beside the heavily rugged-up coachman. It was still raining and freezing cold. I protested, for my ticket clearly stated I was to ride inside, and I wasn't wearing a heavy coat or gloves. At that, a well-dressed gentleman of commanding appearance, seated by the door, spoke up on my behalf. I'd sat next to him the day before and he'd taken a fatherly interest in my story.

'No,' he said sternly to the officious fellow, 'he will *not* ride outside. The lad will freeze to death up there.' He stepped out of the coach and insisted the other inside passengers, all men as it happened, do the same. 'Now, my man,' he commanded my tormentor, 'read out the names of the passengers from the top of the waybill. We will enter in order of purchase.'

My name was first on the list, as he well knew—he'd embarked behind me in Chillicothe. I took my seat, my new champion seated beside me. At no further hotels or on the coach did I suffer any further discrimination.

In the past, having always traveled with older guides, I'd never been so directly attacked. Of course, I'd seen many examples of prejudice and heard many slurs against people of color, but this was the first time I'd been so cruelly used. It gave me a tiny taste of the indignities suffered by so many of my race.

This nasty experience molded the direction of my life.

CHAPTER 16

1845-49 OBERLIN

I WAS A COUPLE of weeks into the new term when I was hailed by one of the senior students. We'd briefly met in Tappan Hall, where I lodged now I was a freshman.

'Hi there, Langston, can you join me for luncheon? I've something I'd like to discuss with you.'

Surprised, for the senior fellows were lofty beings who rarely seemed to bother with us younger boys, I accepted his invitation. Plate in hand, I found him, already seated at a rough-chiseled table. He waved for me to take a seat. As I straddled the hard oaken bench, he introduced two other young men seated beside him.

'Mind the splinters,' one of them cautioned. 'This table and bench were tall trees only last year. The carpentry skills of some of the students delegated to help turn forest into housing and furniture leave a bit to be desired! We're the unofficial sanding department; random splinters end in uncomfortable places, if you know what I mean!'

The others laughed, ruefully, it seemed. I made a careful inspection and repositioned myself a couple of inches further along.

Ignoring their friendly joking, my host said, 'We're the organizers of the Union Society. George Vashon, a highly valued member of our society, suggested we talk to you. He says you're no slug in the speaking department. We thought we'd get in quick before the Young Men's Lyceum fellows inveigle you away. We'd like you to join, and to prove we're serious, we're inviting you to take part in a debate in just over a week.'

I glanced up from my plate, surprised but flattered by the invitation. I accepted, of course!

'What's the subject?'

'It's a hot topic: *Do the teachings of phrenology interfere with man's free moral agency?* One of our best debaters, Edmund B. Wood, is the lead for the affirmative. We've got someone excellent at summing up, but we still need a second speaker. Think you could do it?'

Aha. A subject I'd just learned about. A week before heading back to Oberlin, I'd taken a holiday in Cincinnati to visit Gideon. To my delight, my buddy, Alf Burnett, had just returned from five months touring with a phrenology lecturer. With his usual enthusiasm, he'd extolled the virtues of this new science. I was confident I could twist my knowledge to suit the affirmative position. As for speaking in public, that was easy. After all, my teachers had been praising my speaking abilities for the past few years. How difficult could a debate be?

'I'd be honored to take part,' I said, trying to look grown-up and mature. Inside, I was silently shouting with jubilation. I couldn't wait to write to Charles about this coup, given his attempts to keep me humble after my wintertime teaching success.

The day dawned. My nerves were doing high jumps, but I was confident.

Edmund Wood gave an excellent address. The opposing speaker did the same. I stepped forward.

'Mr. President,' I began. And stopped.

Nothing would come. Not one word. My mind froze, my tongue jammed, my body turned to sludge. I looked out over the auditorium, terrified. Every thought, every feeling, every word took wing, leaving me a solid lump of inarticulate nothingness. I have no idea how long I stood, but somehow, I eventually stumbled to my seat, mortified beyond belief and awash with tears.

Once the debate concluded, fellow students came up to offer their sympathy. Their kindness only deepened my shame and grief. My handkerchief, my sleeves, and even my cap were drenched by my sobs. I ran away to my room in Tappan Hall, locked my door, and continued to weep—as silently as possible. Now and then the doorknob rattled, and someone would entreat me to open. I ignored them all. I cried all night. It wasn't until the five o'clock morning bell that I finally stopped. Arose. A swollen face and inflamed eyes squinted back from my looking glass.

I looked at this ghastly apparition and made a solemn vow. God helping me, I would never again fail in making a speech. Also, while mental and bodily vigor lasted, I would always accept any invitation to improve my oratory skills.

That same morning, once I'd left the Hall, I met another member of the Union Society. He certainly would have known of my shame.

'Langston, I've just been called home for the week, and I want you to take my place in the society debate next Thursday evening. Don't say no! Do it for me!'

Talk about tested! With my just-sworn vow in mind, I accepted, anxious but determined. A week later, when my name was called, I stepped forward for my ten-minute delivery. As I finished, loud and encouraging applause filled the room.

I never again took success for granted, nor missed a chance to learn and improve.

CHAPTER 17

1849 CHILLICOTHE AND NEW YORK

M Y GRADUATION FROM OBERLIN with the coveted Bachelor of Arts, four years later, did not go as expected. I'd passed all the exams with excellent grades and was excited to celebrate with loved ones. I labored long hours to perfect my oration, and friends and family made plans to be present. But an insidious enemy stole the glory from the day, and it wasn't a foe anyone could fight.

Cholera, that terrible scourge, was rampaging through the entire country. And not just America; it greedily stole lives throughout the known world. The staff regretfully canceled our usual commencement celebration, for the risk of spreading the infection was too high. Instead, our professors officiated at a very modest ceremony.

When travel restrictions eased, I could finally return to Chillicothe. By now I was the proud owner of a modest house; my brothers had helped me purchase it. They felt it important I had somewhere to call home. We'd rented it to a family on the understanding that a room was mine when I needed it. It wasn't uncommon for me to come home on leave and find 'extras' temporarily in the secret room off the basement—we'd chosen our tenants based on their active support of the Underground Railroad.

I'd been home only hours when William and Charles called.

'Right, young brother, you've had all this 'spensive edication,' William said. 'What you goin' do now? You quite sure you don' wanna work with me?'

Such a trier! He smiled wryly as he said it and Charles just grinned. They both knew the answer to the second question.

I'd given much thought to this over my years at college. I'd been influenced by many things. Gideon's revelations about our parents' relationship. What Papa could and couldn't do with his own slaves. The demeaning actions of the stage coach agent at Neil House in 1845. The discrimination I'd observed, heard of, and read about since I'd been old enough to take notice. I was not a tall man, (though by now I had an inch or two on Charles) but inside I burned with a giant determination to better my race. The laws of the land were wrong!

'I'm going to be an attorney.'

William looked at me, incredulous. 'You're dreamin', boy.' He turned angrily to Charles. 'I knew that darned school was a fool idea. What nonsense. No-one'll hire a black lawyer!'

Charles ignored his outburst. Rubbed his chin thoughtfully. 'Well, John, your oratory skills would be a useful tool for any court lawyer, and your professors tell us you're now a skilled debater. But are you sure? Are there even any black lawyers in this country?'

'Only three, all in the East. I'm determined to help break the color bar that grinds our people down in poverty and hopelessness.'

'It won't be easy,' cautioned Charles. 'Where will you get the training? I don't know of any other institution as open-minded as Oberlin, let alone a law school. They'll all have only white students.'

The next few months tested my commitment.

My first choice was to find a university or law school. If that didn't work, the next option was to find a lawyer who'd both employ and train me. Everyone tried to talk me out of such an impossible idea, including some of my professors.

One of them said, 'I hate to say it, John, but even if you find a school to train you in legal skills, you'll struggle to make a living. A black person who needs a lawyer would almost certainly seek a white attorney. He's got so much stacked against him with white jurors, a white judge and laws written to favor whites, that it would be a brave person of color who'd risk hiring a lawyer of his own race, for fear it counts against his case. And few white men are likely to hire a black lawyer, I'm sad to say.'

My stubborn streak of 'I'll show them' determination was needed again.

First, I wrote to a prominent lawyer, a great friend of the black community and an abolitionist, asking if he would allow me to work in his practice as a student. His answer came back, 'Don't waste your time. I'm really sorry, but I can't employ you. The only place you might get work is Haiti, where they have a black government, or the British West Indies.'

Next, I wrote to Mr. J. W. Fowler, who'd just opened a law school at Ballston Spa in upstate New York. It provided practical training and academic lectures and sounded like an institution in which I'd flourish. One of my good friends from Oberlin had just gained a place there and highly recommended it.

I informed Mr. Fowler by letter of my education, the grades I'd received, that I could afford the tuition and that I was a man of color. His reply was ambiguous. He'd put the matter to his board of trustees and board of faculty and they refused to consider a black student. However, he invited me to visit him, with the possibility that if they could see me, perhaps they might be persuaded to change their minds.

This sounded at least possible. I made my way north to New York state, by coach, paddle steamer, canal packet and train. After nearly a week of arduous travel, I reached Mr. Fowler. He promised to speak to his boards again.

The next day, he came to see me at my hotel. 'I'm really sorry, Mr. Langston. The answer is still no.'

My jaw dropped. 'Why, sir, did you drag me all this way if nothing's changed?'

'May I be completely open with you?' he replied, looking embarrassed. I bit my tongue and nodded; I'd learn nothing by showing my frustration.

'It's a commercial decision, I regret. I've just begun this school, as you know, and its success is dependent on attracting enough students. Last year, Senator John C. Calhoun from South Carolina visited here to give the commencement speech. He promised to encourage a good number of students from his state to enrol here. The boards are fearful, if he discovers we have a student of color here, that he'll withdraw his support. You know Mr. Calhoun's hardline position on slavery and integration of blacks, I assume?'

Did I what! It was he who'd flung down the challenge that anyone with Negro blood was incapable of learning Greek or Latin. I hated, with a passion, everything that man represented.

'If he, and others of the same opinion, withdraw their support, there's a good chance the school might not survive,' continued Mr. Fowler.

I was so angry I couldn't speak. What a waste of time and money in coming so far.

He continued, 'You have my sympathy, and I would be pleased to help you on in your studies. Here's what I can do. I will let you edge your way into my school. If you will consent to pass as a Frenchman, or a Spaniard hailing from the West India Islands, Central or South America, I can accept you as a student. Your skin color is light; you could easily pass as someone from those countries.'

'What do you mean by 'edge my way into the school'?' I forced out.

He answered, 'Come into the recitation room, take your seat apart from the class, ask no questions, behave yourself quietly, and if after a time no one says anything against you, but all seem well inclined toward you, you may move up nearer the class and so continue until you are, in due time, accepted in full membership.'

I could contain myself no longer. I jumped up from my seat, deeply offended.

'Mr. Fowler, however much I wish to be accepted into your school, on no account will I accept such humiliating conditions. Nor will I yield my American birthright to gain that objective. I expect to live as I hope to die, in my own country and in the service of my fellow citizens. I would rather take my life than consent to such a degrading proposition. I am proud to be a colored American and I shall not prove false to myself, nor neglect the obligation I owe to the Negro race!'

I couldn't wait to brush the winter mud of Ballston Spa off my boots. I turned for home, fighting mad and deeply upset. I'd show the arrogant bastards!

Chapter 18

1850 Oberlin

IF I COULDN'T GET into a law school in the state of New York on fair terms for a black man, what was left? I'd heard of a well-regarded law school in Cincinnati, so I wrote to the owner, Mr. Walker, listing my credentials. It would be pleasant to live in Cincinnati again, with Gideon and many old friends close by.

The only good thing about Mr. Walker's reply was the speed with which it arrived.

'I am very sorry, but I cannot take you. My students would not feel at home with a Negro, and you would not be comfortable with them.'

I threw the letter in the rubbish bin and took my woes to one of our most loved Oberlin teachers, Professor John Morgan. He'd encouraged me all through college; I thought of him as a surrogate father.

He took one look at my gloomy face as I stood at his front door, shivering in the biting wind barreling down from Lake Erie, and quickly ushered me into his book-lined study. Instead of taking his usual seat behind the paper-laden desk, he waved me to the easy chairs situated to enjoy both the garden and the fire. The room was cheerful and snug, with firelight reflecting off the glass-covered bookcases and an exquisite oil painting of an eagle in flight.

'Tell me what's wrong, John. I thought you'd gone to law school in upstate New York.'

I told him my dismal tale of rejections.

'I don't know what to do. It's so unfair! Must black talent be buried? I *know* education's the pathway to Negro equality and progress, but it's getting harder, not easier, the more schooling I get.'

He reached over. Gave my hand a consoling pat. 'You know I wholeheartedly support your ambition. We'll think of a solution. There's always a road less traveled waiting to be discovered. Give me a minute.'

He sat combing his fingers through his thick white beard, while I gazed mournfully out the bow window at the frosty garden, patches of snow piled up in the shady spots. I felt a bit like the robin outside, scratching hopefully in a bare patch of hard-packed earth. Was I also scratching in barren soil, wasting my time? Was there no hope for any black with talent? Was the dream of equality with whites to remain buried?

Suddenly, he snapped his fingers. 'I have it. Let's look at the skills a budding lawyer needs, especially if he wishes to take cases to court. He must speak powerfully and extemporaneously. You're already displaying gifts in that direction, but there's always more to learn. A good lawyer needs the ability to use logic and reason to good effect. He also needs a deep knowledge of many subjects, compassion for his fellow men and, of course, a sound knowledge of the law.'

'That's a pretty good summary,' I said, wondering where he was going.

'Instead of trying to find another institution to take you on, how about you do a degree in theology here, where your talents are known and appreciated? Apart from law, all the other subjects will be developed to a fine degree with our theology program.'

I looked at him in surprise. 'That's different! Would I qualify? Have I got the right foundation? And I have no desire to be a clergyman.'

'Yes, you'd certainly qualify. And no, you don't have to commit to a career in the clergy. As to foundational topics, I hear you excelled in Greek and Latin. Any Hebrew?'

I nodded. 'Yes. I enjoyed it.'

'Right. You'll be at no disadvantage in languages. Remind me of other topics you've studied that might be relevant.'

'Both mental and moral sciences with Professor Mahan. I very much enjoyed his classes.'

'Yes, he's one of the greatest teachers of those topics in the country. To understand values and morality and what makes a healthy and well-balanced society is an important topic for men who desire to help their fellows. And the way our brain and consciousness work—well, that's a very worthwhile science, though I doubt we'll ever completely understand it. For a man who desires to be a lawyer, both sciences will be of value.

'I know you've also had an excellent grounding in classical and English literature, logic and criticism or you wouldn't have graduated with such outstanding marks. And, of course, your debating and rhetorical skills are already well-marked. For such a young man, your ability to hold the audience in the palm of your hand is remarkable.'

Perhaps it was inevitable, given my experiences thus far, but around the same time, I became political. If I struggled, with so much support and financial resources, how much tougher it must be for those without champions, money or education. I was ready to get into battle on behalf of my race. The laws had to change.

A couple of days after Professor Morgan and I settled on my unusual pathway to law, I received a letter from Charles. He had become my role model. He was a powerful orator and always energetic in the fight for black rights. While I'd been at school, he'd become an impassioned leader in what we later knew as the National Negro Convention Movement. Their purpose? Enfranchisement and equality for all blacks.

Dear Brother

I know you hadn't expected to be in Ohio at this time, but now you're back and have a gap before your studies recommence, can you attend the Ohio Black Convention in Columbus next week? A crisis is upon us. A revision of the Ohio constitution is imminent. There's precedent in other states—New York, Pennsylvania, and Illinois—that we could lose some, or all, of the few rights we have. It's critical that we act now. The convention next week is to focus on what we can do.

Currently, most northerners see our people as a side-issue, about as important as their woodpiles. We must bring the matter to their attention. It's critical we open their minds and hearts, make them aware of the injustices we face daily. We must get out of their woodpiles and into their parlors! Get them talking. Get them acting. Get them fighting for us.

Send a note when I can expect you. I've arranged lodgings for us with one of our supporters.

In haste, Charles.

Fired up by the hurtful rejections from lawyers and law schools, I couldn't wait to get into the fight—with words, not guns.

By the end of the three-day convention, I had an important task.

'It's agreed,' said the chair of the convention. 'Six lecturer-agents will take a petition around the state, seeking signatures for equal rights. The men we appoint need to begin as soon as possible, so we're fully prepared for the Ohio Constitutional Convention. John Mercer Langston, would you take the southern region? With your close connections in Cincinnati and Chillicothe, we're confident you'll easily get people to sign. We'll reimburse you for board, travel, and associated expenses.'

I bounded to my feet. 'I'd be honored to assist.'

The next day, I left. The task had to be completed before I began my new studies at the beginning of March.

I was back on the road again during the summer break, with the unforgettable Frederick Douglass. a man who became another mentor. (There's more to that tale, but it's years into the future.)

Runaway slave. Leader of the black convention movement. Charismatic. Crowd-puller extraordinaire! I felt honored that Mr. Douglass had chosen me as his assistant; I even spoke regularly on the same billing. I rather think he enjoyed my hero worship—admiring young protégées enhance the aura of a high-profile person.

'We'll reach Cincinnati in a month,' he said one morning, as we took breakfast in a small mid-Ohio town. 'You've got so many connections there. Please write to your brother, Gideon, and your old landlord and employer, William Watson, and ask if they'd mind promoting my visit.'

'I'll be glad to,' I replied. 'And I'll send a note to my friends, the Burnetts. Mr. Burnett is very close with all the local abolitionists.'

Four days later I got a quick scrawl from Alf.

My dear friend

How wonderful you're coming to the Queen City. Father has passed on details of Mr. Douglass's visit and there's great excitement in the old town.

You'll be amazed at the change in attitude of this old 'home of the mob'! More and more people are open to helping the Cause, and not afraid to be seen supporting it. My mother and sisters regularly join with other ladies to raise funds for runaways, and their bazaars have become so popular we have to restrict the number of people in the hall at any one time.

Can you believe it—I'm a responsible (well, mostly) married man with three children and two shops. But I confess, I do still enjoy flirting with the pretty young ladies who come in to buy our bakery items, confectionery or ice creams. I tell my wife, "Don't growl, dearest. It's good for business." She sighs! I can't understand why!

Your old buddy is champing at the bit to see you. Your favorite cinnamon buns will be waiting!

Your incorrigible friend,

Alf Burnett

The visit was outstandingly successful. For eight days Mr. Douglass stirred the hearts of the people of Cincinnati. Most events were for blacks only, but we also held a splendid mixed-race event which turned out to be a Who's Who of the local Underground Railroad.

Mr. Chase came. Quaker Mr. Levi Coffin, who'd become the informal leader of the local white abolitionists since his arrival in the city, was there. And of course, so were most of the Burnetts.

Alf sat near the front with a young, pretty but tending to plumpness, blond woman–his long-suffering wife, as I later discovered. She looked less than happy at the way both men and women crowded round him before and after the event, laughing, jesting, touching. Did she feel somewhat ignored, I wondered?

I visited him and his new shop twice during my stay. The cinnamon buns were as good as I remembered!

We didn't get as successful a reception in Columbus, the capital city of Ohio. On July 15, we both spoke in the Senate Chamber of the State House to a packed crowd, with five hundred disappointed would-be attendees unable to get in. However, it turned nasty. Troublemakers broke up the meeting, causing a stampede with a bogus fire alarm. As we left, agitators threw stones at us until friendly whites diverted their attention. Mr. Douglass and I escaped, ruffled but unhurt.

'How often does this happen?' I asked.

'Quite normal, John. You'll get used to it,' he replied.

The next day, in front of Neil House, the very hotel I'd been refused admission to when making my first solo journey to Oberlin, I learned a valuable lesson in publicity. Mr. Douglass knew of the segregationist policy of the operators who still controlled the coach loading at Neil House. So, he paid for a first-class ticket and boarded the coach one stop before the hotel. Sure enough, on arrival at the hotel, he was forcibly ejected from his seat by two hefty employees. They insisted he sit on top. He angrily refused. Demanded a refund. They refused.

Newspaper men 'just happened' to be witnesses to the scene.

Out of sight of the journalists, he laughed, giving me a jovial slap on the back. 'Did you hire the buggy I asked for?'

I had. It was waiting for us at a livery stable a street away. We loaded up our bags and continued on our way, speaking at communities in eastern central Ohio as we journeyed to Pittsburgh.

We made an interesting study in contrasts. He was a rich copper-colored, well-built man of about six feet, with an imposing head of hair and an aura of power and strength. I was thirteen years younger, eight inches shorter, of slim build, and a lighter complexion. I could not call on physical size to hold an audience. However, when I spoke, people listened. My ability to ignite passion in an audience was expanded by traveling and working with Douglass. Every day I learned from him subtle tips on how to vary the range of my voice, how to move my body on the stage, how to use wit and pathos.

Traveling with him was a masterclass in eloquence.

CHAPTER 19

SEPTEMBER 1850 OBERLIN

I 'D COME INTO THE dining hall for an early lunch when Henry, one of the senior men, stormed in, waving a newspaper.

'John, look at this! Congress has passed the Bloodhound Bill.'

White-faced, he flung the paper down in front of me. A bold headline dominated the page.

September 18, 1850
Fugitive Slave Act Passed by Congress

Anger flooded my body. 'Damn the bastards! I hoped enough right-thinking congressmen would block that bill.'

We scanned the page together, discussing the main points. It made devastating reading for anyone of color, or any abolitionist, black or white, fighting for the end of slavery.

Henry said grimly. 'What a travesty of justice! It'll turn honest people into law breakers!'

'Absolutely,' I replied. 'I can think of hundreds of decent men who'll refuse to bow to such laws. This is a dreadful day for not just my race, but the entire country!'

Other men gathered around, attracted by our raised voices and obvious distress.

Richard, a theology fellow-student, skimmed the page. 'From what I see here, no black man will be safe anywhere. The law is too wide-sweeping.'

'Any runaway now settled in the north had best get themselves to Canada, or they'll never be safe,' added another of my friends.

Joshua, a young black boy who worked in the kitchen, was clearing a nearby table. He reminded me of myself in the days I worked for Mr. Watson, sweeping the barbershop floor and running errands. He looked up, alarmed at the last comment. His stack of plates was in danger of slipping to the floor. I waved the lad over.

'Do you understand what this is about, Joshua?'

He shook his head, looking worried. 'Not really, sir. Jus' that blacks be in more danger.'

I was pretty sure his family were runaways; many blacks stopped running north when they landed in our town, confident the staunch abolitionist position of almost all our population would protect them.

'Take your plates to the kitchen, then come back here. We'll explain so you can tell your parents. All blacks need to know how this bad law will affect us,' I said.

My friends and I took turns to summarize the clauses for him, referring to the paper to check our interpretations were accurate. Sometimes we stopped to explain the big words and their impact. I knew he was keen to learn–I'd seen him going to Liberty School.

A deposition or affidavit from a court of the state from which the fugitive has come is sufficient to prove a runaway's identity and arrest them. (This is very dangerous. Any slave catcher could get a bunch of affidavits, with broad descriptions that could apply to many blacks, sworn in front of a corrupt official. Then all he need do is ride around looking for someone to fit the description.)

Law enforcement officers everywhere are required to arrest anyone accused of being a runaway, based on the claim of the owner, or supposed owner. If an official refuses to execute a warrant, they will be fined $1,000, paid to the claimant. (Too bad if the official believes it's an unfair claim or doesn't agree with the Act.)

Officials can command any by-stander to aid them in appre-hending someone accused of being a runaway. (Any such official trying that in Oberlin would scrape the dregs of our society to find someone prepared to obey. Only a few anti-abolitionists, all of them unsavory characters, lived in our town, but those few could be lured by the reward. Be very wary of strangers.)

If someone obstructs the official, they will incur a fine of up to $1,000, imprisonment for up to six months, and pay to the claimant $1000 for each fugitive lost. (High penalties for anyone who tries to stop a man-catcher.)

The same penalties apply for any person who shall rescue or attempt to rescue a fugitive from custody. (Try to rescue someone the law has decided is a runaway and, whoever you are, you'll end up in prison. And you'll pay!)

If a person has escaped from service or labor, his claimant may pursue and reclaim him without process, then take him before a tribunal. (No search warrant needed.)

Any suspected fugitive has no rights. They can be held in prison indefinitely—no writ of habeas corpus is allowed them, and no jury is permitted. (A nation allowing such injustices has no right to call itself civilized. Also, it's against the Constitution, which states habeas corpus can never be suspended except in cases of rebellion or invasion.)

In no trial or hearing under this act shall the fugitive's testimony be admitted in evidence. (Nothing they say will be listened to. They could be free, and wrongfully captured, but unable to speak in their own defense. Presumed guilty on the say-so of men of dubious character.)

The case will be decided quickly. Once the decision is made by the authority, the claimant can use such reasonable force as is necessary to carry him back to slavery. (Whips, dogs, chains, beatings. We'd seen them all used, many times.)

If a fugitive should escape, the official will be charged the value of the slave or his labor. (Let someone escape, deliberately or accidentally, and you'll pay—a lot!)

The official who upholds the slave-catcher's claim is paid ten dollars. If a case comes before him and he deems it not proved, he only gets five dollars for his time. (Even well-meaning people can be sometimes swayed by money. This was a bribe to encourage the corruption of justice.)

Joshua looked up at us when we'd finished, alarmed.

'Will dis happ'n to us? My Daddy tol' Oberlin a safe place.'

I answered. 'As safe as we can make it, young man. Few men in this town will buckle under this evil law. We're law-abiding people, but you'll see—we'll be proud to defy this one.'

'Why de Congress make a bad law?'

Henry jumped in. He went teaching every Oberlin winter holiday and loved simplifying things for youngsters. 'Did you know that between 1846 and 1848, America was fighting against Mexico?'

Joshua nodded.

Henry continued. 'It was a bad war, many agree. In '45, Texas, once a Mexican territory, fought for and won independence from Mexico, then aligned itself with America. Next, the border between Texas and Mexico came under dispute. Simply put, America caused the fight with Mexico. Went to war with Mexico, now their neighbor. Once they'd won, they took control of large chunks of Mexican territories, including New Mexico and California. Slave states want those new territories to be allowed to have slaves; the northern states do not.'

I picked up the story. 'The lawmakers have come up with five laws they're calling a Compromise Package. The worst one is this.' I tapped the paper. 'Congress has now accepted it, so this tells us. These conditions destroy every safeguard of personal liberty and affect every level of society, not just runaways like your family.'

Joshua returned to his duties, looking terrified. Not long after, I spotted him running out the door.

It was as bad as we feared. Colored people everywhere were unsafe. Kidnapping had always been a problem, but this ghastly law escalated the numbers all around the country. Many free blacks were illegally captured and shipped south for sale, with no legal recourse. The kidnappers employed devious means to carry this out. For example, a letter written by a southerner was discovered saying, 'Go among the niggers; find out their marks and scars, make good descriptions and send to me, and I'll find masters for 'em.'

The Fugitive Slave Act forced people to take a position. Throughout the north, folk who normally went quietly about their daily affairs, with no firm position on slavery, rose in protest.

Clergymen told their congregations to ignore it. 'God's Law takes precedence over the Fugitive Slave Act. We must trample it underfoot, no matter what the consequences.'

Abolitionists in many northern states, for so many years considered to be dangerous fanatics, gained credibility. The abolition movement gathered momentum. Cities that, in the past, had been antagonistic to emancipation began to turn around. Even in border cities like Cincinnati, with its pro-slavery civil authorities, newspapers and residents, public opinion shifted.

We heard later it was the final straw for writer Harriet Beecher Stowe, so incensed that she penned her runaway best-selling book, *Uncle Tom's Cabin* as an exposé of the vile trade. Her book shook the nation, bringing the evils of slavery into homes across the land, forcing well-intentioned people with no direct exposure to the issues to take notice.

As opposition mounted in the north, southerners ranted just as hotly–about our reaction. They shouted about secession from the union. Was it just a threat, in order to make the resistant north back down and leave their property rights alone (property meaning slaves) or would they really secede?

That was fighting talk. Armageddon was thundering towards us.

CHAPTER 20

1850-1852 OHIO

T O MARK MY 21ST birthday on December 14, 1850, Charles hosted a supper party at his lodgings in Cleveland. A few of my closest Oberlin friends came, and to my delight, my old Cincinnati school friend, Peter Clark, was in town. He was now an up-and-coming leader in the black convention movement, and also our brother-in-law, for Gideon had married his sister in 1844.

Charles began a round of 'remember when' as we sat down to a fine spread of glazed ham, roast turkey, oysters, potato salad and baked vegetables, finishing with lip-smacking loganberry pie and cream.

'I remember you, a little tadpole of a child, traveling over the Alleghenies to Chillicothe when you were not quite five,' he said. 'One time we'd stopped for lunch by a pretty stream, but when it was time to get back on the road, we couldn't find you. I ran to check the stream, terrified I'd find you floating face-down. Gideon dashed down the road a-ways, for someone had seen you chasing a butterfly in that direction. The other men went in different directions. We all called. Nothing. We reconvened back at the vehicles, really worried. Gideon and I were beside ourselves, thinking of having to tell the Goochs we'd lost our baby brother.

'Uncle Billy said, "Has anyone looked in the wagon?" At first glance, there was nothing to see. Then, Arthur, with keener eyes than the rest of us, saw a dirty little foot sticking out from under a blanket. There you were–sound asleep.'

Everyone laughed, and it started a round of stories about childhood pranks and escapades.

Then Peter said, 'Remember when we used to compete for top place in our class tests, John?'

'I hated to be bested, Pete, but you often did. Looking back, I think our teachers encouraged the competition.'

His slim face lit up with a smile. 'Agreed. Perhaps we wouldn't have worked as hard if we'd not had each other. I didn't like being beaten either!'

Henry, one of my Oberlin friends, chipped in with, 'I remember you being so determined to win top place in an exam that you forgot to eat. After a couple of days, we became worried. The others sent me to check if you were ill. You were asleep at your books. When I woke you, you were so faint you could barely walk. But you didn't want to put your pencil down.'

'Perhaps you didn't know what drove me in those first two years,' I replied. 'If my legal guardian, our older half-brother William, had had his way, I'd be a carpenter by now, probably back in Chillicothe. I had to work hard to prove I was worth educating. I guess it became a habit!'

'Just as well for customers you didn't go that route, John,' quipped Henry. 'I saw your efforts at carpentry once. Let's say I wouldn't have wanted to put my weight on any chair you made.'

Charles and I continued talking after the others departed to their beds.

'You're a man of means now, John. Gideon's done a skillful job of managing your inheritance. It's now up to you how you use your assets–bank accounts, shares, and property. Have you given the matter much thought as to how you'll proceed?'

'I'll keep things as they are for now,' I replied. 'I don't have a lot of expenses. If I come across good property deals, I'll probably expand that portfolio. The biggest change is that I won't have to spend my winter vacations working to pay next year's tuition. I can put more time into working for black rights instead.'

'We'll be glad for any extra help you can give, I assure you. There's always more we could do, and never enough hands. Trying to change this state's Black Laws is like trying to push an exhausted cart horse up a mountain single-handed!'

As he leaned forward to bank the fire for the night, he added, 'Gideon's sent papers for you to sign, but it's getting late. Shall we sort it out in the morning?'

From then on, whenever I could fit them around my other commitments, I took every opportunity to attend conventions that worked toward black rights and the end of slavery. Opportunities were many, though the black convention movement went through ups and downs. Schools of thought clashed, sometimes heatedly. From time to time, my mentor, Frederick Douglass, was at the center of controversy. He was a man of forceful opinions and didn't like to be contradicted or criticized. I did my best to understand, but wondered why there was so much fuss over pedantic points when the main issue needed our full focus.

My hobbyhorse was education. I *knew* it was the key to unlocking repression; an educated black population would have the confidence to fight for voting rights.

Though a regular church attendee, I was not a particularly religious person so was surprised at how much I enjoyed the three years of theological studies. I also confess, it gratified me to learn I was the first colored student in the country to enter a theological college of higher learning. Even though I gained good competency on all topics, the one that gave me the most value in years to come was the training in sacred rhetoric and sermonizing. The refined skills in speaking extemporaneously were invaluable, and the intellectual rigor required to dissect sacred texts, then speak to them, extended my intellect and ability to analyze information in a way nothing else could have done.

Professor Morgan's unexpected suggestion to study theology had turned out to be the perfect solution, though even at Oberlin I wasn't without opposition. Scoffers who inclined to the Calhoun school of thought expected to see me fail, believing as they did that such intense theological and metaphysical studies, treated as a science, would be too profound and intricate for a Negro brain. My fellow scholars and professors did not, I'm glad to say, subscribe to such an opinion. I was treated no differently to the white students, and was proud to graduate with my class in August 1852.

There was one more attempt to derail me at the very end. It came from an unexpected source.

At the closing of the commencement ceremonies, Rev. Charles Finney, by now president of the college, prayed mightily that I open my heart, forget law, and go into the ministry.

'Lord, we pray this young man will see his calling to work in your fields. Incline his heart to your ways, oh Lord. Let him see his skills must be used to serve you, be it parish or mission field. The work is mighty; the hands are few. Speak to his heart, dear Father God.' And more of the same. His prayers were never short.

That chat with the Lord, in front of the entire gathering, didn't work. The next day, he summoned me to his office.

Looking over his half-glasses, a frown creasing his high-domed forehead, he tried every tactic in his powerful arsenal.

'Mr. Langston, I know you've been offered several parishes. I've had letters begging me to persuade you to accept their offers. The Almighty has seen fit to bless you with exceptional gifts.'

He got louder. Thumped the desk. The ink bottle sitting beside his blotter rattled.

'You owe it to our Heavenly Father to minister to his people. Would you deny the Lord?'

I sat there, stubborn. Shook my head. I might be young, he might be the powerful president of my beloved college, but I wasn't going to be pushed into a career I had no desire for. I refused to be swayed by his theatrics.

Finally, disappointed, he stopped haranguing me. Accepted I wouldn't budge. But he still had the last word.

Shaking my hand in farewell, he said sadly, 'I'll continue to pray your heart will one day open to the Lord's direction. However, even though I believe with my whole heart that you're making the wrong choice, I give you my blessing. You're an exemplary representative of your race and it's been our joy to educate you in this college.'

I took a big breath as I walked away, appreciative of the blessing but annoyed at how he tried to derail my long-held dream. Stubbornness is both my greatest strength and my greatest weakness. In this case, it served me well.

A weaker man might well have crumpled!

PART THREE

CHAPTER 21

1852 ELYRIA

ONCE I'D FINISHED MY theology studies at Oberlin, I started looking again for somewhere to learn the specifics of law. I found the solution only about ten miles away. Judge Bliss of nearby Elyria, another town with many supporters of black rights, invited me to join his practice. At last, a white man in the legal fraternity was prepared to give me a chance! He and his generous-hearted wife became my champions for the next step of my career.

Mrs. Bliss opened the door, a gracious smile on her rosy-cheeked face.

'John, you are so welcome. Come you in. The judge will be back shortly; he'll take you over to your accommodation in the courthouse, and you'll eat your meals with us. Let me show you where everything is–you must treat our home as yours.'

I'd only been working in Judge Bliss's office a very short time and barely fifty pages into the first law book he'd given me to study, when the first challenge to my oratory skills came, but not from work.

It started at church. A spokesperson for the American Colonization Society came to preach to our large Methodist church, seeking funds for his society's work. I sat through his speech, squirming with distress at his logical-sounding arguments. He and his society wanted us to believe their colonization program would solve the slavery problems of our country. They wanted to ship the colored people of America off to Liberia in Africa.

In earlier years, I'd accepted their ideas as a way out of persecution. However, as I matured, I'd changed my views to the opposite camp. America was our home. The laws of the land we were born in needed to change. Instead of voting with our feet, we needed to be allowed to vote with our voices and our pens.

By this time, almost all American people of color had been born in America; Africa was a place we only knew of in stories told by the old people. This colonization plan would rip people away from extended families, homes, and all they held dear.

I could see many of the congregation being swayed by the speaker's eloquence. With dismay, I noticed people around me nodding in agreement at many of his points.

He made one mistake, however. Confident in his success, instead of inviting people to pledge their support that night, he finished by saying he'd be in town for the following week and would call individually on people to get their contributions.

As the minister was about to pronounce the benediction, I jumped up and asked if I could make a quick announcement. He nodded, a little surprised. Stepping to the front, I invited all who were interested in the subject to attend a meeting at the Court House two days later–before they contributed.

I went home in a state of nerves and barely slept that night. Over-turning his arguments was a big challenge, though I felt sure I could do it–my ten years of training in debate, making eloquent speeches and deconstructing obscure points of scripture gave me confidence that I could persuade at least some of his budding supporters to change their minds. But that wasn't what stole my sleep. Rather, it was what Judge and Mrs. Bliss would say. Would they see me as a viper in their nest?

Next morning, I was first to the breakfast table, anxious about what the good judge would say. Was I about to lose the position I'd worked so hard to gain?

'Good morning, sir,' I said, as my employer entered the room.

He took his seat, spread his napkin over his lap, and reached for the toast. I could feel my knees knocking, hidden under the tablecloth.

He looked up—and smiled.

'John, my boy, I'm proud of you. I've heard what you did. It took guts to throw down the gauntlet to that fellow. I'll be glad to preside over the meeting. You can be sure I'll give you a most glowing introduction.'

I took a deep breath. The knot in my stomach unraveled.

'Oh sir, I've been so worried you'd not approve. I can barely express how grateful I am.'

'And I'll be there to support you as well, son,' said Mrs. Bliss, coming into the room behind me. 'I'll help decorate the speaker's stand. You're an example to us all.'

The fellow from the Colonization Society left town with very few donations. I was invited to give the same speech to several other communities in the county, and it was reported most favorably in the local newspapers.

Chapter 22

1854 Elyria

1854 WAS A WATERSHED year. So many things I'd dreamed of and struggled with for so long came to fruition. I'd say it was one of the best years of my life–ever.

Although I was exceptionally well prepared for it, my admission to the Bar of Ohio in September was yet another test of my determination, or shall we say my stubbornness, to succeed in my chosen career.

After two years of thorough study, practice, and coaching by Judge Bliss, examination day arrived.

At breakfast that morning, the judge gave me a caution. 'Most, if not all, the men you'll be in front of today, John, will be against you because of your color. You must ignore any slights. I know you'll excel in your examination. That's the first stage. But the examiners can only make a recommendation.

'The second stage is to get past the rest of the panel. If they try to refuse you on grounds of color, I'll throw the 'nearer white than black' Ohio Supreme Court ruling at them.'

I knew the legislation he was referring to. 'But I want to be accepted on my merits, sir,' I protested.

He leaned forward, pointing at me to emphasize the importance of his words. 'John, there's no argument from me about that. But you *must* get inside the legal system first. I can't help you change things if you can't gain your license to practice.'

Nervous, I arrived at the court. Three of the best lawyers in the region were appointed to evaluate my knowledge.

'We're not accustomed to seeing a black man before us,' said one of them, frowning as he looked me up and down. His colleagues nodded agreement. They then tried to trip me up. They failed. After hours of grueling questions, they agreed I had an excellent grasp of all the requisite knowledge and skills. From there, the next step was to submit their report to the court. When they did, I noticed they took care to point out the candidate was colored.

The chief judge for the day, presiding over four other senior judges tasked with deciding my fate, was a member of the Supreme Court of Ohio and hailed from the southern part of the state. Down there, the feeling against people of color was intense. He made it clear his preference was *not* to appoint a lawyer with any black blood.

'However, it's of no consequence to me,' he said, looking at me as though I were a beetle on the path.

He turned to his colleagues. 'You fellows decide. Being as you're the ones working these northern circuits, you're more likely to have to work with him–if he's ever engaged by anyone. You're the ones who'll have to manage disruption when people see a nigger acting like a white man in your courts.'

I could see Judge Bliss only just holding onto his temper. He asked permission to speak.

'With respect, sirs, I have tutored this young man for the past two years. In my many years of training young lawyers, Mr. Langston has been the most diligent, hardworking and committed candidate I've ever had the pleasure of working with. His work is exemplary. He deserves to be admitted to the Bar.'

Then one of the examiners, Mr. Gerry Boynton, also addressed the chief judge. 'When I began to examine this applicant this morning, I had the same reservations as you, sir. However, I've never reviewed anyone with better mastery of the required top-ics. He is widely read, erudite, can explain obscure points of law with clarity, and his oratorical skills are outstanding. He will bring credit to our profession.'

Then Judge Bliss spoke again, quoting the legislation he'd men-tioned at breakfast. 'Sir, again with respect, may I remind you of a ruling by the Ohio Supreme Court in 1842 regarding color? This young man is nearer white than black. Therefore, he should be considered a 'white man'.

Crossly, the chief judge asked an odd question, given I'd been sitting in front of him the whole time. 'Where is Mr. Langston?'

The court officer answered, 'He sits within the bar.'

'Stand up, young man,' demanded the judge. He peered short-sightedly at me. 'Hmm.' Turned to his fellow judges on the bench and had a whispered consultation.

I stood there, anxious. What else could they think of to throw at me? I'd answered all their questions perfectly. The examiners were happy. Could these powerful men still refuse me?

The men holding my future in their hands nodded.

'Very well. Come forward and be sworn.'

Trying to suppress a smile as wide as the Mississippi, I did as instructed. Once formalities wrapped up, the room erupted. My friends sprang forward to shake my hand and pound me on the back. I was a lawyer! And the first black one in Ohio!

Later, I asked the chief judge why he asked me to stand up.

'I needed to be sure of your color.'

I boiled with anger inside, but forced myself not to react to the offensiveness of his comment.

I left the court that day, September 13, 1854, a fully-fledged attorney, counselor-at-law, and solicitor in chancery. It was a fine celebration in the Bliss household that night!

CHAPTER 23

1854 Brownhelm, North Ohio

FOR SOME TIME, MY doctor in Oberlin had been concerned about my health. I'd had ten solid years of intense study and, more recently, also crammed political activities into every spare minute I could carve away from my books. Nearly every weekend I was on the road, speaking, attending conventions, and gathering support for whatever black rights issue needed the most attention at the time. With so much important work, I figured sleep and exercise were a waste of time. Unfortunately, my body didn't agree, and I'd been to the doctor several times in the last year of my internship with Judge Bliss, complaining of a racing and erratic heart, a cough I couldn't shake, and extreme fatigue.

I was back at the doctor's again in early 1854 with more of the same concerns.

'Forgive the crassness of the question,' he said after checking me over, 'but have you the necessary to buy yourself a farm?' He knew from town gossip my father had left his sons well provided for, but we kept our private matters close. Few knew just how well off we were.

'Yes,' I replied, surprised at his question.

'Well, here's my prescription, Mr. Langston. You need to get away from your books. Buy a farm and go work on it for two years. You've told me you plan to become an attorney. Forget lawyering for a while. You need to be out in the fresh air. If you want to amount to anything in life, you must have good health. At the rate you're going, you'll be dead before you're forty. It's utter foolishness to think you can abuse your body so–and I thought you were supposed to be intelligent!

This was *not* the advice I expected to receive, but I have to admit, I was exhausted. I didn't admit it to many, but I also carried an underlying anxiety that, even if I gained acceptance to the bar, I'd struggle to establish a law practice. Repeatedly I'd been told, even by Frederick Douglass, that it was highly unlikely anyone would hire me.

I decided to follow my doctor's advice. I certainly wasn't about to stop my studies with Judge Bliss, so close to achieving my dream, but I employed an agent to look for suitable land. A profitable farm would give me a fallback position, should I need it. He found fifty gently rolling, fertile acres at Brownhelm Township, only about nine miles from Oberlin, fourteen from Elyria, and very close to Lake Erie. It was equipped with everything needful to farm successfully, and also came with a very well-constructed spacious two-story frame house. Also, and this was important to me, the community was abolitionist in sentiment, though no Negro had lived there before. I purchased the farm for $3,000 and entered into a lease agreement with the Slaters and their adult son, a hardworking immigrant English family. They ran the farm and we split the profits.

With great pleasure, I moved into my new home, boarding with the Slaters, only days after I'd passed my bar exams.

Would I be able to stay away from scholarly pursuits and professional endeavors for two years, I wondered?

I'd bought the farm with the full intention of doing so, but my resolve was quickly tested and found wanting. Within a few weeks of moving in, I had a visit that changed the course of my future.

It was the beginning of October and I was working in the turnip crop with John Slater, the son, when a white stranger approached, asking for 'Lawyer Langston.' I said, 'Come with me, sir. I'll take you to Mr. Langston.'

I left him with Mrs. Slater, dashed upstairs, had a quick wash and scrubbed my nails to remove the soil, then descended to the parlor dressed in my Sunday clothes.

He looked at me, surprised, then burst into laughter. 'Nice touch! You sure fooled me!'

Joke over, he introduced himself and we got down to business. 'I'm Mr. Perry. Before I explain the reason for my call, may I congratulate you, Mr. Langston, on being admitted to the bar. My friends tell me you passed the examination with flying colors.'

I made a suitably modest response, wondering where this was going.

He went on. 'I'm also a lawyer, and I need an assistant for a really interesting case. Even though you're yet untried, I'd like to give you an opportunity. Would you be available?'

'Most certainly! What's the case?'

'It's a dispute over possession. The owner of the property wants it back; the occupant, our client, is refusing to vacate. It's a hotly contested case, and the opposing lawyer is a highly skilled young lawyer, who's won most of his cases. You'll get a lot of publicity'. He added, 'All parties are white.'

I could hardly believe my ears. To say I was overjoyed didn't even *begin* to describe my delight. So much for the Doubting Thomases who'd said I'd get no clients. Here was a white lawyer, not so well-known, to be fair, giving me a wonderful opportunity.

On the day of the hearing, the Brownhelm justice of the peace, who was to preside over the matter, looked around at the crowd trying to fit into the large office in his house. More men were tying up their horses further along the road and heading in our direction.

'This won't do,' he said. 'We'll have to move the matter out to my barn.'

Everyone traipsed across the yard, stepping carefully around horse and cow manure. We attorneys carried our notes and a chair each. Other men helped carry Justice Curtiss's desk, his wife's kitchen chairs, and a table each for the two opposing legal teams. His wife looked anxious as we stripped her house of most of her movable furniture.

As we set up the desk, tables, and a chair each for judge and attorneys, onlookers moved bales of hay and equipment so they had somewhere to sit. A couple of brindle cows looked over their stalls, patiently chewing their cud. Hens occasionally wandered in, looking for bugs disturbed by the many feet. They squawked indignantly when forcefully ejected.

As many people as could fit, mostly men but a few women, clambered up on the farm wagon. Manure and animal smells overpowered the clean aroma of fresh hay. Thankfully, it was a fine day and we could keep the barn doors open, both for light and ventilation.

Our client, the defendant, had requested a jury, which was selected from those present. Mr. Perry and our opposition made their opening statements. Then witnesses were called.

'Mr. Langston, I'd like you to begin the cross-examinations, if you please,' instructed my colleague.

He observed closely. Twice I bent down to check details with him. 'Superb work,' he whispered each time.

I finished my first cross-examination and went to sit down as the next witness was called, expecting Mr. Perry to take over.

'You're doing an excellent job, son. Keep going.'

He let me interview all the witnesses!

Eight hours later, and all parties heard, we were ready for the summing-up. To my further surprise, Mr. Perry also asked me to present our closing statement.

He was a generous man; once he'd established I could do the work, he gave me the chance to shine.

The jury didn't even bother to leave the room to deliberate. While still in their seats, they gave a unanimous verdict in favor of our client.

The next day, while the Slater family and I were still at breakfast and enjoying the splendid success of the day before, we heard a knock at the door. A white man was standing there.

'Is this the house of the lawyer, Mr. Langston?'

'Indeed,' said Mrs. Slater, who'd gone to the door.

'Please may I speak to him?'

Mrs. Slater ushered the caller into the parlor.

He stood up as I walked in. 'I heard what you did yesterday, young sir. I'd like you to represent me.' He had money in his hand.

'Tell me about your case,' I asked.

'It's like this, young sir. I'm a purveyor of liquor. My customers enjoy relaxin' with their neighbors over a whiskey of an evenin' at my establishment. Them bastards what make the laws 'ave gone and changed 'em. Say it's illegal for me to let fellas enjoy a wee tipple on my premises. T'aint right, you know, takin' a man's livelihood away from him. Confounded temperance people, interferin' like that!'

I wrote down the details, took his deposit, and set an appointment for further consultation.

As I was shutting the door, another fellow rode up to our gate. He also wanted representation–for the same issue. And so it continued until sundown. By the end of that day, I had so many liquor purveyors seeking my services that I had enough work for several weeks and a pocketful of money in retainers. They were all white.

If Mr. Perry had not requested my services that fateful day, I may have been a farmer for a lot longer than two weeks. Instead, my law practice flourished, and I had to leave the farming to Mr. Slater and his son John. Every case I took to court, I won. Interestingly, my clients were all white–English, Irish and American. It became apparent that winning was more important than the skin color of the lawyer. I wondered where the black clients were, but with work and money pouring in, I had little time nor need to ponder that question.

CHAPTER 24

1854 BROWNHELM AND OBERLIN

THERE WAS ONE OTHER really significant and life-changing event that year.

'I'll be off to Oberlin this afternoon, as soon as we finish work,' I said to the Slaters at breakfast one morning, a few weeks after we'd moved in. 'I'll stay over with friends, so I don't have to drive home in the dark. Don't want one of the horses breaking a leg in a pothole.'

Mr. and Mrs. Slater looked at each other and smirked.

'Seems there's quite a few of these trips after work to Oberlin, John. Anything you're not telling us?' joshed Mrs. Slater. 'Might I be sharing the housekeeping duties at some stage soon?'

I flushed with embarrassment. I'm one to keep private matters close. I mumbled a vague reply and excused myself from the table.

Three years earlier, just before college broke for the year, I'd happily accepted an interesting assignment from our Oberlin Young Men's Anti-Slavery Society. The members were mainly fellow senior students.

They said, 'John, would you be interested in spending your winter vacation doing an inspection of the black schools of the state? We'd like to know how they're going. How many students, what equipment they have, the quality of the teaching, how fit for purpose the buildings are, and anything else noteworthy? We also want to encourage more schools to open. You're a persuasive fellow–if you could get more communities to set up winter schools, we'll undertake to send them student teachers. And although we have no funds, there may be some things we can find donors for–if we know the needs.'

'You know I'm passionate about black education,' I replied. 'I'd be delighted to take that on. I've got my own horse, so transport's easy. Do any of you have contacts around the state where I can stay?'

Some put up their hands, and one member offered to list them for me. I also asked for the names and locations of as many black schools as we collectively knew about.

'I'm sorry we can't pay you,' said our chair.

I shrugged. 'I can manage that, thanks.' Charles was the only one who knew just how well-off I was, for I continued to live almost as frugally as when a poor student. However, it wasn't a secret that I no longer needed to earn my tuition during the holidays. I sent a grateful thank you heavenward, addressed to my father.

Charles was at the meeting; he often had business in Oberlin. 'I'll cover the Cleveland area for you, John. And here's a thought–if you train to Columbus and maybe Dayton, you could do them before you start on the country areas.'

By mid-November 1851 I was crisscrossing the state, bundled up in warm winter clothes, tall riding boots and wool-lined leather gloves. Heavy rain gear was strapped behind my saddle and spare clothes, wrapped in oilcloth, went into a couple of saddlebags.

Once I was east of Cleveland, much was new, for I'd had no reason to visit the little villages dotted through that part of the state. It was fascinating to observe at first-hand how commercial opportunities and prosperity followed transport lines. The villages and towns near railway lines, or the two Ohio canals, were prosperous. Farms, hamlets and towns within a couple of days' ride of transport lines had also benefited, for producers now had a way to get their produce to bigger markets. However, those far from transport or good roads were little more than a huddle of log cabins, hard-scrabble farms and poorly clad, uneducated people, black and white. Few of them had any schooling for their children.

Within a couple of weeks, I was in a comfortable rhythm. My horse and I made a good team. Occasionally I had to get her a new shoe, but without too much hassle we quietly jogged along, heading always southwards. By Christmas, I planned to be with friends and family in Cincinnati.

I was happy. Doing interesting work. Meeting a wide variety of people, mostly well-intentioned towards black education. Sure, many schools lacked resources and there was immense need, but we were doing something about it. For a young man with a passion to elevate his race through education, what could be better?

And then something happened. Seemingly simple. Unexpected. Momentous.

It was mid-December when, about 50 miles north of Cincinnati, I rode into the pretty village of Harveysburg, set in an elevated position and looking down the valley to Caesar's Creek. I knew it to be a special place. Settled mainly by Quakers, it was well-known to nearby Underground Railroad conductors as a safe way-station for fugitives making for Canada. It also boasted the first black school in Ohio, founded in 1831 by white Quaker Elizabeth Burgess Harvey, with the support of her husband, Dr. Jesse Harvey.

I'd been invited to stay with one of those relatives. They apparently had a large home and an open door for people of any color.

The afternoon was drawing in as I rode into town. My hosts' house was easy to find, they'd written. 'Look for the large cream two-story house in the main street. It's got blue shutters and an old oak tree hangs over the gate.'

I tied my horse to the post and rail fence and approached the well-maintained property. Gardens hugging the bottom trim boards of the house were covered in straw, hinting at color and perfume in summer. As well as the mighty oak tree they'd mentioned, a scattering of elms dotted around the lot, though leafless at this time of the year, suggested welcome summer shade. Toward the back of the lot I could see another area of garden, dug over ready for spring planting–the vegetable patch, I guessed.

The clip of my boots on the neatly paved path announced my arrival. As I stepped up onto the porch, the door opened. To my surprise, in front of me was a stunningly beautiful young black woman I'd met briefly on campus the year before.

'Welcome, Mr. Langston. I see you've found us,' she beamed. 'Do come in.'

As she reached to shake my hand, she added, 'We have met, but you might not remember me.' Her dark brown eyes twinkled, as if daring me to admit I'd forgotten her. 'I'm Caroline Wall and a senior in the Ladies' Department. You know my older brother, Orindatus, I believe.'

I made some mumbling remark about her brother, but who cared about him! Of course I remembered her! Her smile had nearly distracted me when I'd spotted her in the front row of one of my debates. I'd engineered an introduction and desperately wanted to know her better. However, exams had been looming at the time and I'd dared not get distracted. I'd seen that happen to a couple of other chaps, so derailed by pretty faces they'd had to repeat a year. If I failed any exams, I'd never hear the end of it from William! Distractions I *couldn't* allow. I'd ignored my wayward heart and thrust my head back into my books.

And here she was! As breathtaking as I'd remembered!

'Is this your home? I understood I was to stay with a white Quaker family,' I stammered.

'She laughed–a joyous rich laugh that sent another fish hook into my heart. 'Yes to both. My younger siblings and I live with the Dixs. They're Quakers *and* white. Come you in, and I'll go fetch my foster mother.'

Over dinner I noticed how gentle, yet firm, she was with the younger children in the house, four of them her siblings. When she gave her attention to the adults, she sparkled with intelligence and witty repartee.

After dinner, she excused herself to help put the children to bed and my hostess disappeared to the kitchen. I sat in the lamp-lit parlor conversing with my genial host. He had grand tales of close shaves with runaways and man-stealers. Apparently, the secret room in their barn was well-used.

'Some come from Cincinnati, but many of our 'guests' have passed through the hands of Reverend Rankin in Ripley, up-river from Cincinnati. You'd know of his work for the cause, I imagine?'

I nodded. 'I certainly do. He and his large family are famous for the way they refuse to be intimidated. Their home is in a great location–so high above the village of Ripley that fugitives on the Kentucky side of the Ohio can see the signal light in the Rankins' parlor window. If there's danger, it's not lit. I've heard many a tale of them hearing a posse of slave catchers riding up their track, and the Rankin boys spiriting desperate runaways off through the forest to the next safe house.'

Chores done and children abed, the women came back into the room. I moved over on my fashionably upholstered settee, hoping Caroline would choose to sit by me, rather than the empty chair a few feet away. She noticed my move, smiled serenely, and chose my settee! I felt a rush of excitement. My whole body tingled. It was suddenly difficult to focus on the story my host was telling.

The evening passed in delightful conversation, ranging across many topics of interest. I noticed my hostess and her husband smile knowingly a couple of times as Caroline and I vigorously debated points of interest. She was not only very pleasing to the eye, with luxuriant thick dark-brown hair tastefully arranged to show off her slender neck, oval face, and even features, but gracious, well-spoken, and intelligent. I was hooked!

Too soon, it was time to seek our beds.

'I'll show you to the school in the morning if you like,' Caroline said as we stood up. I accepted with alacrity.

I was issued with a candle and headed off to the guest room. It took a long time to fall asleep.

It was tough to leave two days later, but I had places to be and people expecting me.

I was smitten, but I still had one more year of study, and no promise of work. It was not the time to go courting. But no matter how much I tried to put her sweet smile and clever conversation out of mind, my famous willpower did not prevail. Once we were both back at college in the spring of '52, I kept finding opportunities to spend time in her company. And whenever I saw her talking enthusiastically with other men, a hot flash of jealousy flared. I desperately hoped some other lucky fellow wouldn't beat me to the prize that was Caroline, before I felt secure enough in my future to speak to her of my heart.

Her family story was very similar to my own. Her mother, Jane, had been a slave and her father, Colonel Stephen Wall, a wealthy planter of North Carolina, had a great affection for his mulatto children, born by three of his slave women. Before he passed to his long sleep in 1845, he'd removed his children from the dangers of their slave state to the free state of Ohio, emancipated them and settled them with all comforts in Harveysburg.

From what she told me, I suspected Colonel Wall and my father would have got along famously. Her father also acknowledged his mulatto children and did everything possible for their education and welfare. He bequeathed them property in Ohio and left instructions they were to advance their education at Oberlin.

I began my courtship with cautions from my brothers rattling around in the back of my head. In earlier years, I'd had more than an idle curiosity about their slowness to embrace marriage, for it had impacted my life, not always for the better. If Gideon had been married when I lived in Cincinnati, I'd have lived with him rather than been boarded out. If Charles had been married when I was taken from the Cincinnati school and returned to Chillicothe, he would likely have been appointed my guardian. But looking back at might-have-beens was a waste of time!

Over the years, I'd asked them several times why they hadn't yet taken wives. Typically, they gave answers such as, 'No rush,' or 'Have to find the right woman', and as I got older, they'd expanded their comments to include brotherly advice.

Gideon said, 'There's plenty of gold-digging women out there, and many know we Langston fellows were left well-provided for. Be very careful—a besotted fool and his money are quickly parted.'

Charles said, 'Don't be a Johnny Beadle, made a fool of by unsuitable women or designing mamas.' Johnny Beadle was a humorous character portrayed in popular magazines as a buffoon who rushed into courtship and matrimonial expectations, with disastrous results.

At various times, they made further contributions, such as: 'See your prospective mate in as many circumstances as possible. Visit her home. Watch how she talks to her immediate family and servants. Is she a tidy and organized person? Is she a careful and frugal manager of her portion, or spendthrift and frivolous?'

'Notice whether your conversation is easy. If you struggle to find topics to talk about while courting, imagine looking across the dining table or sitting beside the parlor fire for years with nothing to say to each other. Notice what she reads. Can she discuss a wide range of topics? Do you share any interests?'

'Have a good look at her mother, if possible. What you see in the mother indicates what you'll probably see in your bed in another thirty or so years.'

Now and then one of them would share the latest horror story of a friend who'd been caught by a pretty face, only to find the object of his affections was shallow-minded and could only talk of trivial things, or she was mentally unstable and kept the household in a state of endless crisis and turmoil. Other cautionary tales were of careless mothers who left the raising of their children almost entirely to paid staff while they spent their husband's money faster than the poor fellow could earn it. And a common tale was of cold women who, once they'd fluttered their eyelashes to good effect and got their shoes under a fellow's bed, then pushed him out of it with complaints of tiredness and sick headaches.

All of this was fine advice, and I tried to work through my brothers' checklist, but love is a powerful mistress. I confess to not thinking of *any* of their criteria as I observed my heart's desire. So, it was good luck rather than good management that my Caroline was all the things they recommended—a firm yet loving mother figure to her four younger siblings, a gracious hostess, a fascinating conversationalist with firm opinions and as passionately interested in black rights and education for our race as myself. She could hold her own in any discussion on any topic. We would certainly *never* run out of conversation. This last was not surprising, given that she was being educated at Oberlin—we were exposed to some of the best critical and open-minded thinkers in the state.

Besotted as I was by my dream woman, I became, if possible, even more driven to establish my career so I could ask her to be my wife. First was to pass the Bar examination. Then find a home. The farm fulfilled the second part of that plan, and if I'd not had the wonderful good fortune to be introduced to the community by Mr. Perry, with the resulting flurry of ongoing work, I would at least have had my flourishing and profitable farm to support a wife and future family.

On that basis, and with anxiety, I was ready to propose. However, shyness dogged me. Would she accept? Here was I, becoming known for my ability at speechifying, frightened to speak to a woman. Not any woman. The woman of my dreams.

I came up with a plan. I was good with a pen. Perhaps if I put my proposal in writing, I wouldn't risk tripping over my tongue and ruining my chances. With much anxiety, and many sheets of paper consigned to the fire, I finally found words I hoped would give the desired result. I gave my precious epistle to a close friend to deliver by hand. Then waited. The desire for sleep and food took a holiday, along with my ability to concentrate.

This state of extreme anxiety lasted for two days. At lunchtime on the second day, Mr. Slater came into the house carrying a letter for me. I almost snatched it out of his hands and disappeared into my office, heart pounding, stomach churning, and my nerves all aflutter.

She said YES! I whooped with delight, jumping around my office in a poor imitation of an Indian war dance.

A knock came at my door. Mrs. Slater put her head round, looking worried. 'Anything amiss, John?'

She took one look at my face, grinned broadly, and said in her broad Somerset accent, 'Mebbe not, by the looks o' your face. Anything you want to share?'

I ran over and hugged her (and I'm not usually a demonstrative fellow.) 'I'm to be married!'

A delighted Mrs. Slater clapped her hands in joy, and Mr. Slater came to join the party. He shook my hand enthusiastically. 'We suspected there be a young lady behind all these trips to town, young fella me lad,' he said, pounding my back with his broad farmer's hands. 'Well done, John boy. We wish you happy.'

Our dear Professor Morgan, teacher, friend and mentor, agreed to conduct the ceremony. On October 25, 1854, in a simple ceremony at Oberlin and surrounded by friends and family, my precious Miss Wall became Mrs. John Langston. We then headed south on our wedding-tour, first to Cleveland and then on to Cincinnati to introduce my bride to my childhood friends and for a visit with Gideon.

CHAPTER 25

OCTOBER 1854 CINCINNATI

T HE WIND WAS WHIPPING up foam on the Ohio River as my bride and I strolled down the wide streets of Cincinnati, her hand tucked under my arm.

As we turned into Fifth Street, I thought of my boyhood friend, Alf Burnett. In the brief times we'd seen each other over the years, I knew he'd become a successful businessman and also catered for many major city events–state fairs, important banquets and the like.

From time to time I'd also seen his name on posters or newspaper advertisements, promoting either lectures or his comedy routines. The publicity usually mentioned how far afield he went with his performances–all over the country, it seemed. His acting success, despite his mother's early objections, did not surprise me.

While I was lost in boyhood memories, a poster caught my eye. Steering Caroline over to the wall, we read, in large bold text:

Alf Burnett, comedian, entertainer, and humorist– performing in Cincinnati for a few nights only

I pointed to his name with delight.

'How remarkable. I was just thinking about this very fellow. He's a few years older than me, but we were great friends as lads and I've seen him a couple of times since. I'd love to meet up with him again. You'd like him. I heard he took over his family shop. I wonder if it's still there.'

As I spoke, a tall, fleshy fellow, thick nut-brown hair brushing the collar of his smart black astrakhan coat, came toward us. As he drew near, I looked closer. No! What a coincidence! Unless I was much mistaken, it was the very person I'd been thinking about.

I stopped. 'Alf?'

He glanced our way with the non-committal smile a well-known person makes when accosted by members of the public. Then looked again.

His polite acknowledgment changed into a delighted grin. 'No. It can't be! Johnnie Langston, if I'm not much mistaken.' He reached to shake my hand. 'Well, well. What a surprise. And who is this beautiful woman by your side?'

As he beamed at her with warm approval, Carrie couldn't help but smile back.

Our reunion caused interest to the passers-by. Some stared to see a white man and a black couple so happy to see each other. Others, who appeared to know him, waved cheerily, said 'Good day,' or tipped their hats as they walked around our huddle. He responded politely to those who spoke while trying to stay focused on Carrie and me.

After the third interruption in less than a minute, he gave a laugh. 'What am I thinking of? Why are we standing on the street? Come and have coffee with me.'

He led the way to the very building I'd been heading for. How different it was from the shop I'd visited as a lad! Gone were the small bubbly panes of glass in the front window. Instead, a large plate glass window with a skillfully written sign drew the eye. A wide doorway stood invitingly open, and inside we could see a queue of customers at a marble counter. Delicious-looking cakes and cookies were attractively displayed under glass covers, and baskets behind the counter held a wide selection of breads. Further down the counter was a board listing ice cream flavors, and men and women perched on stools or sat at small tables, enjoying ices in stylish cut-glass coupes.

Toward the back I could see another open door and a sign inviting customers to a tearoom. Alf ushered us in, gave a genial wave to the two girls serving in the store, and gestured for us to walk through.

We were greeted by a buxom coffee-colored waitress with a twinkle in her eye. Her dress was a crisp white, a frilly cap perched on her thick black hair, and a blue gingham pinafore protected her dress. She guided us to an empty table. Two other young women, also of my race, were busy with other customers.

I scrutinized the room, my mouth open in astonishment. Chandelier. Elegant wallpapers. French doors allowing a glimpse of outdoor seating. 'Wasn't this your family parlor?'

Alf chuckled. 'You won't find anything in this building that looks like what you'd remember, old friend. I've also renovated the kitchens and the living quarters upstairs. I believe I've the most elegant tearoom west of New York.'

I spent far more time in churches and community halls than tearooms and ice cream parlors, but could well believe his claim.

As we took our seats he demanded, 'John, I want to know everything that's happened to you, and how long you're in town.'

Our discourse ranged over many topics—there was so much to catch up on. An hour later, as we stood up to leave, he asked, 'What are your plans for the next couple of days?'

'I believe the Watsons are planning some entertainment for friends at their home tomorrow night.'

He ran his fingers through his unruly curls. 'Here's a thought. I certainly don't want to gate-crash anything they've organized, but I have a free night tomorrow. I'd be delighted to contribute to the evening's festivities with two or three of my most popular pieces, if they'd like.'

'That's a very generous offer.' I paused. I didn't want to commit my hosts to extra expense, and judging by the quality of his garments, and the crowds and places he'd just been telling us about, he was clearly used to high fees for his skills.

He must have sensed my concern. 'My gift to you. No charge. Sorry, I should have made that clear.'

The next night his comedic characters and droll recitations had my friends in stitches of laughter. What a gift the man had.

Not everyone in Cincinnati was as friendly as Alf, unfortunately.

Mrs. Watson and Carrie were off meeting other women, so Mr. Watson and I decided to call in to the Melodeon Hall. I wanted to support one of my Oberlin theology classmates, Antoinette Brown. She was speaking that afternoon to the Temperance Association.

The previous year, she'd become the first female minister of any recognized denomination in the United States and, although she chose not to remain with the original congregation, she was in high demand as a speaker. All round the country, women's rights, temperance, and anti-slavery conventions asked her to address their delegates, even though it was still uncommon for women to address a public meeting. I was looking forward to hearing her speak.

We got no further than the door.

'No-one of your complexion will be admitted,' said the burly fellow at the entrance.

We stopped in surprise. 'I'm a friend of the speaker,' I argued.

'It don't matter how many friends you got, mister. You two ain't goin' in.'

I demanded pen and paper and dashed off a note to Antoinette. It turned out the exclusion was the decision of the proprietor, and nothing to do with the Temperance Association. In the heat of the moment, they could not persuade him to relax his restrictions.

It bounced back on him. Antoinette delivered a scorching rebuke from the platform, and the association vowed not to use the hall again until the color bar was dropped.

Too late for Mr. Watson and me—we had no option but to go home.

CHAPTER 26

1855 BROWNHELM

Apart from being the location of my farm, there was something else very significant about Brownhelm Township. Like Oberlin and Elyria, its early settlers were New Englanders with firm opinions about respect and fairness to all. There were a few exceptions–the most notable being one of my nearest neighbors.

At first, he was dismissive and rude. Refused to engage in conversation as he rode past my fence.

'I don't talk to darkies,' I heard him say.

Over time, using humor and good manners, I won him over and we became great friends. Most residents, however, were for the abolition of slavery and some were also conductors on the Underground Railroad. I quickly became well known in the community and enjoyed the open acceptance of most.

In March 1855, the township needed to elect a new clerk. I was riding to a meeting to help choose a candidate for the Liberty Party, at that time the most supportive of black issues, when my friend, Charles Fairchild, trotted up. As we jogged along, he said, 'John, I'm going to nominate you tonight for the position of town clerk.'

I pulled on the reins, bringing my horse to a stop. I looked at him in shock. 'Oh no, you mustn't do that, Charles. My name, I fear, would kill our ticket. We can't afford to take such risk. We must nominate men who have a chance.'

Charles refused to listen. 'I don't care what you say, John. No-one has better qualifications for the job than you. It would be beyond wrong not to put your name forward.'

Flabbergasted, I ceased arguing, sure that the rest of the nominating committee would reject his nomination.

But he was right, and I was wrong. That night they chose me as the Liberty Party's candidate, and on polling day, to my amazement and surprise, I was elected with a sound majority. It's not putting too fine a point on it to admit I was beyond delighted; I was the first Negro in the nation to be elected to public office in an open contest with whites. The publicity did no harm to my career!

'Mr. Langston, I'd like you to take on my case.'

'Mr. Langston, there's a matter of law I need to discuss with you.'

'Mr. Langston, my neighbor's trying to steal some of my land. He's planted trees on my side of our boundary. Can you help?'

Day after day, new private clients came to my door, and in my role of Town Clerk I had to attend to many legal matters as well. I was so busy I had no time to help on the farm. Thank goodness the Slaters were such excellent managers.

Then, one day, an opportunity of a different stripe arrived by letter, post-marked New York.

Dear Mr. Langston,

We hear you've become the first black man in America to be elected to a civic position by a white community. We tender our most sincere congratulations. Your achievement is hugely significant for the promotion of equality between the races.

The American Anti-Slavery Society invites you to speak to our twenty-second anniversary conference, to be held May 1855 at the Metropolitan Theater, New York. Your time slot, should you accept, will be for thirty minutes on the morning of May 9–the anniversary of our founding. Exact time to be confirmed.

If you can join us on this important occasion, we will pay you an honorarium of $50, plus cover all expenses of travel and accommodation.

Yours respectfully,
Edmund Quincy
Corresponding Secretary
American Anti-Slavery Society

No one had ever paid me for a speech before. I could scarcely contain my excitement! This request to speak to the AASS would put me in front of many of the most high-profile abolitionists in the nation, people I was keen to meet.

I thought about who might be there–people I'd either read about, or Frederick Douglass had mentioned. William Lloyd Garrison, one of its founders and the publisher of the abolitionist paper *The Liberator*; Wendell Phillips, lawyer and such a brilliant orator that people called him 'abolition's golden trumpet'; John G. Whittier, poet, Quaker and abolitionist; Gerrit Smith, the wealthiest landowner in New York State, who believed his wealth was a divine gift to be used for the oppressed. He'd already spent at least a million dollars on freeing slaves and supporting abolitionist causes. Perhaps Harriet Beecher Stowe or her brother, Henry Ward Beecher, might be there? And James and Lucretia Mott, Lucy Stone, Stephen and Abby Kelley Foster? Heady stuff for a twenty-five-year-old black lawyer from a modest village in North Ohio!

Charles Fairchild called into my office while I was still holding the open letter, my brain spinning at the possibilities and opportunities it would open up.

'Look at this, friend!' I passed the letter to him. 'If you hadn't insisted on nominating me, this would never have happened!'

He clapped a hand on my shoulder. 'John, you so deserve it. How did they hear about you, I wonder?'

I tried to look modest. 'I dropped a note to Mr. Douglass, telling him of the election result. As you know, he's been my mentor in political matters for the last few years. He's on the AASS executive committee. Perhaps he put a word in.'

'Of course he did! Couldn't happen to a better fellow! Tell me, what do you know about their aims and objectives? There's many abolition societies now.'

'Mr. Douglass tells me the AASS don't just fight for abolition. They also work to elevate the character and condition of people of color by combating prejudice and discrimination throughout the nation. He's been wanting me to meet these people for over a year.'

———◈———

May 9, 1855 New York

With a cold rain washing the streets of New York, three thousand people crowded into the Metropolitan Theater.

I began my speech with, "*There is not, within the length and breadth of this entire country, from Maine to Georgia, from the Atlantic to the Pacific Oceans, a solitary man or woman who is in possession of his or her full share of civil, religious, and political liberty. ... Why? Because slavery is the great lord of this country, and there is no power in this nation today strong enough to withstand it.*"

I talked about the unfreedom of black and white, northerners and southerners, rich and poor. Of how the evils of slavery contaminated the entire nation. Of how prejudice infected everyone. And I shared an example I knew intimately.

"*I wish to speak now of ... the class which I have the honor to represent—the free people of color. What is our condition regarding civil, religious, and political liberty? In the state in which I live, Ohio, they do not enjoy the elective franchise, and why? It is owing to the indirect influence of American slavery. Slavery in Kentucky, the adjoining state, says to the people of Ohio, 'You must not allow colored people to vote and be elected to office, because our slaves will hear of it and become restless, and directly we shall have an insurrection and our throats will be cut.' And so, the people of Ohio say to the colored people that they cannot allow them the privilege of voting, notwithstanding the colored people pay taxes like others, and in the face of the acknowledged principle that taxation and representation should always go together.*"

I finished with a challenge. "*Shall our free institutions triumph and our country become the asylum of the oppressed of all climes? ... May God help the right!*"

As the audience rose to their feet, cheering and clapping, my heart raced. I'd done it! I'd spoken to this mighty crowd, and they liked what I had to say! For the rest of the day, I was walking on air. The next day's New York dailies printed my speech in full, as did all the main anti-slavery papers and journals around the country.

After that huge congress, nothing was the same. Everything I'd done until then had been a training ground for the wider fight. My ability to influence others for the good of my race increased dramatically because of that speech.

CHAPTER 27

1856 BROWNHELM AND OBERLIN

As my one-year term as the Brownhelm town clerk drew to a close, I began to talk about my next career move with Carrie. Logically, my law practice should be based in Oberlin with its larger population, but it meant a long drive to work every day. In August 1855 our first baby, Arthur, had been born and I couldn't bear him to grow up with a father he hardly saw.

One morning, over breakfast, Carrie said, 'Mercer', (she liked to call me by my middle name), 'if Oberlin is the best place for business, what say we move into town?' As she spoke, she spooned porridge into Arthur's mouth.

When she paused to look for my reaction, our curly-mopped little darling wriggled in his highchair, reaching for the spoon in his mother's hand. We both laughed as his mouth opened and shut like a baby chick, squawking for more, more, more.

'I've been thinking that very same thing, my love. I'm confident of making a living as a lawyer now, so I don't need the income from the farm. And in winter, the nearly two-hour ride each way is a chore. Shall I start looking around for a suitable residence?'

She clapped her hands with joy. Arthur copied her, making us laugh.

A few days later, as I was heading to Oberlin, Caroline asked me to take her best Sunday boots to her brother's cobbler shop for repair. Once Orindatus, whom his family called Datus, had finished at college, he'd learned the shoe-making trade and now was a partner in a flourishing business. He was well respected in the town—had even been a village marshal for a short time.

As he tap-tapped the new toe and heel plates, I took a seat so we could catch up on family news.

'Did Carrie tell you we've decided to move into town?'

Datus, a thickset man with skin a couple of shades darker than his sister's, looked up. 'She did. Dropped a wee note to Amanda yesterday. What are you planning to do with the farm?'

'I've decided to sell. It's a desirable property, as you well know. I doubt it'll linger long on the market. My next call, when I leave you, is to get the realtor to find somewhere suitable. We won't sell the farm until we've got something else.'

Datus finished the repair, brushed his hands on his well-worn leather apron, and carried the boots over to the counter. As he wrapped them in brown paper, he looked at me from under his thick eyebrows. 'Amanda and I talked of little else last night. Fact is, we've a proposition for you.'

I was curious. He was a thoughtful man and considered in anything he took on. Not one for idle chat.

He didn't speak further until he'd tied the parcel, finishing with a neat string bow. Then, leaning on the counter, he said, 'We were going to come out this weekend to discuss our idea with you. Would you consider exchanging your farm for our new house? We've talked about owning a farm for some time, but thought it would be a few years off. However, when we read Caroline's note, it was as though the idea jumped off the page. We could barely sleep last night for thinking about it.'

'But you've just finished building that lovely house. You've not even moved in! Why would you want to go out to Brownhelm?'

'We wouldn't. We'd put a manager on it, like you did. We'd spend weekends and holidays there. We want to give our children a country upbringing like I had. Even though we Wall children were born enslaved, our father never treated us as such. We had a great childhood; the run of the plantation, streams to fish and swim in, animals to play with, freedom to roam.'

Reliving the joys of a country upbringing–I could see how that would appeal to him. But I was still perplexed.

'I thought Amanda was excited about moving into her new home?'

'She was. But we can build another house. We really love your place. It's in such a beautiful location and it seems too good an opportunity to miss. If you say yes, there's no contest in her mind between the farm and the new house. Every time we drive back to town after a visit, she wishes she could stay longer. Obviously, the farm is worth more than a house in town. We'd include another parcel of bare land in the offer.'

'Well, that's unexpected.' I rubbed my left ear, the habit I'd had since my youth when faced with complex questions. The idea was intriguing. 'I guess it might work. We'd have to get all properties valued and make sure there's a fair exchange. But first, I need to check with Carrie. I wouldn't make a decision this important without discussing with her. I suspect she'll be amenable; each time you've taken us to see the progress of your house she's been most complimentary.'

After much organizing and negotiating, the exchange was transacted. The two sisters-in-law managed the domestic details, such as what furniture and curtains stayed at Brownhelm. Datus and I spent time in the sheds and other outbuildings, agreeing on what equipment and stock he would take over and what I would sell. Carrie also had a grand time ordering new furniture for our much larger new home.

On a beautiful spring morning, with mixed sadness and excitement, we left our country home. I took a nostalgic glance at the verdant pastures as we wheeled out the gate and onto the muddy, rough road for Oberlin, but it was the right time to go. The two well-matched chestnut sorrels stepped out eagerly, as if they knew this was no ordinary day and Carrie sat beside me on the driving seat, holding nine-month-old Arthur. Stowed behind us, in the tray of our light wagon, were the last household items and foodstuffs we'd not sent ahead with the heavy gear.

Apart from one surly fellow, our new neighbors in East College Street, the best part of Oberlin, made us very welcome and our local friends were delighted to have us close to them again. Being so far away in Brownhelm, regular socializing had been limited to either daytime visits or longer stays. To visit with friends and be back home in our own beds at night was a real treat.

Our little family quickly expanded. It was the custom for Oberlin families to take in boarders, for the town lacked sufficient accommodation for all who wished to be educated. I received a letter from a wealthy white Louisiana planter.

Would it be acceptable for you to board my three sons for the duration of their education at Oberlin Preparatory School and possibly College? They and their mother, a woman of your complexion, are dear to me, but it is not possible for me to protect my sons from the disadvantages of mixed-race heritage in this place.

I wish them to be given every advantage of education and I understand Oberlin is the best place to achieve this. I have been informed that you and Mrs. Langston might be sympathetic to their situation.

Within the next year, another boy of similar parentage, and then our next baby, Ralph, also joined our family. It was as well we'd bought a large house—we needed it for this household of boys!

'The property swap has worked out wonderfully, Mercer. This house is perfect for our needs,' Carrie said one night, as we stood on our wide veranda to farewell Professor Henry Peck and his wife. They lived right across the street and had been our supper guests. Henry had been one of my principal teachers during my three years of theology studies and was now one of my best friends.

With my arm around my beloved wife, I looked past Carrie's now well-established vines growing up the porch supports and along the street. Everywhere I could see large two-story houses, of similar size to ours, each surrounded by their own well-laid out gardens. Although I appreciated the luxury of our beautiful home, there was a bigger reason I'd wanted to live in the best street in town. I felt a responsibility to live to the same standard as my white neighbors as a way of carrying the flag for others of our race. I wanted to show the world that blacks were as good as whites, that we could achieve to the same standard–if given education and opportunity.

CHAPTER 28

1857-58 OBERLIN

I'D HAD MY SHINGLE up in Oberlin for about a year, and business was flourishing, when a deputation of local gentlemen came knocking on my office door.

'Mr. Langston, we'd like to nominate you as Township Clerk for our district.'

I'd been given the nod that such a move was contemplated, so it didn't take me by surprise as much as the Brownhelm honor. This position covered a bigger region than the little community of Brownhelm, so it was gratifying to be considered. However, I knew not everyone in the Russia Township district, of which Oberlin was part, was in favor of black integration.

'I'm very honored, gentlemen, but are you quite sure? I would hate my nomination to mean a Whig or Democrat got the vote.'

'We're sure. You've all the right credentials for the job and you're highly respected. We need a good candidate to get rid of the current fellow. Anson Dayton's sympathies are not compatible with our town.'

And so it happened. Even though Oberlin was so pro-freedom, they'd never before elected a Negro to public office. Congratulations from supporters of black rights flooded in from far and wide. Dayton was *not* happy. Two years later, the town's rejection of him had far-reaching consequences.

A couple of weeks after the Russia Township election, the local Board of Education chose me as Acting Manager of the Oberlin schools. That was followed by election to the Oberlin City Council. Heady days for a black orphan boy who'd been told he was crazy to think he could be a lawyer!

However, Oberlin and her nearby communities were rare in their acceptance of people of color. Every day, national newspapers reported harsh and unfair judgments heaped on my persecuted brethren.

One of the most inflammatory judgments was the Dred Scott affair.

I'd been following Dred and Harriet Scott's complex legal case since it began in 1846. I wasn't the only one. As the challenges and counter-challenges mounted, their story came to the attention of every abolitionist and black rights advocate in the country.

Dred Scott, born a slave, had been taken from Missouri in 1833 to the free states of first, Illinois, then Wisconsin, by his owner, Dr. Emerson, a military surgeon. During this time he was allowed to marry. The Scotts were in Wisconsin for about nine years. In 1842, they were removed back to Missouri with Emerson and his wife of about four years. Emerson died in 1843 and Scott attempted to purchase his family's freedom from Emerson's widow. She refused. In 1846, based on his long-time residency in a free territory, which supposedly gave him the right to be free, he decided to go to law for the freedom of his family. He was aided by abolitionist lawyers.

For eleven years, the Scotts battled. The case bounced around from district court to the Circuit Court of Appeals, and eventually to the United States Supreme Court.

Enter Chief Justice Roger Taney, the most powerful judge in the nation. He made headlines, and not in a good way!

On March 6, 1857, following a very convoluted line of reasoning, he decided persons of African descent were not citizens of the United States! Therefore, they had no right to take a case to court. On that basis, the Scotts had no right to sue for freedom.

What an uproar that caused!

As I was leading my horse into the blacksmith's shop for new shoes, black clouds suddenly dropped their load. Bullets of hail pelted the wooden shingle roof. Outside, the street turned to soft glue. The rain was so heavy I could barely see First Church, right across the road. I'd intended to walk along to my office while the job was being done, but the rain changed my mind. Instead, I shifted some horseshoes off a stool and sat down to watch the burly blacksmith, Allen Jones, weave his metal magic.

He lifted up the horse's back leg and, resting it on his thigh, removed the old shoes and trimmed the hoof. As he worked, he spoke loudly above the noise of the rain. 'What say you 'bout this Dred Scott rulin'?'

'It's evil. Of all the civil liberties we've lost recently, this is the worst!'

'Why you think the judge do it?'

'I suspect Taney thought he was settling the matter once and for all, but I predict it'll do just the opposite. From what I read, anyone with any fairness in their veins, not just the abolitionists and we blacks, is boiling with anger.'

'I cain't read, but I hear people talkin' when they wait for their hosses. You're the lawyer. Can you 'splain to me?'

'We're fighting an uphill battle for black rights, Allen. This ruling pushes us even further back. In the south, even before Judge Taney's ruling, some states already had laws forbidding citizenship to free blacks.

'And in the north, blacks in some northern states had more rights when the Declaration of Independence was signed in 1776 than now. Back then, five northern states gave free blacks voting rights. Now we're down to three, and in one of them, New York, black rights have been reduced. And though the number of states has more than doubled, no new states allow blacks to vote. We have to pay taxes, but if we can't vote, we've got no say in how we're ruled.'

Allen reached for a new shoe and tried it against the horse's trimmed hoof. Satisfied, he lowered the leg, gave the horse's haunch an absent-minded pat, then, gripping the shoe with long tongs, carried it over to the red-hot furnace.

'I've no book learnin', he said, 'but seems to me somethin's gotta be lanced. If a horse's hoof gets an abscess, you gotta drain it. Let the poison out. With this slavery, seems to me there's so much anger, it gotta be lanced too.'

'How do you suggest we do that, Allen?'

As the metal turned white hot in the flames, he said, 'Those southern fellas ain't gonna give up their slaves. Ifn' the government allows such an unfair law, seems to me they want slavery everywhere. If the north be serious 'bout stoppin' the wrongs done us peoples by fellas like this Taney, I think there'll be war. Like fittin' a shoe, gotta trim away the old stuff an' reshape the shoe afore fittin' something better.'

Uneducated he may have been, but people everywhere echoed his down-to-earth opinion, in the south as well as the north. Southerners were talking secession–they wanted freedom to live on their terms without the north telling them they couldn't have slaves. Northerners had two main reasons to maintain the status quo–the union of states was sacrosanct, and the south had no right to force the rest of us to accept slavery or allow such an evil to extend to the new territories.

The controversy brought some unexpected names to the fore. I kept hearing of Abraham Lincoln, a prairie lawyer from Springfield, Illinois.

'What do you know about him?' I asked Judge Bliss one afternoon. I'd been representing a client at a court hearing he'd presided over. As we often did after completing official duties, we were enjoying coffee and catching up on the news.

'As a lawyer, he's known as Honest Abe and I hear he's an up-and-comer in the new Republican party. He hates slavery,' replied my friend and mentor.

'Has he any political experience?'

'Yes. As a Whig, he served in the Illinois House of Representatives and also had a two-year stint in the U.S. House of Representatives in the late 1840s. I believe he gave up politics for a while and went back to his law practice, but he couldn't sit idle watching the high possibility of slavery spreading to the new western territories.'

'Good for him. What else do you know about him?'

'Not a lot, but I understand he's a plain-spoken man. Those who know him seem to respect him. I hear he has a particular skill in explaining complex topics in words even a person with no education can understand.'

That got my attention. I was always ears-open for ways to make my speeches as effective as possible. I resolved to take more notice.

Soon after, a newspaper reported one of Lincoln's speeches to an Illinois audience.

'Listen to this fine turn of phrase, dear,' I said to Caroline, who was relaxing with some embroidery in her rocking chair. Our two boys were in bed, our boarders were busy with their studies, and we were enjoying a rare quiet evening together.

"... it is asserted to be true in letters, newspapers and public speeches, and borne by every mail, and blown by every breeze to the eyes and ears of the world."

'I love the imagery,' she answered. 'Truth blown on the breeze—I can see it! Who's the writer, and what's he talking about?'

'Abraham Lincoln. A Republican lawyer from Illinois. He was critiquing a speech by Judge Douglas about state and territory rights, slavery, the troubles in Kansas and the shocking Dred Scott ruling.'

I kept reading. 'And here's another of his pithy phrases. *"... see what a wreck-mangled ruin it makes of our once glorious Declaration."* He sounds like a good thinker as well as a wordsmith. I'd be interested to meet the man.'

'Well, since you've joined the Republican party, perhaps you will.'

The next time I heard of Abraham Lincoln was after he'd spoken at the close of the Illinois Republican State Convention June 16, 1858. They'd just named him as their candidate for the senate.

'Do you remember last year I mentioned Abraham Lincoln, Carrie,' I asked. I was reading the paper while finishing my breakfast coffee. 'He really has a remarkable way with words.'

I read out:

"We are now far into the fifth year since a policy was initiated, with the avowed object, and confident promise, of putting an end to slavery agitation. Under the operation of that policy, that agitation has not only NOT ceased, but has constantly augmented. In my opinion, it will not cease until a crisis shall have been reached, and passed. 'A house divided against itself cannot stand.'

"I believe this government cannot endure, permanently half slave and half free. I do not expect the Union to be dissolved–I do not expect the house to fall–but I do expect it will cease to be divided. It will become all one thing or all the other."

'Let me see,' she said, pushing her chair back and coming to lean over my shoulder. We read the full speech together.

'You're right. He's eloquent without being flowery. The simplest laborer would understand what he's saying. Perhaps it's his plain speaking that makes his words so powerful.'

I frowned. 'His prediction of being 'all one thing or all the other' sounds fine if the north prevails, but think what horror would be unleashed if slavery were to extend to all states.'

Carrie grasped my shoulder. She was a clear and objective thinker. 'God help us, but there'll be war if they try.'

PART FOUR

CHAPTER 29

1858 OBERLIN

MONDAY, SEPTEMBER 13, 1858, was crisp and sunny. As I headed off that morning to see a client in a nearby county, I reflected with pleasure on how, four years ago to the day, I'd been admitted to the Ohio Bar. Those years had brought many blessings in both my personal and professional life. The nursery now included Chinque, our precious first daughter, my wife was content, and business was expanding. It was a good day, warmed with happy memories.

The end of the day was anything but tranquil.

Riding back into town in the late afternoon, through the dappled shade from the tall trees bordering the road, I was looking forward to a pleasant evening with my wife and family. To my surprise, I found the center of Oberlin almost deserted. At that hour, the place was normally humming with people wrapping up their business for the day, children enjoying their last games before being summoned for their supper, men chatting on the street and students moving from class to home. What could have happened? Had the Second Coming occurred while I wasn't looking?

I saw a feeble old man sitting on a porch. Without dismounting, I called out. 'Where is everyone?'

'Gorn t' Wellington t' rescue John Price,' he replied.

I looked at him, perplexed. I didn't know the name.

He expanded. 'He's a runaway. Man-catchers come 'n dragged 'im back t' Kentucky. A mighty wot-for. Everyone who cud find a way o' gettin' there grabbed guns, jumped on hosses, climbed inta wagons, took orf in a bustin' 'urry to stop them damned southerners gettin' the poor lad on the train south. I'd've gone mesel' but what cin I do?' He gestured to the black hickory walking stick leaning beside his rocker.

I turned my horse and set off at a canter, south to Wellington. I'd only gone four miles when I saw a buggy racing toward me, dust rising from the wheels. As it got closer, I spotted Simeon Bushnell, a local printer and bookshop clerk I knew well, at the ribbons. Squashed in beside him were Richard Winsor, an Oberlin student, and an ill-clad black man with a smile as wide as Kansas.

Simeon called out excitedly as I rode by. 'John is safe; here he is; I have him.' As I slowed down, I heard him say, 'Come back, Mr. Langston!'

I nearly turned my horse, but I could see a huge crowd, hundreds strong, coming our way. They were singing, shouting, and enthusiastically waving a motley array of weapons. At their head, I spied my brother, Charles, and my brother-in-law, Datus. I gave Simeon and his exulting passengers a congratulatory salute, but kept riding.

As I drew near, Charles called out.

'What a day we've had, John. You missed a good one!' I was swept up in the rejoicing crowd, everyone retelling the events of the day and what they'd seen, heard, or taken part in.

I had seen our fugitive in the town, but his story was new to me. Turns out he'd been living in Oberlin for some time. In our community, all runaways were accepted and supported. The Liberty School was set up for people of any age who wanted to learn to read and write, they were allowed to live openly in the community, and no barriers to work were raised other than their own skill and ability. John was a casual farm worker and well respected by those who knew him, including his Sunday School teacher.

The stories were flying from lip to ear; it was difficult to piece it all together.

'I'll take my horse home to her stable and be back soon,' I said to Charles as we tried to talk. Delighted people kept coming up, making conversation difficult.

'I wish I could come too,' said Carrie wistfully, once I told her what was going on, 'but the children are in bed and the maid's gone for the day. Don't leave me too long in suspense, Mercer!'

'I'll be back when I can,' I promised, gave her a quick kiss, crammed my top hat on, and hastened back to the excited crowd.

By the time I returned, our fugitive had disappeared and those who knew weren't saying where he was. I heard later he'd been hidden in a back upstairs room in Professor Fairchild's home, one of our most respectable and law-abiding professors and not known to be an abolitionist. No spy in the community would think to direct the law there. Nonetheless, it was a relief to learn, a couple of days later, that he'd been safely escorted across the lake to freedom in Canada.

Stories were told and retold as folk moved from group to group in the center of town, sharing the drama of the day with those who'd not been present. The cool fall day had slipped into evening before I had a reasonably clear picture of the events of the day. My training in logic and investigation stood me in good stead as I listened and questioned.

One of my best sources was my friend Henry Peck, who'd been one of the rescuers. I heaved a sigh of relief when I found him, for many wild stories were flying round; I was confident he'd have a coherent view of the matter.

'Do you know how it all began?' I asked.

'I had plenty of time to find out as we raised the dust back and forth between Oberlin and Wellington,' he laughed. 'As you know, we're always alert for strangers in town. About three weeks ago, some locals noticed an unfamiliar fellow staying at Wack's Hotel, a southerner from his speech. They immediately became suspicious.'

'As they should,' I replied. 'There can't be a body in town who doesn't know about the attempts last month to steal the Wagoner family. That devil, Anson Dayton, was behind that. He's a nasty excuse for a lawyer.'

'He's involved with this as well,' replied Henry. 'I tell you, John, it was a good thing for this town when you began your law practice here. He's sore against you, though. Hates your "black guts", he's been heard to say.'

I shrugged. I'd heard worse. I knew Anson hadn't forgiven me for winning the Township Clerk role, let alone giving him competition for regular legal work. I was younger, more successful ... and black. He hated blacks. Unfortunately for the town, after losing the clerk position, he'd secured another post with power—as the local U.S. Deputy Marshall. And, he, like Chauncy Wack, was a Democrat and deeply unsympathetic to fugitives.

Henry went back to his story. 'The fellow people noticed, Jennings by name, was seen talking to Dayton. It was also noted that Jennings was trying to look inconspicuous. Given he's tall and with a strongly built bull-necked physique, that made them even more suspicious.'

'Such a combination would send alarm bells ringing for any abolitionist or black!' I chuckled. 'Chauncy Wack, Anson Dayton, and a southern stranger! That's a particularly nasty combination!'

Wack was as disreputable as his establishment, and very unpopular with most of the townsfolk. Since the Fugitive Slave Act in 1850, no runaway was completely safe, even though few from the south visited our town—our nation-wide profile as an abolitionist hotbed kept most pro-slavery people away. However, for opportunists with no morals, it was a tempting source of income. A strong farm worker was worth around $1,000. Kidnapped and sold, everyone involved made serious money. Set him free and they got nothing. People like Wack were always after easy money.

'Jennings disappeared for a while,' said Henry. 'Seems he'd originally come for someone else, but recognized our John Price as belonging to a neighbor back in Kentucky. We gather he sent word back to the owner, who organized a power of attorney. Next thing we know, another stranger was spotted; he'd brought the paperwork from a Kentucky court. The two fellows finally connected back here at Wack's, then two more strangers showed up.'

I said, 'Let me guess. Were they government agents?'

Henry nodded. 'For sure. That became obvious in the melee down at Wellington. Makes sense for the officials to send out-of-towners. They'd have known very few Oberliners would assist them.'

'So how did they get hold of Price, with so many people keeping a look-out?'

'Unfortunately for our lad, he seems not to have realized how serious it was. To be fair, someone he knew betrayed him.'

'I heard the Boynton boy's name mentioned, but I've not had the details. Was it him?'

'Yes. Shakespeare Boynton, only thirteen, saw the chance for profit. The kidnappers enlisted his help; they had to get their target quickly away from Oberlin or their plot might be foiled. Boynton's an opportunistic lad with no moral code or compassion. His old man's no better.

'It's well known that Price does casual farm work, so he saw no cause for alarm this morning when Shakespeare arrived at his lodgings, driving a horse and buggy and saying, "Hey John, my Pa wants help with digging taters. Hop up and I'll take you there now."

'Apparently John said, "Can't, thanks. I'm looking after my friend Frank. He got hurt on the weekend. Fella over New Oberlin way might want work. I can help you find him, if you want."

'Young Boynton said, "Thanks. I just gotta see the blacksmith first. I'll be back". That was an excuse to rush back to Wack's Hotel and update Jennings. This set the next stage of the kidnap in motion.

'The rest is how I imagine it played out, but from what I've heard, I'm not far off the mark.

'Our young Judas went back and collected Price, who, all unsuspecting, climbed up on the buggy seat alongside his betrayer. But the plan nearly failed. They'd only just set off when they came upon the man they were seeking. He declined the offer; he already had work.

'The quick-witted boy said, "Tell you what, John, let's go for a drive, while I got my Pa's buggy. Not often the old buzzard lets me take it. Bet you don't often get out for a trot neither. I'll bring you back soon. Your mate Frank won't be long on his own."

'Price agreed. The two jogged along the dirt road leading to the Boynton farm, chatting idly. About noon, they reached the town boundary. Boynton heard hooves. Looking back, he saw a two-horse vehicle coming toward them. In it, he spotted his accomplices.

'He steered the buggy to the edge of the road so the approaching vehicle could draw alongside. A few minutes later, it was on them. One of the three captors jumped down, grabbed the unsuspecting Price even before Boynton fully stopped his horse, and thrust him into the back seat of the wagon. They then headed immediately the nine miles to Wellington. They planned to board the 5.13 pm train direct to Columbus and from there south to Kentucky.

'And there it might have ended for the luckless runaway, but for an observant passer-by. A local man spotted Price, jammed in tight with a bundle of unknown white men, heading south. This could only mean one thing. As soon as he reached Oberlin, he gave the alarm.'

Others in the crowd shared how quickly the town responded to the call. It was as if someone had tipped over a beehive. As the old man had told me, hundreds of our worthy Oberlin men and boys grabbed horses, commandeered passing buggies and wagons, snatched up their guns, and were rapidly on the heels of the kidnappers.

My other reliable source was Charles, who'd been in the thick of the events in Wellington. He painted a vivid word picture of the events, filling in sketchy details I'd gleaned from others.

Once the captors arrived in Wellington, they hustled John into Wadsworth's Hotel, in the middle of the village. They wanted food, plus somewhere quiet and out-of-sight while they waited for the train.

Little did they dream of the uproar about to overtake them. It was only 2 pm and they'd not even finished their meal before the hotel was surrounded by the Oberlin rescuers, determined to wrest the poor captive back. The public square in front of the hotel filled with people. Men milled around, shouting and waving guns. The crowd was fired up with righteous indignation, but at first no-one took the lead.

Wagons and carts carrying curious observers came from nearby communities until there was no space in the square to tether their horses.

'The leaves of the forest seemed to carry the news,' said an eyewitness.

Onlookers cheered each new group of arrivals. Women crowded the sidewalks, stores, all adjacent windows, and the nearest roofs. This was better entertainment than a circus!

One quick-thinking fellow came up with a plan to turn the tables on the kidnappers. He headed to the Town Hall for a warrant to arrest the captors—the two southerners and the federal deputy marshal and his assistant from Columbia. Others, including Charles, managed to get inside the hotel to try and reason with the kidnappers.

The captors rushed John upstairs to an attic room, out of reach of anyone trying to snatch him away.

As the uproar on the street grew louder, someone inside suggested Price be allowed to speak to the crowd. The captors led him downstairs to the second floor. Leaving him inside, Jennings stepped out onto the balcony. Below him was a sea of angry people, many waving guns.

The Kentuckian tried to placate the crowd. 'I want no controversy with the people of Ohio. This boy is mine by the laws of Kentucky and the United States.'

'There are no slaves in Ohio,' shouted someone in the crowd.

'The boy is willing to go to Kentucky,' replied Jennings. John had reluctantly agreed to return, sure he would never be able to escape again.

'Let him come out and speak for himself,' came the reply.

They pulled the captive out to stand beside Jennings.

'Do you want to go back to Kentucky?' called another man.

John shuffled. Looked anxiously at his captors, clearly afraid. 'I s'pose so. They got the papers on me.'

The questioning went on for a few minutes but suddenly stopped when one of the crowd pointed his gun at Jennings and shouted, 'Jump down, John. I'll shoot that damned old rascal.'

With that, the kidnappers pulled John in and ran back upstairs to the attic, which only had a small fanlight window.

The 5.13 pm train to Columbus came and went—without captive and captors. They could not get out of the hotel.

The next few hours were a confused mess of claims and counterclaims. Charles was one of a small group trying to force a resolution without violence. Eventually, some of them were allowed into the upstairs room to negotiate.

Finally, a handful of men pushed their way into the hotel and forced their way up the stairs, past guards sympathetic to the captors. With clever trickery, they got the door open. As they reached for John, the top of a ladder shattered the small attic window on the other side of the room. In the confusion, the rescuers snatched John and hustled him back down and out into the square.

A roar of delight met them as they emerged with their prize. A buggy standing near the door was commandeered. While Price and Winsor, the one who'd grabbed him, scrabbled for their seats, Simeon Bushnell gave the restive horse its head. They took off as though the hounds of hell were at their heels. As they galloped out of the square, they heard Winsor yelling, 'All is well'.

Everyone cheered, hats were flung in the air, and the assembled Oberlin crowd ran for their conveyances and took off after them, shouting in triumph.

The would-be captors gave up. They figured there was no point in trying to claim back their victim; they were more concerned for their safety. The remaining crowd agreed to give them safe-conduct if they left immediately, but threats were made if they returned. They slunk out of town on the next train.

CHAPTER 30

1858-1859 OBERLIN AND CLEVELAND

ALTHOUGH LIFE IN OBERLIN seemed to fall back into its normal easy pattern, the forces against us were mounting.

Only six weeks before John's rescue, I'd been appointed president for the all-black Ohio State Anti-Slavery Society, with Charles voted executive secretary. We'd formed the society specifically to fight against the Fugitive Slave Act. The rescue brought us even more supporters. I was also one of the fund-raisers. Printed matter for our audiences was needed at our many meetings, so I was a regular customer of the printer's shop where Simeon Bushnell worked.

'Do you reckon they'll come after us?' he asked one day, as he parceled up a big bundle of leaflets. 'I'm real glad we rescued John Price, but I'm wondering what consequences we might face. Have you heard anything, Mr. Langston?'

Freeborn cabinetmaker and undertaker, Wilson Evans, another of the rescuers, was also in the shop. He spoke up while I was considering my answer. 'I can't see it attracting much attention outside of Ohio, Simeon. Who cares about a little backwater town so far from Washington?'

I shook my head. 'Sorry, Wilson, but I don't agree with you. I think this is just the beginning of a much bigger fight. Our town has thrown down the gauntlet. I can't see President Buchanan allowing us to get away with it. Everyone knows Ohio is primarily Republican, and we've got Governor Chase supporting us, but Buchanan and his pro-slavery Democrat cronies will want to teach us a lesson. We're seen as a defiant hotbed of abolitionism that dared to challenge their precious Fugitive Slave Act. The president will look weak if he doesn't punish such an overt act of civil disobedience.'

The other two looked serious. 'Well, let them try to make an example of us. We've got you to support us, sir,' said Simeon, looking determined.

I was flattered by his belief in my abilities, but I knew the case needed far more than just my skills, should it go to court.

Sure enough, to court it went.

The rescuers were deluged with offers from highly experienced lawyers—nearly every member of the Cleveland bar offered his services for free.

Some of the senior rescuers and supporters came to me. 'We've got all these highly experienced men offering to take on our case, John. Who do you think we should select?'

'You can't go better than Rufus Spalding to lead the defense,' was my response. 'Look at his credentials. He's a former Speaker of the Ohio House of Representatives and has been a judge on the Ohio Supreme Court.'

'But isn't he a Democrat?' asked Professor Fairchild.

'He doesn't agree with their stance on slavery,' replied James Fitch, a local bookseller and printer and one of the rescuers. A devout man, he was also the much-loved superintendent of the Oberlin Sunday School. 'He left them a few years ago over the slavery issue. He's a leading light in the Republican party now. A sound fellow with vast experience.'

'He's also a good friend of Governor Salmon P. Chase,' I added. 'You can bet your bottom dollar the Governor will provide advice behind the scenes.'

Our fellows ended up with four outstanding attorneys.

As soon as the case began, heavy-jowled Democrat Judge Hiram Willson showed he was deeply prejudiced against Oberlin and its leaders. It also became glaringly obvious that the legal confrontation was not really about the rescue, but politics; the ruling Democrats were determined to make an example of us. The strongly southern-supported Democrat party stood for slavery; racial equality threatened the very fabric of their slave-based society.

Many unjust and illegal things were allowed by the stern-faced judge. For example, the pool of forty possible jury members needed for the arraignment had been carefully chosen by the court officials to suit their cause. Even though our part of Ohio was overwhelmingly Republican, thirty of the forty possible candidates were Democrats. Since each side could reject twelve candidates, Belden, the prosecuting attorney, was making sure he'd have no Republican juror to persuade. And one member of the jury was the father of 'Judas' Boynton, the lad who'd tricked John into his buggy. Impartial? I don't think so!

On Tuesday December 7, 1858, the arrest warrants began to be served. Charles, Datus, Simeon Bushnell, Richard Winsor, Henry and Wilson Evans and thirty-one other men, both black and white, many of them prominent and influential men from both Oberlin and Wellington, were charged under the terms of the Fugitive Slave Act for aiding and abetting in the rescue of John Price. Some were out of town, but those who received their warrants were requested to get themselves by train to Cleveland the next day to be charged in court.

Rufus Spalding, a past judge on the Ohio Supreme Court, led our men's defence, aided by three outstanding lawyers from Cleveland. Legal tussles began immediately. Judge Willson was reluctantly persuaded to let our men return home on their own recognizances, without bail, despite the objection of Belden, the prosecuting lawyer.

The officials tried to scoop me up in their accusations, but everyone agreed I was in neither Oberlin nor Wellington when the business took place. A number of others who *were* involved were also not charged—a quick look showed they were Democrats. I became well known for the motto I used at every rally and meeting: 'The Democrat party must be destroyed'.

Winter recess was on us, so they set the trial date for March 1859.

You might suppose things would quieten down over the next three months, but another incident brought the case back to the forefront of public attention for a few weeks. It related to William Lincoln, one of the college students who'd taken a leading role in the rescue.

One cold Saturday evening in mid-January, I was reading by a crackling fire in the parlor when I heard a knock. Being closest to the front door, for my wife was upstairs with the children, I went to open it.

There on the doorstep was my brother-in-law, Datus, and an exhausted-looking and disheveled William Lincoln. Datus's horse and trap stood at the gate.

'Come in, come in.' As far as I knew, William was teaching down at Dublin, near Columbus, for the winter term. I'd made it my business to know how many of the rescuers had been served their warrants to appear in court, and I knew he was in the group not yet officially notified. By the look of him, something was dreadfully wrong. His clothes needed a good press, he'd not shaved in a couple of days, and he smelled as though he'd been rumbled in dirty hay.

I called for the maid to bring us hot drinks and food, and seated my unexpected guests by the fire.

Once they settled, I asked, 'What's up, fellows?'

Datus spoke first. 'I was driving past the train depot a short while ago, and who should stumble out but William, off the Cleveland train. He's been given a right run-around by the constabulary! I thought you might have some idea whether there's anything we can do legally about the way they've treated him.'

William, holding his hands to the fire, took up the tale.

'Mr. Langston, you've no idea the trials I've had the last 36 hours. Early yesterday afternoon I was drilling my pupils on their times tables when two men burst into my classroom with a pistol and manacles. One of them was one of the two out-of-town federal agents we'd bested. With no explanation, he clapped the handcuffs on me. Told my terrified students I was a 'bad man'. Only gave me time to exchange my gown and slippers for an overcoat and boots, then hauled me out of the building, into a carriage, and off to Columbus.'

'What!' I was horrified. 'Was this to do with the warrant to appear in court?'

'They didn't immediately say so, but yes, it was. I tried to reason with them. I said, "You need not put these manacles upon me. I shall make no resistance" but even though I asked several times over the next some hours, for my wrists were soon severely galled, they refused.'

Datu had only heard some of the story; he sat as shocked as me.

'Once we got to Columbus, I begged my captors to take me to friends to seek legal help, but they refused. Took me straight to the jail. Deputy Marshall Lowe, the other federal agent involved with kidnapping John Price, was waiting for me. He wouldn't let me contact my friends either. Said there was no point—I'd be on a 4 am train to Cleveland to be arraigned. He also wouldn't remove the manacles. Had me thrown in a stinking cell.

'After Lowe left, the first fellow finally took off my handcuffs. Promised me food, but nothing came. I tried lying down on the dirty straw pallet, but the cell was full of rats. I had to drive them out before I could sit down. The stench was so awful I stuffed my nose with a handkerchief. I'd only just dropped off to sleep when, in the middle of the night, they woke me to go to the train depot. Only then did I get a cup of coffee and a piece of stale pie.'

Just then, our maid came in with sustenance. William looked at the plate of cookies and ham sandwiches longingly, then at his grubby hands.

'Would you like to use the facilities?' I asked.

'Oh, thank you. They gave me no chance to clean up.'

Once back from the washroom, and with food and drink inside him, he sat back with a contented sigh. 'That's the first food I've had since 3 am this morning. Now, where was I?'

'About to get on a train to Cleveland,' reminded Datus.

'That was a repeat of Columbus–clapped in prison again and no food. It wasn't until four o'clock this afternoon they took me before Judge Willson, entered my plea of not guilty, and I could go free on my own recognizance, same as you and the other fellows, Datus. I didn't even have the fare to get here, let alone back to Dublin. I had to beg Lowe to give me a dollar. Otherwise, I'd be still on the streets of Cleveland.'

'They treated you like a common criminal!' burst out Datus. 'That's disgraceful! Every one of those authorities would've known you'd be allowed to depart on the same terms as the rest of us, awaiting the trial! Can we do something about this, John?'

'We'll certainly complain about it. And publicize it.' By now I'd become quite skilled at generating publicity for worthy causes.

Before William returned to Dublin, we held a public meeting so he could tell his story. A resolution was passed, condemning 'the illegal, cowardly and insulting use of official authority'. Publications further afield wrote about it, and William Lloyd Garrison's Boston newspaper, *The Liberator*, even commented on it. Our supporters in the press used every offense against decency to stoke the fires. Evil Goliath (the federal authorities) against tiny David (the small-town rescuers)–great story, great imagery!

They milked it for all it was worth.

CHAPTER 31

1858-1859 OBERLIN AND CLEVELAND

WHILE THE COURT WAS in winter recess, the lawyers on both sides were preparing their cases. Aside from the many twists and turns the attorneys had to navigate in the court case, our lawyers also came up with a cunning plan to turn the tables and tangle the prosecution. They filed a case against the accusers, and Lorain County, of which Elyria was the county seat, played an important part in the scheme.

The Lorain County Grand Jury issued warrants for the four men who'd captured John, charging them with kidnapping under an Ohio state statute, which made the arrest, imprisonment, kidnapping or decoying out of Ohio of any *free* black or mulatto an indictable offense. The gist of it was that trying to take a black out of Ohio before they *proved* him to be a fugitive slave was a crime. As far as Ohio law was concerned, anyone stepping foot in Ohio was free. Therefore, by definition, John was free. The clever wording of the charge against the kidnappers was that John's status as property hadn't been tested in court. That was now impossible to prove; John was out of reach!

The Lorain County officials then set about to try and capture the four kidnappers, who had to come north for the trial. It became a long-drawn-out game of cat and mouse. At the root of it, our lawyers were messing with the volatile issue of federal versus state rights, and challenging the validity of the Fugitive Slave Act. It caused a lot of extra work for the prosecutors as they tried to keep their chief witnesses out of the Lorain County jail.

Some months later, this ploy played a very important part in bringing the trials to a conclusion.

In March 1859, with the winter recess over, the opposing attorneys met to select the jury for the trial. I was exceptionally busy with work, so opted not to attend the preliminaries in Cleveland. I wanted to clear as many cases as possible so that, when our men were required to appear, I could be there in the spectator gallery to support them. However, we all kept well-informed of events. Every morning, the previous day's update, as reported by the Cleveland papers, arrived in Oberlin by train.

Another of the rescuers, Ralph Plumb, was, like me, an Oberlin lawyer. I liked him and valued his sharp mind; we often got together to discuss interesting cases and finer points of law. Until they recalled him to the trial, Ralph was at liberty to continue working, so we fell into the habit of reviewing the news from Cleveland each morning over a cup of coffee.

'Look at what they're doing with the jurors again, John,' he said the day after the judge opened the case. 'They've stuffed it with Democrats, just like they did at the arraignment.'

'You're right,' I replied. 'Not one Republican and not one person from Lorain County.'

Another example of bias, once the trial had begun, was allowing Chauncy Wack, owner of the disreputable hotel where the abductors met, and therefore one of the witnesses, to sit in court through all the evidence. When our lawyers protested, for witnesses were not allowed in court until called, the judge waved it away as inconsequential.

Tuesday, April 5, 1859, the trial finally began. I was there with my pregnant sister-in-law Amanda. I looked around the courtroom of the imposing new Cleveland County Court House as I helped her take a seat in the gallery. It was a bitterly cold day, for snow had fallen in the morning, but it didn't deter anyone; the high-ceiling room was packed with supporters, reporters and the curious. The pack of bodies soon warmed the room, though the smell of damp clothing and body sweat was unpleasant.

We exchanged greetings with a goodly number of our neighbors, including many of the rescuers' wives, for Oberliners had turned out en masse to support family and friends. As we shuffled past people already seated, heading for empty chairs further from the aisle, we had to dodge not only knees and handbags, but also knitting needles and embroidery hoops. I suppose sitting for days listening to lawyers drone on was a perfect time for industrious women to catch up on handiwork.

Down below, reporters with notebooks in hand and pencils perched behind their ears vied for space at the reporters' table. The latecomers had to take their chances in the main gallery. They'd come from far away, including Massachusetts, New York, and Pittsburgh, and many were sending their reports to more than one paper. Many editions published the commentaries verbatim, for the case had stirred a hornet's nest of debate everywhere. With the invention of Pitman's shorthand, the telegraph stringing further across the land, and our rapidly expanding railway system, reports flashed from top to bottom of the country in a few hours.

Each rescuer was to be tried separately. Simeon Bushnell was first, perhaps because no-one disputed who'd galloped John off in the buggy, back to Oberlin.

The legal wrangling, witnesses' testimony, cross-examinations and summing up went on for ten days. Belden, the prosecuting attorney, complained that our defense attorneys were playing to the public and the reporters at least as much as the jury. He was right. They did it deliberately; it was a brilliant chance to whip up public sentiment against the Fugitive Slave Law and the Buchanan administration. As soon as we'd seen how they'd rigged the jury, we knew it was impossible to expect an impartial trial; the more realistic of us didn't even expect an acquittal. So, our attorneys made political capital of the situation whilst doing their best to defend our brave champions of freedom.

Lawyers' arguments concluded and the judge's last remarks made, the jury was excused to reach a conclusion. They reconvened after lunch, the foreman stood, and the courtroom hushed.

Solemnly, the judge asked, 'Do you have a verdict?'

'Yes, your Honor. We find the defendant guilty.'

Around the room people gasped. Shifted nervously. Glanced at each other. A few cheered and were glared at. Simeon sat there, silent. His poor wife sobbed.

No sooner was the verdict pronounced than Belden, the prosecuting attorney, called, 'Charles Langston will now be tried.'

The judge then announced the same jury would hear all cases. The roar of disapproval was so loud it startled the pigeons perching on the window ledges outside.

'It is an outrage to try another very similar case with the same men who've just rendered a verdict,' said Spalding. 'Their minds are made up. How can they possibly be impartial? It's unheard of. A villainous outrage. We will not attempt a defense before such a jury.'

The other three agreed.

'Very well,' said Belden petulantly. 'I ask the court to order all the accused into the custody of the marshal.'

The judge accepted his request. 'Let the accused be called.'

All the defendants' names were read out and the twenty who were in court rose. They were led off to prison, carrying the carpetbags and valises they'd expected to be taking home for the weekend. The judge left and the courtroom burst into a babble of dissent—alarmed, annoyed, and angry.

We family members walked beside our men to the Cuyahoga County Jail, located only a few steps from the Court House. It was raining and we all had to wait outside the prison; the sheriff was reluctant to accept his prisoners without written orders. Perhaps he wouldn't get his fees otherwise? We stood there, getting steadily wetter, while the marshal, leaving my brother-in-law in charge, went off to get the necessary paperwork. Clearly, he didn't expect his charges to run away!

Sheriff Wightman, a good man, stood on the doorstep of the county jail, looking worried as he surveyed his unexpected visitors. 'Gentlemen, I open my doors to you, not as criminals, but as guests. I cannot regard you as criminals for doing only what

I should do myself under similar circumstances. Come in out of the weather.'

We supporters were left outside. As the prisoners filed inside, James Fitch turned to a friend. 'Please get someone to take charge of my Sabbath School next Sunday. You've four hundred children and youth to look after in my absence.'

While officials argued about whether to accept the prisoners, Sheriff Wightman and John B. Smith, the jailer, another sympathizer of our cause, made the men as comfortable as possible. Once their stay was confirmed, Mr. Smith and his wife gave over their own apartment on the top floor of the jail, plus other adjacent rooms, for their stay. Surely this was one of the most unusual confinements in penal history!

Then began a remarkable, frustrating, and lengthy battle of wills between the judge and prosecuting attorneys on one hand, and our attorneys on the other. Although bail had not been required earlier, it was now demanded, or the rescuers would not be released. They refused.

It was clear to us all that Belden acted out of malice. He was determined to humble not only the men on trial, but also our abolitionist communities. He delighted in throwing some of the leading citizens of Oberlin and Wellington–professors, teachers, students, farmers and businesspeople, including my brother, my brother-in-law and many of my friends–into jail.

The stand-off reverberated throughout the land. These men were not common criminals; they'd already proved they were willing to appear whenever the court required them. However, they wouldn't be intimidated. They united on the principle of fairness, even if that meant prison.

That Sunday, six or seven hundred people gathered inside the large yard of the jail and on the street outside. Others stood in the windows of nearby houses. They were there to worship with the rescuers; the service was led from just inside the doorway of the prison by my friend, Henry Peck.

The following Monday, before Charles' trial began, we all expected the first order of business would be to reverse the injunction that had kept them in prison over the weekend. To our dismay, an incorrect wording in the court records said the rescuers had *chosen* to surrender their recognizances and be taken into custody. No matter what our attorneys said, the judge refused to change the wording. Our men dug their heels in. Refused to pay bail. It was a standoff. If they wouldn't pay bail they had to stay in prison until the case was concluded.

'How are you finding it, Charles?' I asked my brother a week later.

'We're very comfortably situated, thanks to Mr. Smith and his wife. Apart from the fact that we can't leave, we're treated most generously. Friends and visitors come and go whenever they like. We're well fed, not only by the Smiths and their staff but also with contributions from visitors. I'm almost better fed here than at home!'

I chuckled. 'I won't mention that to your housekeeper! How do you keep yourselves occupied?'

James Fitch, Simeon Bushnell's employer, was sitting with us and answered. 'We've got plenty of activities, thanks. Friends bring us books, papers, and all manner of other activities. Shame they can't bring in a printing press—they're a bit large—or Simeon and I could carry on with our work.'

We all laughed.

Datus came over to chat. 'If we're still here next week, John, could you bring in some of my shoe-repair tools? I'll give you a list of things I could use here. If I set up shop, I know visitors will bring their shoes and boots for mending.'

Others started making harnesses and cabinets. Professors and teachers took the chance to prepare lessons and do more study. The place was a hive of activity.

And so it continued—for nearly three months.

Belden thought he'd won a victory by sending them to prison. Instead, by making them martyrs for the abolitionist cause, he added ammunition to the fight for the end of slavery.

The impasse created further complex legal tussles. A motion was submitted to the Ohio Supreme Court for writs of habeas corpus to release the rescuers, and Governor Chase tried his darnedest to influence the Supreme Court judges on our behalf. If possible, this case ignited the nation even more. Hotheads were even prepared to march on the prison and release our men.

One anonymous writer said, 'We must no longer submit to the despotism of the federal government. Our wrongs we must right, if we can, through the ballot box, and if this fails us, through the cartridge box.'

There was even talk of federal troops being used if Chase authorized state troopers to release the men. This was fighting talk. Newspapers around the country took sides. If possible, the nation became even more polarized. The situation was compared to the siege of Boston by English troops in 1775 that triggered the War of Independence. But, to our shock and dismay, on May 30, the Supreme Court judges reluctantly turned down the application for habeas corpus. They chose not to inflame the already angry debate that might have led to a full-scale battle about state rights versus the federal government.

In fact, the battle they were afraid of was only two years away. But–the first bullets were not fired in our state.

CHAPTER 32

APRIL-JULY 6 1859 OBERLIN AND CLEVELAND

WHILE THE JOCKEYING WENT on to have the rescuers released from jail, Judge Willson finally accepted the need for a new jury and my brother's trial went ahead on April 18. While it was in progress, charges against two of the rescuers were dropped because of mistakes in their indictments. To our family's delight, one of them was Datus. He headed home the night of April 25. He'd served only eleven days in jail. There was much rejoicing in the Wall household that night, though I missed it; I was still in Cleveland, close by to support my brother.

On May 10, the last day of Charles' trial, I took my seat in the court again. It had dragged on for over three weeks. The accusations, witness statements, and evidence were very similar to Simeon Bushnell's trial. As he'd done at the first trial, the judge showed his bias in his address to the jury before sending them off to deliberate. Given what we'd been witness to for the previous five weeks, no-one was surprised when, half-an-hour after they'd been sent off, the jury came back with another verdict of 'Guilty'.

A collective sigh went round the room. Our supporters looked gloomily at each other. Charles looked up at me and gave a resigned shrug as officials escorted him from the dock.

'Court dismissed. Tomorrow I will pronounce sentence on Bushnell,' announced Willson. He nudged his glasses back up his broad nose, adjusted his gown and strutted self-importantly from the court.

The next day, May 11, they led Simeon into the prisoners' dock. His wife, Elizabeth, sat beside him with their baby daughter. The courtroom was packed, for word had gone out that today was his sentencing day. The maximum sentence was six months in prison and a fine of $1,000.

Judge Willson asked him, 'Do you have any regrets to express for the offense of which you stand convicted?'

Bushnell looked at him levelly. 'No.'

As we watched the white-wigged judge lean forward and deliver him a lecture, we could tell he wasn't going to be lenient.

'You've broken the law. You express no regret for the act done. Instead, you're exultant in the wrong. Sixty days in prison, starting now. You'll also pay $600 plus costs.'

Simeon's face drained of color. This was a vast sum for a young family man on a low wage. He said nothing. His wife dabbed her eyes. As the marshal led him away, the baby reached her arms out for her daddy, crying as he disappeared. The room erupted into a hubbub of noise.

The judge banged his gavel. 'Silence in the court!' he yelled.

The rest of the day was filled with disputes between the lawyers and Judge Willson. Charles' sentence was deferred to the next day, Thursday May 12. I was impatient to get home to family and business matters, but nothing would make me leave Cleveland until I knew my brother's outcome. Poor Charles, his fate hanging for yet another day. Given the severity of Simeon's sentence, we were all disheartened.

As soon as the wrangling in the courthouse finished, I hurried to see if I could assist Charles. 'You know you'll get a chance to speak before Willson sentences you. Would you like me to do it on your behalf?' I asked. I knew him to be a powerful speaker, but I was itching to help. I'd had five years of continuous practice at speaking to courts, besides the intense training in oratory at Oberlin. I felt I could raise a worthy argument for leniency.

'No thanks, John, though I thank you for the offer. I know you'd do a great job, but this is my battle and I have things I wish to say.'

The next day, the small black school teacher faced the portly, powerful white judge.

'Do you have anything to say?'

'Yes, your honor, I do.'

The judge looked surprised. He was used to prisoners being so intimidated by this stage of the proceedings that they just wanted it ended, but given he'd invited Charles to speak, he leaned back in his chair, fiddling with a pencil.

I smiled to myself. The man had no idea what was coming.

Charles squared his shoulders, took a breath, and began.

'I know the courts of this country, the laws of this country, the governmental machinery of this country, are so constituted as to oppress and outrage colored men, men of my complexion. I cannot, then, expect any mercy from the laws, from the constitution or from the courts of the country.'

He gave a brilliant speech, painting a vivid picture of the racial injustices all blacks, whether free or slave, faced in the United States. He talked about how mothers '... *dare not send their children to school, for fear they would be caught up and carried off ... [by]... slave catchers, kidnappers, Negro stealers'.* He described the history of the black race in America. And he shared the words of our father, who'd fought honorably the whole way through the Revolutionary War.

'My father always told me he fought for my freedom as much as for his own... [and for] ... the fundamental doctrine of this government, that all men have a right to life and liberty...'.

His speech was remarkable. At the finish, the whole room burst into such long and loud applause that Willson ordered the room to be cleared if the noise didn't stop.

Despite his prejudice, it seemed the judge was affected by Charles' words. His sentence was only twenty days in prison and a fine of $100 plus costs.

As Charles was led from the court and back to the jail, the audience again cheered him. The irate judge scowled as he banged his gavel, trying to restore order.

CHAPTER 33

JULY 1859 CLEVELAND, ELYRIA, AND OBERLIN

THE END OF THE affair took us by surprise.

While Simeon and Charles were on trial, a range of legal loopholes secured the freedom of the eleven Wellington rescuers, spread over some weeks. Once they were gone, it became even more obvious that the real accuser was the mighty U.S. government and the real entity in the dock was tiny defiant Oberlin. The president and his henchmen were determined to humble our small town. The fourteen men still in prison, twelve of them yet to be tried, were but pawns in a bigger battle.

So how could Oberlin get free of such an adversary?

It was our cohort of highly experienced lawyers, all working for free, who managed it.

Behind the scenes, ongoing legal pressure against John Price's captors had continued. It became another stand-off, but this time the power was on our side. Our friends in Elyria had continued to work with the legal system, toying with the minds of Belden and his anxious key witnesses, the two Kentuckians and the two federal officials. The kidnappers were arrested as soon as they'd testified in Charles' trail and whisked off to Lorain County jail. There they languished for eight days. By May 19, wealthy

Democrat supporters had paid their bail of $800 each and they were released, but they had to agree to appear when required. They were scheduled to go to trial in early July.

Belden was tired of the extensive support the rescuers were getting; he planned to finish the trials of the remaining twelve Oberliners in the next ninety-day court session. He also got federal writs of habeas corpus to release his witnesses from Lorain County's jurisdiction. However, this was not as easy as he'd expected. The writs were only valid if the men were in custody, and they could only return to custody if the officials of Lorain County were there to receive them. The sheriff had to revoke their bail and accept them back into custody, and they also needed a judge to accept the writs.

The Lorain County sheriff was given a tip-off. His solution was beautiful in its simplicity–he would disappear for the day to a remote part of the county on business. When Attorney Belden, the federal marshal and the four kidnappers arrived, thinking it would be a simple task, no sheriff was to be found. They cooled their heels in Elyria all day, waiting for his return.

Finally, they saw the sheriff riding into town. It was seven o'clock at night.

'I've got to put my horse away and attend to some other business first,' said the sheriff. The six went to the courthouse to wait for him. He didn't turn up.

The next day was Sunday. Belden and the marshal located both judge and sheriff. They, however, refused to do business on the Sabbath. The judge, not a pious man, was seen 'fixed up' in his best suit and heading to church.

Monday morning, determined to outwit the recalcitrant locals, Belden rang the judge's doorbell at sunrise, about 4.30 am.

'Sorry,' said his wife, 'he's not at home. He won't be back until Tuesday.'

'I have an appointment with him,' complained Belden. The lady at the door just smiled. She, like so many in Elyria, was an abolitionist and very happy to play along with this cat-and-mouse game. Her husband had left home two hours earlier.

Tuesday rolled around, and again neither official was in town. Frustrated at the wasted time, Belden and the marshal finally gave up and went back to Cleveland with their unhappy kidnappers.

Meanwhile, the Kentuckians had wired back to Kentucky for help. They were staring down the barrel of a long time in an Ohio prison and just wanted the nightmare to go away. Ten months ago, they'd set off to Ohio, expecting to make some easy money by capturing a defenseless runaway, but their lives had descended into chaos. They were terrified of the charge sticking. One of Maysville's most prominent attorneys arrived by train to see if he could negotiate a conclusion.

With calm intervention and careful wording of petitions so Attorney Belden, a difficult and contentious man, could save face, a compromise was proposed. If Lorain County officials would drop their charges, and Belden would release the remaining twelve Oberliners, both cases would be considered closed.

Eventually, in great frustration, Belden agreed to negotiate. He'd had enough of the wrangling, strategies, and counterstrategies. The situation was a shambles. Judge Willson didn't like the settlement either, but finally agreed to dismiss the case. On July 6, after eighty-three days in prison, our men were free, except for Simeon Bushnell, with five days of his sentence left. At five o'clock that afternoon, they finally left the prison. Traveling with them was the kindly Cleveland sheriff and Mr. Smith, the jailer who'd done everything possible to ease their incarceration. Hundreds of Cleveland folk escorted them to the train station. A band led the procession and everyone cheered as a hundred-cannon salute was fired off on the foreshore of Lake Erie.

What a party we held in Oberlin that night!

'Carrie, where are you?' I called as I dashed in the door from work. 'I've just heard. The men are coming home! The town's organizing a welcome. Can you get the maid to sit with the children?'

She ran through from the kitchen. 'I wouldn't miss it for the world! How long have we got?'

The sun was setting, and the heat of the day had eased to a soft warmth by the time the train pulled in. Caroline and I were at the station with nearly 3,000 of our fellow townsfolk. The birds settling to sleep in the nearby trees rose in alarm at the tremendous cheers and shouts as the men stepped down off the train. They'd left for Cleveland in the chill of mid-April, with snow still on the ground. Now it was July, gardens were abundant with flowers, and oak, elm and birch leaves whispered in a pleasant breeze.

People made speeches, banners flew, the town's fire companies lined the route, flowers were strewn in the path, and the Oberlin Brass Band escorted us all to First Church. We celebrated their release with prayers, songs, and hymns from the 125-strong choir, and there were many speeches. I knew most of the details, but many in the town had only heard parts of the story. They listened enraptured as our friends from Elyria shared how they'd played cat-and-mouse with the authorities. Then the sympathetic jailer and sheriff talked about how they'd enjoyed turning the gloomy old Cuyahoga jail into a pleasant temporary home for our fellows, at least as far as the environment would allow. Everyone cheered and laughed at their tales.

This lengthy episode, coming on the heels of a decade of outrages against black equality and abolition of slavery, united the northern states in a way nothing else had. The publicity went on for so long that people were forced to sit up, take notice, and choose sides.

Educated and respected whites had united with blacks, some well-educated, others with minimal learning. All the rescuers were prepared to put themselves in harm's way for the sake of a persecuted brother. All suffered emotionally and financially. Young families were denied their fathers. Businesses were left without their owners. Students were left without their teachers. Pulpits were left without their preachers. But even those with the least resources counted it worthwhile, for it exposed the wholesale corruption of civil liberties, and how slave power advocates were plotting to destroy freedoms previously taken for granted.

I liked how a Massachusetts newspaper summed it up. "The persecution of Christian men for showing kindness to runaway Negroes is a losing operation, socially and politically."

The newspapers were our friends. Controversy sells papers, and we'd given them plenty to loosen the pockets of potential subscribers.

CHAPTER 34

1859 OBERLIN

I T WAS A HOT August day, and I was busy with a client. The windows were all open to try and catch a breeze when I heard a man's voice in my outer office.

A minute later, my assistant knocked. He knew not to interrupt, so I concluded it must be important.

'Sorry, Mr. Langston, there's a Mr. John Thomas to see you. He insists it's urgent.'

I looked at my desk calendar. Sighed. The only gap was my lunch break.

'Very well. Tell him I'll see him at noon.'

At the appointed hour, in walked a tall, well-proportioned white man of pleasant demeanor, sporting a well-groomed brown beard and whiskers. I estimated him at around forty years of age.

'I'm due at home for lunch, sir,' I said, standing up as he came in. 'I can give you a few minutes now or, if you'd like to walk with me as far as my house, you can tell me what you want. That should be enough time to establish whether I can help you.'

He chose to accompany me to my gate.

That short walk reshaped my afternoon. It also had extreme consequences for Oberlin and a number of its residents.

As soon as he was sure we couldn't be overheard, he said, 'I confess, sir, my name is not John Thomas. My father is John Brown of Ossawatomie in Kansas and I'm his oldest son, John Brown Jr. Perhaps you've heard my father has a plan which, in his words, will 'strike a blow which shall shake and destroy American slavery'.'

I stopped in my tracks. 'I have heard whispers that he's planning something. I know no details.'

Pretty much everyone in the country knew of John Brown Sr. Some called him a saint. Others were convinced he was a fanatical madman. One thing I knew for sure—he was no shrinking violet! When it came to ending slavery, he was prepared to stand and be counted.

He and some of his sons, including the one standing in front of me, had been at the center of a number of bloody battles in Kansas three years earlier, when Free Soilers fought against slavery supporters who wanted Kansas to be admitted to the Union as a slave state. In one retaliatory raid, they accused Brown of murder; the uproar was heard nation-wide. In another battle, a band of between 30-50 Free Soilers led by Brown fought off 250 border ruffians. That exchange cost him dearly—Frederick, one of his seven sons who'd lived to maturity, was amongst those killed.

Immediately, I knew this would not be a quick conversation. I said, 'I assume, given you've sought me out, you know I've been active for the last decade in the fight for black rights and the end of slavery. I'm very interested to hear what you have to say, Mr. Brown. Join us for luncheon, and after the meal you can tell me why you're here.'

He accepted with alacrity; I suspect the tempting aromas of steak and kidney pie wafting down the pathway had something to do with it. We didn't talk business over the dining table, for Caroline, our children and some of our boarders were present.

As soon as the plates were empty, I invited Young Brown, as I was already thinking of him, to join me for coffee and conversation in the parlor.

Once the coffee pot was on the sideboard, cups in our hands and the door shut, I asked, 'So, what do you wish of me?'

'I'll speak plain. We believe the time for talking is done. The southern despots refuse to listen. They dominate the federal government and gain more power every year. It's time to change tack. My father has come up with a plan to spirit huge numbers of slaves to freedom, but to do it he needs men.'

I stopped stirring the lump of sugar in Caroline's elegant coffee cup and looked at him, startled.

'You'll have to give me more details.'

'He's going to trigger a slave uprising near Harper's Ferry, Virginia. I'm instructed to ask if you know of any Ohioans, white or black, who'd be prepared to join in guerrilla warfare. To strike and, if necessary, die for the American bondsman. Father's convinced this is now the only way to stamp out the curse of slavery.'

I set my cup down carefully, taking a moment to gather my thoughts. This was clearly not a conversation to be transacted in half an hour. 'Bear with me, John. I want to give you my full attention. Let me send a note to my office to postpone this afternoon's appointments.'

Once I'd dispatched our maid with the message, I returned to my coffee and guest. My mind was racing with the implications of what he was asking. Whilst I was fully supportive of using force where necessary, I had big concerns about what sounded like a major insurrection.

'If I understand correctly, this plan of your father's would be regarded as kidnapping at the least, and probably treason. Anyone involved could be strung up for such activity.'

His dark eyes glowed with fervor. 'Correct. We're all prepared to pay the ultimate sacrifice, if that's what it takes. We need brave men to join our ranks. Men with the same conviction. Men prepared to die for freedom for all blacks. We have some very wealthy supporters helping to fund guns and ammunition, but we need brave men to fire those guns if needful. We believe that once the revolt begins, the slaves in nearby plantations will cast off their shackles and join. I ask again, do you know any Ohioan, black or white, who would join us?'

'The intention sounds admirable, but I need to know more about this plan.'

'Father will organize small groups of liberators, well-trained and armed, to guide slaves to freedom through the Virginian mountains to Pennsylvania and then north to Canada. He believes it will be so attractive a proposition that slaves will come in droves. Because of this mass migration, the slave owners will suffer economically and the evil system will be crushed.'

It seemed an idealistic and crazy idea, but–crazy ideas sometimes succeeded. Who was I to stamp on this man's vision? It worried me though. I knew the slave oligarchs wouldn't just roll over and let their property disappear.

I hesitated, then gave him two names.

'I know of two young black men of great physical courage who might be prepared to join you. Sheridan Leary is a freeman. A harness-maker. Earlier this year I heard him say, when addressing the Oberlin Anti-Slavery Society, "Men must suffer for a good cause." That wasn't just talk; he's been shot at for trying to help a slave escape, but it hasn't stopped him. He's now a married man with an infant daughter. I don't know whether that has modified his zeal for danger–only he can answer that.

'The other is carpenter John Copeland Jr., Leary's nephew. He's said to be an excellent shot. He's a tall, muscular young man. He was at the forefront of the Wellington rescue. One of the small group that overpowered the guards at the hotel door and wrested John Price from the kidnappers in the attic.'

My guest sat up enthusiastically. 'Would it be imposing too much to ask them to meet me today? I need to be on my way at the earliest opportunity. I've other people to see, and then must return to my farm in West Andover, Ohio. My role is to work from behind the scenes to keep men and supplies flowing. Father and other members of the party are already secretly assembling on a farm a few miles out of Harpers Ferry.'

'Consider it done.'

I swiftly wrote two notes, giving no details but asking the men to come to my home on a pressing matter. Such messages were common enough in our circle—they usually meant a runaway needed urgent help. The employers of both men were as committed to the Underground Railroad and black rights as their staff; the lads would have no problem leaving work.

They didn't give Brown an instant answer, but after discussion with their loved ones, the two men opted to join John Brown Sr. They were prepared to lay down their lives for a righteous cause.

They left Oberlin on October 6 on the pretext of looking for better paid work and reached the Virginia farmhouse hideaway near Harpers Ferry on October 15.

On October 16, 1859, John Brown Sr. led a raid on the U.S. Armory and Arsenal at Harpers Ferry to supplement his supply of arms. Did John Jr. know his father intended to raid it? I don't believe so. It was a crazy idea, and the son was a gentle man, which is probably why his father delegated him to manage the background work. He'd already suffered imprisonment and a serious mental breakdown because of the Kansas conflict.

Two days later, dreams and bodies smashed, the grand plan was no more. Of the twenty-one men who raided the armory, only five escaped, including Owen, one of Brown's sons. Everyone else either died then or later. This included Brown himself and two more of his sons, Oliver and Watson. Of my two friends, Leary was shot while trying to escape across the Shenandoah River and Copeland was captured.

As they led him to the gallows on December 2, John Brown smuggled a note to a jailer:

'I, John Brown, am now quite certain that the crimes of this guilty land will never be purged away, but with blood. I had, as I now think, vainly flattered myself that without very much bloodshed, it might be done.'

Fourteen days later, John Copeland followed his leader on the one-way path to the gallows.

A week later, on Christmas Day 1859, a vast crowd of grieving black and white Oberliners gathered at First Church, Oberlin, for Copeland's funeral.

Any sane person would know the government could never ignore such a blatant challenge. The might of the U.S. Army against a handful of men? A sure recipe for martyrdom. Had I known Brown's intention, I doubt I would have sent those notes. This still sits heavy on my conscience.

CHAPTER 35

LATE NOVEMBER 1860 CLEVELAND

NOT LONG BEFORE MY thirty-first birthday, I was with Charles in Cleveland on Ohio Anti-Slavery Society business. With our busy lives and commitments, it was rare for us to have time to relax, but this was one of those unusual opportunities. We'd arrived back at his home early from our meeting and were sitting by his fire, ties loosened, enjoying a quiet chat.

Normally he'd get straight to his desk with its groaning load of paperwork, but tonight he ignored the schoolbooks awaiting marking, and the pile of society and black rights paperwork demanding his attention.

'John, I sometimes think of how you were dragged away from the Goochs back in '39. I know it was devastating for you at the time, but having watched so many black rights chipped away over the years, do you now think William was right to insist you stay in Ohio?'

I eased my boots off and pushed my stockinged feet closer to the flames before I answered. It was a cold night and I'd become chilled during the walk back to his home.

'I don't think I'll ever completely forgive him for the harsh way in which it was done. The Goochs are the only parents I remember. I've tried to find them several times, but all inquiries come to nothing. Maybe they've gone to California. Or perhaps the colonel died and his wife remarried. I'm deeply grieved that I've lost contact with them.

'However, was William right? I didn't want to admit it for many years, but probably yes. If I'd gone to Missouri, it's highly unlikely I would have had much schooling. Or at least, the quality of education I received at Oberlin. By staying here, you and Gideon knew what was happening and made sure I got educated, despite William's objections.

'I take my hat off to the Oberlin founders–they were so far ahead of their time. I don't believe there's *any* other institution in the nation where I would have been so supported and encouraged. I wonder what it will take before we have similar opportunities for blacks and women throughout the country. Probably not in our lifetime, I hazard!'

Charles continued his train of thought. 'We were lucky our father had such a commitment to education. If he hadn't insisted on that, Gideon and I wouldn't have gone to Oberlin either.'

I winced. 'It's tough being the youngest at a school your older siblings attended. Everyone expected me to measure up to you two! The college leaders are very proud you were their first black students. I got your names thrust down my throat regularly!'

'You soon shot past us academically, Little Brother,' Charles answered. When I was younger, he'd often called me Little Brother to rile me up. Now I just grinned. Leaned over and patted him on the head. I was now several inches taller than him, for he stood only a whisker above five feet.

He pushed my hand away. 'Are you suggesting I'm short? I'm six feet tall–on the inside!' We both laughed. He leaned over to stoke the fire, adding more logs from the basket and a shovelful of hot Pennsylvania coal, then got serious again.

'Look at what you've achieved in the last ten years, John. A thriving law practice and civic responsibilities. A happy, healthy family. Well-respected throughout the country as an outstanding orator. Plus, you mix with the intellectual giants of the abolition and black rights movements. Not too shabby for an orphan child from Virginia.'

'But is it enough?' I asked. 'There's still so much to do. Politically, our people are further behind in gaining freedom and equality. It doesn't seem to matter how many conventions we attend, petitions we get people to sign, or how many speeches we give. We still don't have equal rights for free blacks or freedom for our poor southern brethren.'

'Don't despair, John. Things are changing. It's not all gloomy, you know. Look at the increasing number of black children getting educated. And what about that 'nearer white than black' law the Ohio Supreme Court passed in 1842? You might not have been accepted to the Bar if it hadn't been for that.'

I perked up. 'Yes, you're right. It's not just me who's benefited by that loophole. Plenty of other mixed-blood people with reasonably light skins have managed *some* justice and civil rights. Those who've been able to vote have helped influence elections and we know every vote counts. And thank goodness for last year's ruling by the Ohio Supreme Court!'

'I presume you're referring to the Alfred J. Anderson case?'

I nodded. 'I was delighted that affair finally concluded. It's been hanging around the courts for three years! Now election judges can't deny the vote to a man who claims more white than black ancestry. I know it helped bring in a sizable number of the 20,000 Ohio votes Lincoln polled ahead of his opposition. I reckon we can take some credit for that, given the efforts we put into encouraging light-skinned blacks to vote!'

We smiled happily at each other.

'I wonder if we'll ever have black politicians in state or federal government?' said Charles. 'What about you, John? I could see you being a member of Congress one day.'

I raised my eyebrows. 'It'll have to be a very different country for that ever to be possible!'

But the idea landed on fertile soil.

CHAPTER 36

DECEMBER 1860 COLUMBUS

I was in Columbus and seated across the desk from Governor Chase. Although I'd been tutored by some of the best teachers in the country, he'd continued to be one of my heroes and role models since my early years in Cincinnati.

He was a big, broad-shouldered man with a firm jaw and clean-shaven face. His almost bald head with its receding hairline was framed by sparse greying fair hair fluffing out behind his ears. When he looked at you with his piercing brown eyes, you knew you were in front of a man of honesty, intelligence, and uncompromising courage. His sincerity and commitment to justice for all people, with a special love and commitment to blacks, was known across the nation. Sometimes his bluntness offended people, but no-one doubted his integrity. He was one to trust. And his speeches were not flowery puffery and hot air. Like Lincoln, he used straightforward language everyone could understand.

He'd asked me to call.

'You and your brothers are fine people, John. It's been my privilege to have known you all since you were young men. I was trying to remember when you and I first met. I think you were still a lad?'

'That's correct, sir. You probably don't recall the first time–there was a bit going on. I'd dropped into Gideon's barbershop after school for a quick chat. You were there, being shaved, when a posse of man-stealers came storming in. You chased them out.'

He studied my face. Paused. Laughed. 'By Jove, I *do* remember that incident! You were there, you say? I don't recall a small boy.'

'As soon as you'd roared at the would-be kidnappers and they'd hustled off the premises, Gideon told me to make myself scarce. I waited a minute to make sure they'd gone, then ran straight round to my friend, Alf. His family's bakery and confectionary shop was close. I figured I could wait there until it was safe to head home.'

'Do you mean Alfred Burnett?'

I nodded.

'Aha, young Alfred. There's another remarkable young man, though in a completely different arena. I'm pleased to see how successful he is as an entertainer. He's wonderful medicine in this troubled world. I always thought he was wasted behind a shop counter, no matter how successful the business.'

I smiled as I thought of my friend and his droll humor. 'His mother used to growl at him for fooling around, as she called it. For years he had almost as much opposition to being an entertainer as I did to becoming a lawyer. We don't often see each other now, living in such different worlds, but I count him as a good friend. Have you seen him lately?'

'Indeed. My two daughters and I had him take breakfast with us not so long ago. He has a standing invitation to call in any time he passes through Columbus. We enjoy his bright spirit and the joy he brings to the table.'

We chuckled as we swapped anecdotes about Alf's tricks and funny faces.

'But I didn't ask you to call just to share old times, John. I want to thank you personally for your outstanding work in encouraging people to vote—white and black.'

I politely accepted his thanks, and I had my own to give. 'If we're talking about influence, I know I'm speaking for all blacks of Ohio when I thank you for what you've done for this state, not only in your four years as governor, but in the preceding years. Most of our discriminatory black laws are repealed, our people can now testify against whites, our children are guaranteed access to public education and our personal liberty laws have improved. You've been a major influencer in all these matters.'

He smiled but deflected, as was his way. 'That's generous of you to say so, but there's so much more to be done. I'm delighted William Dennison is coming in as my successor. He's an able man and shares the same values. He'll continue the fight, and I'll do everything I can in my new role in the U.S. Senate.'

Our conversation shifted to the Presidential election.

'How do you feel about Mr. Lincoln as President?' I asked.

He sighed. 'Everyone knows I wanted to be nominated for president by our brave Republican party, but the members decided differently. My supporters tell me I missed on the nomination because I'm so hard-line on the slavery issue. I'd never change my stance on that, so perhaps they were right. For the sake of the cause, it was critical we win at a national level. I'm now right behind Mr. Lincoln with my full support. He's an honest man and will need all the help we can give. I fear this next term is looking very fraught.'

I was interested in his perspective. 'Do you think South Carolina will go through with secession? The papers seem to think so. And who else do you think will leave the Union if they go?'

'Sadly, I agree with the newspaper editors. Who else might secede? Let's not crash into that hurdle until we must. I fear for the times ahead, but,' he jutted out his determined jaw, 'we *cannot* allow slavery to prevail. Our country is fast approaching a crisis; it will have to decide between freedom and slavery. Perhaps it will come to civil war, though I hope and pray it doesn't. That would be the greatest tragedy of all.'

'That's a terrible scenario,' I replied. 'Few want war, but when bullies won't back down, what options are left?'

He looked sad. Left the question unanswered and turned the conversation back to me.

'John, I'm thankful we have your energy, abilities, and influence working for the cause in whatever way you can. Four million people in bondage–

it's a crime of the worst kind and I've dedicated my life to wiping out this evil. Men such as you and Charles reach people I can't. And I really applaud you for the splendid work you're doing in bringing education to your people. I foresee a brilliant future for you, young man. Who knows, maybe one day we'll have you in Congress.'

I just smiled. Another one seeing me in the corridors of power! It was a fine dream–if the world were different.

The world as we knew it *was* about to change–but not in a good way.

Goodbye, Dear Reader

I T'S TIME TO SAY farewell–for now. There's much more to tell, but I don't want this to turn into a doorstopper! I insisted we finish before the whirlwind that turned the land of my birth into a terrible bloodbath. I speak of the Civil War, 1861 to 1865.

If you're of an impatient disposition (a trait I've often been accused of!), here's a peek into my future.

In 1863, President Lincoln finally allowed blacks to enlist as soldiers in the Union Army. From then on, I used my eloquence to assist in recruiting three black regiments. We sure showed those doubting Thomases our men were *at least* as good as white! The inclusion of black soldiers helped turn the tide of union losses. Helped us win the war. Helped us throw off the yoke of slavery.

After the war, I was shoulder-tapped to assist with the herculean task of reconstruction. President Ulysses S. Grant honored me with several positions.

Education for all blacks, as you surely know by now, has always been dear to my heart. I was privileged to be the first Dean of the Law School of Howard University, chartered by congress for the higher education of blacks, both men and women. I served from 1869 to 1875, the last two years also as acting president of the university.

Another United States President, Rutherford Hayes, appointed me Minister-Resident and Consul-General to Haiti and Chargé d'Affaires to Santo Domingo from late 1877 to 1885.

And, the achievement that attracts the greatest attention was my election, in 1888, to the United States House of Representatives, representing the 4th Congressional District of Virginia. However, it did not go smoothly! Imagine the uproar when a black man stood for national office in a once-slave state! Because of voter fraud and unethical practices by my white opposition, it was September 1890 before I could take my seat.

Maybe we'll meet again one day. It depends on whether I can persuade my scribe to take up her pen again on my behalf.

Meanwhile, whoever you are, and wherever you live, never doubt the good you can contribute to the betterment of this world.

Be determined.
Never give up.

THE END

For Those Who Want to Know More

WHAT IS TRUE AND **What Is the Author's Imagination?**

This fictional biography is as faithful to history as fiction will allow. All the major events happened and everyone is an historical character, apart from a tiny number of peripheral characters such as Gideon's housekeeper, Mrs. Bird, and Joshua, the young lad clearing dishes in the Oberlin dining room.

The major incidents and events of John's life happened, and so did the mob attack on the Alley/Burnett home and business in 1843. However, I have no evidence the black community helped with the preparations. Some early readers have asked for more detail about how fifteen men beat off a mob of two thousand. Alf will give you a lot more detail in my next book in this series, *Finding Alf*, due out either late 2022 or early 2023.

Almost all the dialogue is out of my imagination, although, where suitable, I've integrated people's words from contemporary sources, especially John's autobiography and newspaper and court reports of the Oberlin/Wellington Rescue. Words in italics attributed to John and Charles Langston, John Brown, and President Lincoln are direct quotes, with the exception of the letter Charles wrote to John in 1850. That was pure imagination, though John did go to the convention described in Chapter 18, and took on the task of getting signatures.

Some explanatory notes:

John Mercer Langston. As John told you in 'Goodbye, Dear Reader', he was the first black representative of the 4th Congressional District of Virginia to the U. S. House of Representatives. Not long after that, as the Jim Crow laws took effect, it became increasingly difficult for people of color to be elected. The second black representative for the same seat was Senator Robert Scott, elected in 1992, over one hundred years later.

I'm often asked if John had any relationship to the famous Black poet, Langston Hughes. Absolutely. He was Hughes' great-uncle. Mary Leary, widow of Sheridan Leary who died at Harpers Ferry, later married Charles Langston. She was Hughes' grandmother.

Republican party. It's worth noting that the Republican party of the 19th century was markedly different from the current party of the same name. It was founded in the 1850s to prevent slavery from being extended to the new territories such as Texas and California. Within a few years, the party extended its platform to include abolition of slavery and equal rights for blacks and other minorities. It's fair to say it represented the social conscience of the United States. Ulysses S. Grant, one of the most effective Union generals in the Civil War, and who did many great things to aid reconstruction, was also a Republican.

Democratic party. Many Democrats of those times supported the status quo, hated the idea of racial equality, and did everything they could, both legally and illegally, to undo the improvements in the lives of black people that the Republicans legislated for after the Civil War. Andrew Johnson, the vice-president who took over after Lincoln was assassinated six weeks into his second term, was one of the worst. He sabotaged as many of the reconstruction measures as he could. Lincoln had appointed him, a southern sympathizer and Democrat, in an effort to re-unite the country at the end of the Civil War. His legacy remains today in many of the dreadful inequities still experienced by African Americans.

Salmon P. Chase, when a young lawyer in Cincinnati, was known as the slaves' lawyer. He battled in the courtroom for justice for runaways and the abolitionists (white and black) who supported them. He was one of the founders of the Republican party, the first Republican Governor of Ohio in 1855, served as Lincoln's Secretary of the Treasury, and from 1864 to 1873 was Chief Justice of the U.S. Supreme Court.

The Burnetts are my distant ancestors. Alf's oldest brother, Joseph Burnett, emigrated to New Zealand (my home) in 1856, bringing with him a tin trunk crammed with family letters, journals, newspaper cuttings and other memorabilia. Many of these precious items are now in the New Zealand National Library. Alf became a nationally known entertainer, despite his mother's opposition, had an open invitation to call on the Chase family, and *did* take breakfast with them in 1859. He mentions it in a letter to brother Joseph, whom he corresponded with until the end of Alf's life in 1884.

The one important detail I've no historical proof of is that Alf and John knew each other, but on the extremely high basis of probability, I've plaited their friendship into my books. My first novel, **It Happened On Fifth Street: A tale of forgotten heroes**, (told through the eyes of a younger Alf) shares the true tale of the Burnett family's courageous stand for abolition and the devastating impact on their family of the city-wide riot of 1841. During the research, I stumbled upon a scholarly article citing John's experience in that same riot. Too good a snippet to ignore!

So why did I choose to write about John? Once I'd discovered him, he started whispering in my ear! Ask any author—we *have* to get those voices out of our heads and through our fingers to your eyes. At first, he was to be a major player in my next book about Alf and his side-kick Abigail (a fictional character). However, John took charge of the story and said, 'I want my own book!'

Other Notes About the Story:

I've researched as carefully as possible to ensure the details are correct. However, there are occasional discrepancies in the various sources. For instance, the birthdates of John's siblings and half-siblings vary. When I've had to make a choice, almost always I've accepted the dates John gives in his autobiography.

I couldn't find exactly when in 1858, John's daughter, Chinque, was born. I made it fit before the rescue for the convenience of the story.

Russia Township, near Oberlin, became known as New Russia Township in 1992.

In the story of the Wellington Rescue, for simplicity I said all four would-be captors left town on the next train. In fact, only three left Wellington immediately after the rescue. Deputy Marshall Lowe was still there the next day and chased two Oberlin students through the streets when they came back to retrieve a weapon they'd left behind. Why was he still there? Probably because he had to start investigations for the future prosecution. The federal authorities couldn't allow the rescuers to be seen to flout the law.

Major Sources:

Langston, John Mercer. *From the Virginia Plantation to the National Capital, or, The First and Only Negro Representative in Congress From the Old Dominion.* 1894. Can't get better than the horse's mouth! However, I discovered some date confusion. Langston wrote his autobiography toward the end of his life. He said the destruction of *The Philanthropist* press took place in 1840, which is out by a year. There are a couple of other discrepancies about how long he was in Cincinnati and how long in Chillicothe the second time. For example, he says he had two winter terms at Chillicothe. That doesn't line up with other confirmed details. I suspect William and Aimee Cheek (see next source) had the same problem. They place him in Chillicothe for only one year, but blur it.

Cheek, William and Aimee Lee Cheek. *John Mercer Langston and the Fight for Black Freedom 1829-65.* University of Illinois Press, 1989. In this brilliantly annotated and meticulously researched book, they mentioned they had notes for another book covering the rest of John's life. I haven't found it and wonder if they ever finished it. If you know anything about this, I'd be thrilled to hear.

Brandt, Nat. *The Town That Started the Civil War.* Dell Publishing, 1990. A gripping tale about the remarkable town of Oberlin and the rescue. It's easy to read and very well researched and annotated.

I've also read many other books, novels and historical texts about the period.

Some online resources you may find interesting:
1850 Fugitive Slave Act: https://www.accessible-archives.com/2017/02/manstealing-law-explained/ gives an excellent summary of the 1850 Fugitive Slave Act. (In those times, 'man' applied to any gender.) *"This enormous collection of African American newspapers contains a wealth of information about cultural life and history during the 1800s and is rich with first-hand reports of the major events and issues of the day."*
The Dred Scott case and how black rights were eroded: https://www.blackpast.org/african-american-history/1857-abraham-lincoln-dred-scott-decision-and-slavery/
Sectional/political issues leading up to the Civil War: You'll find a useful overview at https://www.americanyawp.com/text/13-the-sectional-crisis/
Ohio's treatment of blacks: You'll find more on this at https://core.ac.uk/download/pdf/214083146.pdf *The Strange Career of Race Discrimination in Antebellum Ohio'* by Paul Finkelman. Case Western Reserve Law Review, 2004. John's election to Brownhelm is referenced. See footnote #35, p. 381. On pps. 389, 392, 394 are references to 'nearer white than black' rights.

Any mistakes are mine, and I'd greatly appreciate you dropping me a line to robyn@gettingagrip.com if you stumble across any.

Other Help:
I owe enormous thanks to many generous people.

In particular, historian Beverly Gray of Chillicothe was hugely helpful about John's early life in Chillicothe and his extended family members. I'd go so far as to call her a national treasure! When I started asking questions of various Chillicothe organizations, all roads led to Beverly.

Mimi Daria of Cincinnati, whom I met at the Harriet Beecher Stowe House in Cincinnati in 2017 when doing research for *It Happened On Fifth Street*. Mimi is my first port of call for obscure details about early Cincinnati and residents. An excellent researcher.

Huge thanks to my four wonderful editors: Kirsty Powell–I love your high-level scrutiny. (Well, I don't always *love* it, but it's hugely valuable!) Judy White–your gentle but firm recommendations and careful editing make this a far better book. Michele Zwillinger from California–your support in so many ways is exceptional, including picking up my non-American whoopsies and your careful eye on American spelling, grammar, and punctuation. I'm also truly grateful for your insights into America's confusing political structure and terms. Also, my Kiwi/American cousin, Pam Loan, whose attention to detail is incredible. You saved me from countless too-modern phrases, as well as a bunch of other items I'd missed. You're a star! Teamwork is the name of the game.

I *love* librarians! I just about danced in the street when the Archives Department of Oberlin College sent a copy of John's enrollment details. It verified a tiny but important detail.

Thanks to my many writing support buddies, especially Linda Coles, and my local Book Club cheer squad. You girls are the best! Also, other experienced historical authors who so willing share their wisdom on curly questions–Amy Maroney, Helen Hollick, Deborah Swift, Rob Bauer and Steve Moretti for starters. Abject apologies if I've missed anyone. Also, the many subscribers to my *Robyn's Ramblings* historical fiction newsletter, some of whom are in my Advanced Reader team. You dear people rock–so many have emailed with help and ideas when I've reached out.

A Very Brief Note About Abraham Lincoln (for non-American readers): I originally planned to include more about Lincoln in this book, but where do you start with such an iconic figure? For those who want a quick overview, he was the greatest president the United States has ever known.

If Lincoln had not fought for right, if he had not held the faith, there would have been no *United* States from 1861 on. At best, the United States would have become two countries, and the evils of slavery would have continued for many more years. At worst ... but I don't even want to consider that.

Lincoln was a good and honest man who hated slavery and revered the vision of the Founding Fathers. He'd retired from politics after a two-year term in Congress in the late 1840s, but as the fierce debates escalated through the 1850s, and the southern push for new slave territories gained ground, he could not stay silent. A blind man could see the country was spiraling down into a whirlpool of constitutional and moral crises. Was it to be freedom or slavery? A united country or secession by the slave-owning South?

Using simple words that all men could understand, he both electrified and polarized the nation. Coming from relative obscurity, he became the first Republican president in the country's hour of greatest need. Many would say he was divinely appointed.

Millions (maybe billions) of words have been written about him and his speeches have been reproduced over and over. The following two brief quotes spoke to me:

"Near eighty years ago we began by declaring that all men are created equal; but now ... we have run down to the other declaration, that for some men to enslave others is a 'sacred right of self-government'. These principles cannot stand together. ... Let us re-adopt the Declaration of Independence, and with it, the practices, and policy, which harmonize with it... If we do this, we shall not only have saved the Union; but we shall have [made it] ... forever worthy of the saving."

"When the white man governs himself, that is self-government; but when he governs himself, and also governs another man ... that is despotism ... .The Negro is man. ... **There can be no moral right** *in connection* **with one man's making a slave of another."**

Within days of his confirmation as President of the United States, on November 6, 1860, southern states began plans to leave the Union. On December 20, 1860, South Carolina was the first to vote for secession.

By the time Lincoln took office on March 4, 1861, seven states had seceded and four more followed in the next three months. The Union was no more. Then the southern Confederacy attacked Fort Sumter, a federal military installation. It was war.

Brother against brother. Family against family. State against state. Terrible? Yes. Necessary? Who can say? But once the southern Confederacy attacked Fort Sumter, it was inevitable. Both sides were out of options.

If you love historical fiction and would like to keep up with my future novels, you'll get occasional spam-free news and interesting tidbits (plus giveaways, special deals, and great reads by other authors), at https://www.robynrpearce.com/

For my non-fiction books on time management-related topics, check out https://www.robynpearce.com(No R in the middle of this url.)

If you've enjoyed this book, it would be incredibly helpful if you could leave an honest review on and Goodreads and whichever bookshop you purchased it from, especially if you made an online purchase. For independent (indie) authors swimming in the deep ocean of online publishing, reviews are our oxygen!

Extract From Robyn's Next Book

F INDING ALF: THE ANTEBELLUM *years of Alf Burnett, entertainer and abolitionist.*

Prologue
Cincinnati January 1882

Dear Brother Joseph

My grandchildren found a trunk in the attic yesterday, forgotten in a dark corner.

Cora's lad, Alfie, (poor child, named after me!) came running downstairs, covered in dust and cobwebs. He's five now and always off on some harum-scarum fancy, but I confess to indulging him a touch more than the others. With his impulsive ways and boundless curiosity, he reminds me of my younger self. I don't need to explain that to you, do I?

'Grandpa Alf, we found a treasure chest! Come. Come.'

Sighing, I put down my paper and allowed myself to be dragged away from my chill-chasing fire and up the narrow steps to the cold, dusty attic.

His cousins were trying to open a scratched old wooden box they'd dragged into the middle of the room, under the grimy skylight. We've not bothered to install gas lighting up there and in the cramped space, jostled by three eager young lads, it was difficult to tell whether it was locked or just jammed. By now I was curious too. It was vaguely familiar, but I had no memory of what it might contain. So, the boys and I dragged and pushed it down three flights of stairs, coughing as we disturbed the long settled dust in its ornately carved lid.

With better light and more space, I managed to lever it open. The children hovered around in great excitement, with wild talk of pirates' treasure causing me some mirth. They were comical in their disappointment when, lid finally open, all we found were letters and documents.

But Joseph, it *was* a treasure! In our dear Papa's handwriting were papers about his Vigilance Committee activities– things we'd hastily hidden during the frightening days of 1841 and '43. And letters–so many letters. A big bunch from you after you took your family back to England. Many more once you emigrated to New Zealand in 1856. My rambling scrawls to the family when on my many travels. A fat scrapbook of newspaper clippings highlighting my humble career. And that's just for starters.

I have a proposal. As I sat on my heels in the comfortable warm parlor, jostled by chattering small boys, it occurred to me we have a responsibility. We're old men now and who knows how long the Lord will spare us– so many of our loved ones have passed to their eternal reward. At the very least, we should tell our families the stories of our turbulent times. The significant events we've seen or been part of. The tragedies *and* the achievements. And perhaps, one day, people interested in history will want to know more of the dramas and turmoil we've lived though.

What say we both write down what we recall? Have you still got your old journals? How well I remember, in those youthful years of boarding with you and dear Mary Ann, that you'd take time, every evening, to record the high points of the day.

Please don't tell me you lack time. Now you've retired from business and your sons are running the farm, you probably have more of that scarce resource than I. I'm often still called upon to walk the boards.

Of late, I've been rather alarmed at occasional dizzy spells. Thus far, I've been able to hide them from my loyal audiences and my dear Vandalia, but I suspect my acting days will soon be over. My old ticker has changed its rhythm; it's gone from a steady and reliable waltz to, some days, more of a wild and erratic staccato. I feel a sense of urgency about this project and will start forthwith. Do say you'll do the same!

New Zealand is so *far* away. How I miss you!!!

Your loving brother,

Alfred

Chapter 1

Abi

March 2018 Auckland, New Zealand

I looked around the air-conditioned lecture theater at my fellow students. Class was almost over. A couple of people rustled pages, closed laptops, and packed up their bags, ready to escape into the midday sun.

'Listen up, people,' said Dr. Zwillinger. 'Here's your first assignment.'

Her sharp gaze landed on the guy next to me, his eyes on his phone.

'The red-shirted gentleman in the third row, if you'd be so good as to spare me your attention, it will be to your advantage.'

Students smirked and my neighbor hastily dropped his device, flushing with embarrassment.

Dr. Zee (Zwillinger took too long to say, she'd told us at her first lecture) gave a quirky grin and twirled a curl of her long red hair as she addressed the now attentive class.

'Here's your topic. 1,500 words on some aspect of life in America in the mid-1800s. Before we study the Civil War in depth, I want you to have a sense of the times.

'You can reference some of the main political and economic events, but only if relevant to your chosen theme. Look at how the key issues impacted ordinary people's lives. You're not here to regurgitate what you find on Wikipedia. Dig deeper. What was it like to be an ordinary family? Not the rich, famous, or notorious that most commentators focus on. Also, I don't want a string of boring facts and figures. Spare my eyes and tired brain. Give me something to keep me awake.'

Laughter rippled around the auditorium. We liked Dr. Zee. She turned boring bones of dates and data into dramatic stories.

'Look particularly at the twenty years prior to 1861, when the Civil War began. It was a period of expansion. Huge population growth. The West was opening up. War with Mexico, annexation of Texas, financial crises. And of course, slavery was a political hot potato.'

I knew exactly who I'd write about. It was time to check on Alf Burnett again. First stop, Great Aunt Hanna, whose trunk of family letters had first sparked my deep interest in 19th century American history.

The heat had gone out of the day by the time the bus dropped me close to home. Thinking about how to construct my essay, I bounced into Mum's office.

'Can I borrow the car to pop round to Aunt Hanna's?'

Mum took her hands off her keyboard. Gave me one of those 'looks'. Didn't answer my question.

'Nice day, dear?' Bit of a stickler for manners, is my mother.

I grinned. 'Hello, Mother darling. A good day, thanks. How was yours?'

I tried to listen politely while she burbled on about her latest graphic design client. Finally, she switched channels. 'Now, what was this about the car?'

'I've got a history essay, and I'm hoping Aunt Hanna will let me bring home some of her old American letters.'

'Sure, love. I'm stuck at this desk for the next couple of hours. Take her a ginger loaf as well—I cooked two today.'

I had a secret I'd shared with no one. Three years earlier, while at home reading some of Aunt Hanna's wonderful trove of family papers, an old coin with a hole bored through had fallen out of an ancient paper-thin envelope. I'd threaded it onto a cord and hung it round my neck, planning to show Aunt Hanna the next day.

As soon as I placed the cord over my head, everything went black. When I came to, I was on the floor of an unfamiliar room, as frightened as the strangely dressed stocky twelve-year-old boy staring at me. In his hand was the same letter I'd just carefully put away. One second, I was in 2015 New Zealand. The next, I'd fallen (literally) into 1837 America!

I later worked out the boy must have been my multiple times great uncle, Alf Burnett, and the coin was from his coin collection. It became the passport–to him and his time!

For me, the magic lasted only a few weeks. For Alf, however, my visits spread over a four-year period. Our last time together was October 1841, and their family home and business had just been trashed in one of Cincinnati's worst racial riots. Because their white abolitionist family was widely known to help runaway slaves to freedom via the Underground Railroad, they'd been tar-geted by the violent pro-slavery mob. Angry vigilantes rampaged through the city for over a week, and the Burnett men had to run for their lives.

Why did these magical visits stop? Blame it on my cat. I'd been on my front porch, holding the coin in my hand, when Macavity, chased by a runaway dog, knocked it out of my hand. I was devastated. Searched the garden for weeks. It was gone. My gateway to Alf and his time had closed.

After that, I stopped reading the letters. It hurt too much to know I'd never see him again. Logically, I knew it was silly to be so distressed about the loss of someone who'd died more than a century before I was born. But ... when did logic ever win over emotion?

Since then, whenever I remembered my loss, I consoled myself with the thought that, even if I found the coin again, I might be like grown-up Susan and Peter in the later *Narnia* books–unable to return.

Aunt Hanna was examining a deep red rose. She smiled when she saw me coming across the manicured lawn. An agile 85-year-old, her happy place was the garden. Still holding her clippers, she used the back of her hand to push a stray wisp of white hair out of her eye, leaving a light smudge of dirt on her finely lined face.

'Perfect timing, dear. I was about to have a cuppa.'

She gestured to the half-full bucket of spent flowers at her feet. 'I'll throw this lot on the compost heap. Do you want to pop the kettle on?' I forced myself to be patient until we'd settled into the faded cane chairs on the verandah of her century-old villa. The afternoon sun threw a patchwork of light and shade through the whispering silver birch leaves and a summer breeze sent us whiffs from the richly perfumed gardenias below.

As she reached for a slice of Mum's ginger loaf, Aunt Hanna asked, 'How's uni going?'

'Good so far. Our history lecturer gave us a really interesting essay topic today. I think you'll be able to help with it.'

She looked surprised.

I explained, then asked, 'May I borrow the Burnett letters of the 1840s and 50s for a few weeks? Just to use at home.'

'Of course you can. I've transcribed some of the harder ones, including those crosshatch letters you saw. You'll find my printed versions in the files with the originals. I'd already bent my eyes backwards to decipher them, so figured I might as well save anyone else the same challenge. I hoped one day you'd want to know more.'

'You never told me.'

I felt guilty. I'd been just as excited as Aunt Hanna when she first discovered her mother's tin trunk of letters.

She gave a quiet smile. 'When you said you'd signed up for American History this year, I knew you'd be back for more. History doesn't go away; the stories wait patiently to be rediscovered when the time is right.'

I laughed. 'How wise you are! That time is now.'

I wasn't taking American history just to get a pass. When I'd first discovered Alf and his family, it brought the period to life. Why did his oldest brother, Joseph, emigrate to New Zealand? How did Alf's life turn out? Did their efforts to help runaway slaves pay off? What happened with the abolition issue?

I was deeply invested in learning more.

Back home with the letters, I started searching for highlights that might impress Dr Zee. Where to start? The Burnetts were such prolific letter-writers, my problem wasn't finding sources; it was having too many!

Grabbing a pad, I scrawled out a mind-map. What did I already know? How could I build on it? And what could I do justice to in a 1,500-word essay?

The abolition story was fascinating, but too big a topic.

Who were the people Alf told me about? Harriet Beecher Stowe was one. He'd delivered cakes to her father. I knew she helped ignite public opinion about slavery with *Uncle Tom's Cabin*. No problem to find background on her. But she didn't meet the criteria–too famous.

What about Salmon P. Chase? The Burnetts talked about him many times in the letters, and he was often referenced, scathing-ly, in some of the obviously pro-slavery newspaper articles they'd saved. I knew he later became governor of Ohio, then treasurer in Lincoln's cabinet, then Chief Justice for the entire country. Again, too famous.

I drummed my fingers on the desk.

'Be more specific,' I muttered to Macavity. He replied with a loud purr as he needled my legs with his sharp claws.

What did I know of Alf's life that I could use? Could I do an assignment about schooling standards and expectations?

I did a quick calculation. Alf would have been only fourteen when he, brother Joseph and his wife, Mary Anne, arrived in

Cincinnati in 1839 to join the rest of the family. Alf started working for the family business immediately. His mother wanted him to continue his education, but Cornelius, his father, wanted another apprentice in the bakery.

Alf was delighted, for he and school were not a comfortable match. His teacher regularly sent notes home, saying things like, 'Alfred won't amount to anything if he doesn't cease playing the class clown'.

The letters showed that the whole family, women included, were literate and good at expressing themselves on paper. Several played the piano. They had books in their homes. Traveled often. But I'd seen no mention of formal higher education.

What about people of color, I wondered? Did they even get *any* schooling? And what could they expect to achieve in their lives at that time? I knew it had been against the law in the southern states to teach slaves to read. What about free blacks? Or those in the northern states? And if they had access to schools, were they any good?

I felt a tingle of excitement. A story of contrasts should meet Dr. Zee's request for something different.

I tried to remember if Alf ever mentioned any children in the black community. What about the boy I overheard him talking with after the riot? I'd been hiding behind an old shack, waiting for Alf to be alone. That kid was probably black–I heard him tell Alf he'd run from the mob that rounded up all the men and boys of color they could find. What the heck was his name? John something–that didn't help! Did he have any schooling? I remembered his brother was a barber. If only I could go back and ask.

I sighed. That door had slammed shut.

I needed to get to the university library. Surely, I could dig up enough for comparisons of schooling between blacks and whites. The Burnetts would be examples of white education and maybe I could find a black family to balance the essay structure.

My scrappy mind-map had more question marks than content. I yawned. Perhaps more ideas would surface by morning.

———❈———

To be notified when this next Alf and Abi book is released, just jump on my newsletter list at www.RobynRPearce.com. I promise not to deluge you with garbage :-) It's *very* rare that it's more often than two-weekly and sometimes there's a long gap if I'm head down in finishing mode. And you know the drill–of course you can unsubscribe at any time.

At the same site you'll also find bonus material about this story–maps, photos and background material about John and Alf that couldn't fit in this book. You'll also find the first four chapters of Alf and Abi's first book, **It Happened On Fifth Street: A tale of forgotten heroes.**

ABOUT THE AUTHOR

I live in South Auckland, New Zealand. My peaceful waterside home is a wonderful creative place to be, whatever is going on in the world!

From when I was a small child, I've been in love with stories that bring history to life. This was fostered as a child, when every school day I looked at the oldest European wooden house and the oldest stone building in New Zealand. Their stories romanced me.

Then, in my adult years, older family members began to share letters and journals of intrepid ancestors who'd sailed for this far land, leaving sometimes difficult, sometimes terrible, situations on the other side of the world, all in the hope of a better life for their children.

With such a heritage, no wonder freedom is one of my core values.